# 如何用英文進行
# 國際商務談判

溫晶晶 編著

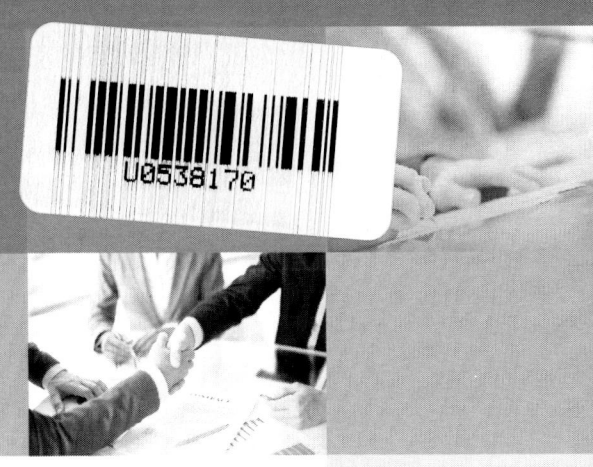

崧燁文化

# 前 言

　　與眾多學科不同的是，國際商務談判是典型的跨文化、跨學科的綜合性學問和藝術。國際商務談判作為國與國之間、企業與企業之間經濟交往的重要環節，在相當程度上決定著交易的成敗，企業的興衰，甚至影響著一個國家的發展機遇。因而，在不同歷史背景、不同民族、不同個性的談判工作者之間，建構起暢通無阻、共贏同進的橋梁，這既是國際商務談判工作者的使命，更是國際商務談判課的宗旨所在。

　　近年來，各類關於「國際商務談判」的書籍層出不窮，編者本人也撰寫了不同層次和類型的相關內容。但是，由於語言和文化的差異難以可克服，國際商務談判這門獨具特色的跨文化課程，在用不同文字表述後損失了相當部分的原始意境，從而也造成了談判效果的耗損。因此，為了能夠讓學習者更好地領悟國際商務談判的精髓，盡可能原汁原味地保留另外一種語言的本真含義，進一步提高國際商務談判人才的培養品質，編者從國際商務談判的實戰性出發，根據國際商務談判的規律，全面地介紹了國際商務談判從準備、組織到談判技巧、戰略戰術的相關知識。

　　相比中文的國際商務談判類書籍，本書以英文寫成，加大了跨文化方面的相關內容，和對談判人才個性化培養方面的知識介紹，突顯出本書國際化、通識化、實戰化的特點。

　　本書理論和實務並舉，知識性與普及性並重，可作為大專院校國際貿易、公共關係、市場行銷、企業管理等專業的大學教材，也可作為政府部門和企業培訓高級商務談判人才的參考用書。

# 目 錄

## Chapter 1  Fundamentals of International Business Negotiation  (1)
1.1  Basic Concept and Characteristics of Business Negotiation  (1)
1.2  Forms of International Business Negotiation  (7)
Case Study  (11)
Exercises  (14)

## Chapter 2  Preparing for Negotiation  (15)
2.1  Establishing Objectives  (15)
2.2  Collecting and Analyzing Information Concerned  (18)
2.3  Forming the Negotiation Team  (21)
2.4  Planning for International Business Negotiation  (25)
2.5  Choice of Negotiation Venues  (31)
2.6  Negotiators Check List  (33)
Case Study  (37)
Exercises  (37)

## Chapter 3  The Process of Negotiation  (38)
3.1  Negotiation Atmosphere and Opening Steps  (38)
3.2  Opening Strategies  (40)
3.3  Bidding and Bargaining  (43)
Case Study  (45)
Exercises  (46)

## Chapter 4  Closing the Negotiation  (47)
4.1  Identification and Means of Negotiation Closing  (47)
4.2  Tactics Towards Agreement  (51)

  4.3 Tips on Contract Signing ………………………………………………… (54)

  Case Study …………………………………………………………………… (60)

  Exercises ……………………………………………………………………… (61)

## Chapter 5 Negotiation Principles ………………………………………… (62)

  5.1 Win-Win Concept …………………………………………………… (62)

  5.2 Collaborative Principled Negotiation ……………………………… (65)

  5.3 Law of Interest Distribution ………………………………………… (75)

  5.4 Law of Trust …………………………………………………………… (83)

  Case Study …………………………………………………………………… (89)

  Exercises ……………………………………………………………………… (91)

## Chapter 6 Negotiation Strategies and Tactics ……………………… (92)

  6.1 Developing Your Negotiation Strategies …………………………… (92)

  6.2 Strategic Considerations ……………………………………………… (97)

  6.3 Useful Negotiation Strategies ………………………………………… (98)

  6.4 Useful Negotiation Tactics …………………………………………… (101)

  Case Study …………………………………………………………………… (105)

  Exercises ……………………………………………………………………… (106)

## Chapter 7 Professional Skills for International Business Negotiation … (107)

  7.1 Skill of Talking ………………………………………………………… (107)

  7.2 Skills of Asking and Answering ……………………………………… (110)

  7.3 Skills of Body Language ……………………………………………… (119)

  7.4 Application of the Body Language in Negotiation ………………… (123)

  Case Study …………………………………………………………………… (124)

  Exercises ……………………………………………………………………… (125)

## Chapter 8　International Business Contract Negotiation (127)

　　8.1　Conclusion and Guarantee of a Contract (127)

　　8.2　Modification, Termination and Assignment of Contracts (132)

　　8.3　Authentication and Notarization of a Contract (135)

　　Case Study (137)

　　Exercises (138)

## Chapter 9　Personal Styles and Negotiation Modes (139)

　　9.1　Negotiators' Personal Styles (139)

　　9.2　Negotiators' Personal Styles and AC Model (140)

　　9.3　Personal Styles vs. Negotiation Modes (142)

　　9.4　Application of Personality Checks (143)

　　Case Study (145)

　　Exercises (146)

## Chapter 10　Different Cultures and Business Negotiation (147)

　　10.1　Definition of Culture (147)

　　10.2　Cultural Change (149)

　　10.3　Negotiation and Conflict Resolution Across Cultures (152)

　　10.4　Cultural Dimensions and Negotiation (153)

　　10.5　Business Negotiating Styles of Different Cultures (154)

　　10.6　Cross the Cultural Gap (158)

　　Case Study (160)

　　Exercises (161)

# Chapter 1　Fundamentals of International Business Negotiation

## 1.1　Basic Concept and Characteristics of Business Negotiation

### 1.1.1　Definition and Characteristics of Normal Business Negotiation

The word「Negotiation」derives from the Latin word「Negotiari」, which means「to do business」. Now in a broad sense, negotiation refers to the action and the process of reaching an agreement by means of exchanging ideas with the intention of dispelling conflicts and enhancing relationship to satisfy each other's needs.

Business negotiation is a process of conferring in which the participants of business activities communicate, discuss and adjust their views, settle differences and finally reach a mutually acceptable agreement in order to close a deal or achieve a proposed financial goal.

Business negotiation is a form of negotiation itself. It presents not only the characteristics of common negotiation, but also the characteristics of business activities. In modern society, the range of business activities is expanding all the time. The subjects of business activities almost include everything from tangible to intangible goods for exchange and sale. That is to say, it includes production factors such as technology, labor, capital, information, real estate and the like as well as the sales of general consumer goods and various materials. Therefore, business negotiation includes all the discussions over institutional or individual interests in business transactions.

Business negotiation falls into the scope of applied science. This discipline covers the study of the forms, principles and procedures of business negotiation, the psychological analysis of the participants, as well as the introduction of specific methods, strategies and skills used in business negotiation. In real situations, business negotiation takes on numerous forms and concerns various contents, involving different procedures and methods in different cases. The Chinese saying「play to the score」well manifests the nature of business negotiation. As a negotiator, you should identify the objective of your negotiation first and then figure out proper methods and strategies to be used. Take the following cases as an example—a university plans to negotiate with a digital company over the price at which to purchase desktop LCD computers, and two large corporations talk about merger. Though both of them are business negotiation, the knowledge, methods and strategies used are different.

Business negotiation demonstrates the following characteristics:

(1) The objective of business negotiation is to obtain financial interest.

It is the financial interests that all parties concerned hope to gain to satisfy their need through negotiation that enable them to negotiate over a matter of common concern. In business negotiation, what the negotiators care are the cost and efficiency involved. The success of a business negotiation is judged by the satisfying financial interest gained from the negotiation. Therefore, financial interests serve the purpose of the negotiation. In another word, a business negotiation without any financial interests and efficiency is of no value.

(2) The core of business negotiation is price.

Now that the purpose of a negotiation is to gain financial interests, the measure used to show how much interest each negotiator can get is the price. And other terms, including the product quality, quantity, delivery and payment, are closely tied to it. Take a taxi company in Nanjing for example. The company placed an order of 100 Santana 3,000 sedans. The unit price for this order may differ from that of a monthly purchase of 50 sedans or an annual purchase of 600. Let's have a look at another example. The reason why air express is more expensive than ocean shipping is that the quotation includes the cost incurred to save time in addition to high air freight. As price is indicative of the profits from the sale with small margin but quick turnover, promptness and security, that makes it the focus and major issue of business negotiation.

But it should be noted that even though the price is the focus negotiators still need to leave room for concession over price. Apart from it, there are some other directly or indirectly related terms. Instead of bargaining over the price, negotiators may try to get corresponding 「compensations」 from other terms. The ability to focus on haggling over the price, to circumvent it if necessary and eventually fall back is a must for every business negotiator.

(3) Its principle is equality and mutual benefit.

The basis of any business negotiation must be equality. It is the only way to mutual benefit. In a negotiation, if one side takes the upper hand, the agreement established is most unlikely to be followed. Only the principle of equality and mutual benefit can lead to 「win-win」 or 「multi-win」.

(4) Items of contract should keep strictly accurate and rigorous.

A business negotiation comes to a conclusion when two sides sign an agreement or a contract. The terms and conditions stimulated in the contract represent the rights and obligations of each side. These terms and conditions are expected to be worded with great accuracy, caution and prudence, which are the prerequisite for the guarantee of each side's interests. A negotiator who has reached a favorable settlement may walk into the trap of a tricky written contract set by the other side, especially when they are not careful enough in drafting the contract, failing to ensure the completeness, vigorousness, correctness or accuracy, equitability and legitimacy of the contract. Once such a 「mishap」occurs, the interests nearly in their hands may get devalued, or they may be totally divested of these interests—unfortunately, the negotiation may turn out to be fruitless and their efforts produce nothing in the end. Such cases are rather common in practice. Therefore, in business negotiation, negotiators should take the written contract seriously as well as the oral commitment, with more emphasis on the accuracy and rigorousness of the former, so as to avoid being deceived or losing money but without any evidence to defend themselves.

### 1.1.2  Definition and Characteristics of International Business Negotiation

International business negotiation refers to the business negotiation that takes place between the interest groups from different countries or regions. It is an important activity frequently involved in foreign trade and other economic exchange, serving a critical approach and method for these interest groups or individuals to confer together to reach an agreement or settle the issues of their interest conflicts.

In addition to the general characteristics of typical business negotiations, international business negotiation demonstrates the following features:

(1) There exists language barriers.

In face-to-face communication, or in written correspondence, one of the first obstacles encountered in international business negotiation is language barrier unless your counterpart also speaks your mother tongue and writes in your native language. English is the most commonly-used language in international trade and business activities while most international trade practices and terms are expressed in English. If the other parties are not from the English-speaking countries, other languages, such as French, Spanish, Russian and Arabic may be used in negotiation. People with multi-lingual skills are viewed as a master key to international business negotiation. However, such talented people are rare. A person who often participates in international business negotiation must at least master one foreign language—for example, English. At very formal and important international business negotiations, all parties occasionally have their own interpreters, and most often hire temporary ones who know the language of the counterparts well—say, immigrants and international students. This can produce an effective communication and reduce the cost of negotiation.

(2) There exists cultural differences.

The differences in culture, customs, religion and belief among countries are greater than those of different areas in a country. These differences manifest themselves more obviously in international business negotiation. If negotiators fail to understand these differences due to different cultural backgrounds, they are more likely to encounter unnecessary misunderstandings, which may even endanger the normal negotiation. For example, when an Indian businessman is shaking his head to show his satisfaction with the features of the product you have just presented, you may be quite puzzled that he has not identified with your quality product; or after you quote a high price to the other side, the Swiss negotiators, waiting in your usual way for bargaining over it, but your counterparts may not be used to this kind of bargaining. They may think that perhaps you lack common knowledge of the prices on the international market, or perhaps you do not have real interest in this transaction. As a result, they will leave you alone. On the other hand, the diverse religious beliefs and social ideologies also have a great impact on the international business negotiation. An experienced business person must know how to circumvent the cultural barriers, try to find out common interests to get along, and deal with these differences with tolerance. If necessary, you may even cater to and compliment the opposing cultures so as to reduce the conflict or barriers produced by cultural differences, or turn these differences into an accelerator for negotiation.

(3) International laws and domestic laws are both in force.

The final outcome of an international business negotiation is the cross-border transfer of the object and the payment, involving not only domestic laws, but also related international business laws and international practices concerning international trade, international payment settlement/international transportation and international insurance. For example, if you are in import and export trade negotiation, you need to master the terms used in international trade and fully understand its implications, and have enough knowledge of the laws in your opponent's country and the regulations and laws imposed by international economic organizations. Additionally, it takes time for you to learn and gain experience from the practice. Finally, an sensitive international business negotiator should be well informed of the new regulations and laws imposed home or abroad, with regard to the negotiation contents, so as to adjust the negotiating strategies accordingly.

(4) International political factors must be taken into account.

Within the scope of business negotiation as it is, international business negotiation is part of the political and economic relations between the countries and regions concerned. Therefore, it will often be related to the political and diplomatic relationship between these two countries or between them and the others. Assume that a company asks you to cooperate with them to start a big utility engineering project on a site under territorial dispute with its neighboring country, which may increase the risk of not only being unable to finish the project, but also inducing diplomatic confrontation. Here is another example: an importer from the Middle East asks a Chinese textile enterprise to manufacture a batch of T-shirts with words of racial or religious discrimination on them. In this case, Chinese negotiators must refuse such an offer, no matter how profitable the deal is. It is thus clear that negotiators engaged in international business negotiation must be highly sensitive to international politics.

(5) The difficulty and the cost are greater than that of domestic business negotiations.

Seemingly, as a consequence of the above mentioned features—that is, as far as languages, social conventions, values, legal environments and political factors are concerned, international business negotiations involve more elements and tend to be more complex than domestic ones. It is more difficult to conduct as well. Additionally, the expenditures on travel, conferences, study tours and entertainments are also higher. For example, to close a deal of an object worth a huge amount of money, we need to visit our counterpart's country and check the goods and so on; occasionally we have to go there again and again for rounds of negotiations to ensure that they have satisfying credit rating, reliable technical standard and efficient implement of the contract. In a sense, international business negotiation is an overall competition of knowledge, skills, perseverance and wealth.

### 1.1.3 Types of Business Negotiation

So far as the types of business negotiation are concerned, we focus on four areas to prepare you for the fundamentals: sale of goods/services, investment, technology transfers as well as business contract.

(1) Sales of Goods/Services

Sales negotiation is an increasingly important part of the sales process. Negotiation starts when a buyer and a seller are conditionally committed to the sale. Negotiation generally results in a compromise between seller and buyer on price, i.e., the seller reduces and the buyer increases the price from their starting positions.

Due to the status differences of the two parties, generally the negotiator shall discuss the export business on the basis of analyzing the relation between supply and demand in international market, making proper strategic objective to achieve the desired results. No matter in what situation, the goal of the negotiators is to provide/get the right product in the right place at the right time at the right price. For the exporter, he must make sure that he gets paid for the product, and for the importer, he must be assured that what he'll get is exactly what he orders.

To achieve desirable results in a sales negotiation, one must consider a variety of factors: product, quality, quantity, packing, price, shipping, quotation, offer and counter offer, insurance, payment, claim and arbitration, etc.

(2) Investment Negotiation

The creation of joint venture is probably the most widespread and complex investment negotiations that exist nowadays. Here, we just quote the negotiation of joint ventures as an example of investment negotiation.

Literally, setting up a joint venture is a long and complicated process that involves four stages: preliminary investigation, pre-negotiation, negotiation and implementation. The preliminary investigation covers the initial approach to the market. This exploratory stage is mainly a phase for collecting information before acting. The pre-negotiation phase includes making the first contacts with the company that could be a partner, assessing the compatibility of the two parties' objectives, ascertaining if they have common views on market strategy, conducting the feasibility study, and signing a letter of intent. When the feasibility study has been approved by the authorities, the full negotiation can take place. At this stage, the parties concerned discuss everything necessary to set up and operate the future joint venture, such as the rights and obligations of each party, as well as the respective contribution of capital, technology, expertise and other resources. The negotiation also addresses issues concerning the management of the joint venture, its decision-making structure, its policy for personnel management and the conditions for its termination. At this stage, parties also explore such issues as domestic and export pricing of the future products for sale. This phrase is rather difficult with more than 50 issues, involving a large number of negotiators, lasting a long time and be subject to multiple unexpected events.

The last stage of the whole process concerns the implementation of the agreement. It would be logical to think the negotiation is over, but this is usually not the case. At this stage, surprises crop up on a daily basis, for instance, the working conditions or supplies of raw materials may undergo dramatic, unforeseeable external changes, as a matter of fact, numerous renegotiation may take place.

(3) Technology Transfer

For different environmental and developmental reasons, technological advances in different countries have always been unequal. The disparate nature of technological progress throughout the world provides the very basis for technology transfer. In the past few decades, international technology transfer has multiplied in leaps and bounds.

Technology transfer is a means of transferring research findings from within the institution to and for the benefit of the public. There are three principal legal methods that can be used to import technology. The first one is through assignment, which is the most expensive one among the three as it entails the purchase from the owner all his exclusive rights to a patented technology, trademark or know-how. The second method through a licensing agreement or contracts is more flexible and less expensive, hence more suitable to our national conditions. The third method is signing a know-how contract. But more often than not, the purchase of know-how alone is not enough. It takes place together with the purchase of equipment or technology and therefore can be included in the license contract.

A number of unique features in technology transfer as following. First, commercial technology transfer is highly monopolistic. Second, a single technology can be traded multiple times, as the transfer does not involve ownership but only the right to use. Finally, technology transfer does not simply follow the basic market rule of exchange.

(4) Business Contract Negotiation

A contract, in the broadest sense, is simply an agreement that defines a relationship between one or more parties. A business contract, in simplest terms, is just an agreement made by two or more parties for the purpose of transacting business. The contract which is generally adopted in import and export business is the formal written contract. Written terms may be recorded in a simple memorandum, certificate, or receipt. Because a contractual relationship is made between two or more parties who have potentially adverse interests, the contract terms are usually supplemented and restricted by laws that serve to protect the parties and to define specific relationships between them in the event that provisions are indefinite, ambiguous, or even missing.

## 1.2  Forms of International Business Negotiation

What international business negotiation involves is extensive and complex, which according to the main bodies, objects, forms and procedures involved in the negotiation, can be classified in the following ways:

### 1.2.1  Classification by Chief Negotiator

(1) Government-to-Government's Negotiation (G2G's)

Two governments negotiate with each other over the issues of mutual concern like the trade of goods and services, economic and technical cooperation, large-scale construction project, foreign exchange and capital transfer, to resolve conflicts and reach consensus agreement. This kind of negotiation is usually conducted by the officers from the Ministry of Commerce and the relevant department. For some important projects, it is up to the top level of decision makers to make a final decision. Sino-US textile negotiation, Middle Europe footwear negotiation and Sino-Russia oil pipe transport negotiation fall into this category.

This category includes the negotiation between a country and an international trade organization, for example, the negotiation over China's entry into WTO and the negotiation between China and the Association of Southeast Asian Nations (ASEAN) over the establishment of 「10+1」Free Trade Area. These negotiations are committed to obey the regulations of the trade organization concerned and eventually revolute to one-to-one negotiations over opening the domestics market. Above mentioned negotiations concerning the interest balance among countries are much more complicated, difficult and lasting much more time than those of international business negotiations.

In addition, the negotiations between two governments over some specific cooperation projects are within this scope. For example, as the city of Shanghai in China and New York City of the US are sister cities, two municipal governments used to have negotiations over Trade Fairs and exchange and display of the exhibits in the museums of the two cities. Though these negotiations also relate economic interests, their major purposes are cooperation with each other therefore they boast a friendly atmosphere.

(2) Government-to-Business' Negotiation

When a country plans to introduce a large set of equipment, but there is a gap in this industry in the country or technical strength is weak, and corresponding enterprise is qualified to do the task, government officers in charge of commercial affairs will supervise the negotiation.

They normally invite related experts to join them in negotiating with relevant foreign enterprise groups. While one side of the negotiation is a country, the other side is usually a large leading business enterprise group; therefore, this is also a kind of equal business negotiation. Its outcome is that technology importer pays for the imported equipment and the loyalty fee and opens part of its market to the other side for mutual benefits. Besides, the negotiation between a local government and foreign company also belongs to this category, such as the local government purchase of vehicles and office supplies on the global market, worldwide bid city transportation and environmental protection projects and the resources of a special region.

(3) Producer-to-Producer's Negotiation (P2P's)

This negotiation usually takes place between the finished or the semi-processed goods manufacturers in one country and the parts and accessories producers in other nations. It may also include negotiations over the cooperative production project of the companies based in different countries, and cross-border mergers of large multinational manufacturers. The finished product manufacturers are often in a stronger dominant position, having the final say in the parts of a accessories purchases while the suppliers usually are placed in a more passive position in the negotiation. But the parties of the cross-border cooperation are usually placed in a more equal position, or offer supplies for producing a product in the same market. A classical example is the cooperative production of the airbus among European countries such as France, Germany and Italy; or using the patent to produce identical products for different markets. such as Ford Automobile Group, which manufactures the popular focus sedans in the US, and has also established joint ventures in Brazil in South America, Germany in Europe and China in Asia, producing the automobiles of the same model.

(4) Producer-to-Trader's Negotiation (P2T's)

Because the international division of labour is increasingly elaborate, quite a number of manufacturers focus only on manufacturing process or assembling process, unable to afford to market or sell their products themselves. Besides, they will experience many differences and barriers caused by the language, legal environment, distribution channels in foreign countries and other factors. Therefore, import and export companies or traders are the bridge between two manufacturers or between a manufacturer and a distributor. Traders serve to provide the foreign manufacturers with raw materials and parts they need, therefore, they do not need to bother to negotiate with a great number of small suppliers. As long as the traders can provide the big enterprises with the parts or the raw materials to the specification, quantity and price they need, or as long as the traders make a quotation to the specification, quantity and price acceptable to the big purchasers, the two parties are quite likely to close the deal.

(5) Retailer-to-Producer's Negotiation (R2P's)

When retailing giants negotiate with foreign manufacturing companies over the purchasing, selling, commission agency, and joint venture, etc., it is usually the company with larger size and more strength that has more say in the negotiation. Multinational retailers, like Wal-Mart,

Carrefour, Metro Group, with their large orders and worldwide buying networks, order directly from manufacturers all over the world to cut costs. Two household electric appliances giants in China-GOME and SUNING, which almost control 60% of the retailing sales on the domestic household electric appliances market, negotiate directly with foreign home appliances producers for agency issues as well as purchase domestic products.

(6) Business-to-Business' Negotiation (B2B's)

This negotiation involves the discussion between importers and exporters, wholesalers and retailers. Its purpose is to resell the goods to get profits. The two sides typically haggle over the trading items, price, quantity, quality, shipment, insurance, payment, service, cooperation and disputes settlement and so on.

(7) Business-to-Consumer's Negotiation (B2C's)

One side of the negotiation is representatives of a manufacturer or a trading company, and the other side is the consumers from another country or other countries. Their negotiation contents are usually concerned about the quality service and product, involving the process to confer how to inspect the quality of the product, how to use it, how to handle refund and replacement, etc. For example, in 2006, about 500 Chinese consumers approached Kodak Company requesting it to refund them for the inferior cameras. In this negotiation, consumers are likely to be in a weak position due to the restraints of language, suing costs and negotiation costs. Nevertheless, consumers with high sense of self-protection may offset their weak position and strive to assure their own interests by various ways. They may present the invoice issued by the manufacturer or to International Quality Warranty, to the local Consumer Organization or appeal media and public supports to defend their rights. Companies aware of their social responsibility tend to resolve this kind of dispute legally and reasonably in view of the corporate reputation and long-term interests.

## 1.2.2 Classification by Negotiation Object

(1) Product Trade Negotiation

It is also called visible goods trade negotiation, the process in which importers and exporters from different countries confer with each other about the buying and selling of a product, the terms and conditions for the transaction, including the relevant quality, quantity, packing, price, shipment, insurance, payment terms, claim and arbitration. Import and export trade negotiations account for absolutely larger part of international business negotiation, taking various forms.

(2) Technology Trade Negotiation

International technology trade negotiation refers to the conferring process in which the technology transferor and the transferee from different countries discuss about the features, price, payment terms and so on of a technology or a set of equipment. A broader definition of technology trade includes the buying and selling of relevant equipment and right to use technology patent, while narrowly defined, it only refers to the purchasing of technology and the patent and the right to use it. Technology trade negotiation tends to be more complex than common commodity trade negotiation, and involves related technicians or experts. During the validity of the patent, the transferor is usually in a favorable position.

(3) Service Trade Negotiation

International service trade refers to the cross-border transfer of a service which does not take the form of a self-contained physical object. Service trade includes labor export, cross-border transportation, international communication, finance and insurance, tourism, advertising, medical care, film, audio-visual records, sports, technological instruction, designing, accounting, auditing, assessing, legal consultation and services, etc. Service trade negotiation can be complex, time consuming, and costly, concerning more additional clause. Except for labor export negotiation, the seller is more likely to be in an advantageous position.

(4) International Project Negotiation

International project negotiation refers to the process in which governments or enterprises from different countries confer about a joint venture project. It involves a joint venture, cooperation, inter-holding, inviting a bid, submitting a bid, leasing, contracting, auction and operation and other activities. For instance, Shanghai Auto Group and American General Motor Company had several rounds of talks over the issues of producing Buick and Chevlet cars in China. They discussed the proportion of shares each side would held, corporate bylaws and transfer of stocks and other concerns for establishing the joint venture. As project negotiation involves many domains and aspects, including production, marketing, market, prevailing laws and regulations in each country, it boasts to be the most complicated of all the international business negotiations: it engages the greatest number of people, the top level of complicity, the highest cost of input and the longest time of discussion. It is not uncommon that a big project takes months and even years from the initial phase of intent negotiation to the final phase of signing the agreement.

## 1.2.3　Classification by Form

(1) One-to-One Negotiation

One-to-one negotiation refers to the situation in which each buyer or seller, or each party in the proposed cooperation project entrusts only one negotiator from each side to confer face-to-face and one-to-one on its behalf. These talks are generally informal ones about the international commodity exchange or small-scale cooperation project or formal negotiation between the top level management of two parties. Negotiators can communicate in the same language or through the interpreter, have an intimate knowledge of the international market of the object or the details of the cooperation project. They are fully prepared for the negotiation. The outcome and objective of their negotiation is clearly definite.

(2) Team Negotiation

Team negotiation is the one in which a negotiating team is constructed each side to participate on behalf of its organization. In international business negotiation, most team negotiations are relatively formal, especially those concerning a large sum of money or a complex content. For example, a Shanghai printing house was planning to purchase a used Hydeburge high-speed color offset printing machine made in German. The Chinese negotiating team was composed of a vice president of production, an engineer and a manager of the, import a export department while the German team included a sales manager and interpreter. Therefore, Chinese side apparently has an advantage when the number of people, the staffing and the related knowledge are concerned. Before the negotiation, more wise ideas may be pooled to improve the negotiating plan; during the negotiation, the team members may back or complement each other, striking at the core technology and making full use of possible negotiation skills. If necessary, a final decision will be made to close the deal quickly. Of course, team negotiation involves more people and more money, especially more traveling expenses to negotiate abroad. Additionally, the failure of the team members to coordinate well with each other would affect the outcome adversely. What is worse, they may even make things difficult for each other, leading to the breakdown of the negotiation.

(3) Multilateral Negotiation

It is also dubbed as 「multi-angles」 negotiation, which refers to the business negotiating situation in which negotiators representing three or more interest groups from different countries confer to reach an agreement. This negotiation covers a wider range of concerns, engages more delicate personnel relations, which makes it hard to achieve effective coordination. Therefore, it is more difficult to carry through than other kinds of negotiations, for example, the Doha Round of WTO negotiations, negotiations over a regional 「free trade area」 of ASEAN 10+3 members, Ariane astronautics project negotiation between Germany, France, the UK, Italy and other West European countries. In the course of the negotiations, one or more gravity centers of interest would turn up and give pressure to other negotiating parties. The consequence thereafter may be that one or more sides refuse to cooperate, leading to the breakdown of the negotiation, or the sides which refuses to cooperate withdraws, leaving the multilateral negotiation less effective than expected.

# Case Study

Analyzes a series of successful deal-making strategies when negotiating with a powerful partner.

Wal-Mart, the world's largest retailer, sold 315 billion USD worth of goods in 2006. With its single-minded focus on 「EDLP」 (everyday low prices) and the power to make or break suppliers a partnership with Wal-Mart is either the Holy Grail or the kiss of death, depending on one's perspective.

There are numerous media accounts of the corporate monolith riding its suppliers into the ground. But what about those who manage to survive, and thrive, while dealing with the classic hardball negotiator?

In 「Sarah Talley and Frey Farms Produce: Negotiating with Wal-Mart」 and 「Tom Muccio: Negotiating the P&G Relationship with Wal-Mart,」 HBS professor Jim Sebenius and Research Associate Ellen Knebel show two very different organizations doing just that. The cases are part of a series that involve hard bargaining situations.

「The concept of win-win bargaining is a good and powerful message,」 Sebenius says, 「but a lot of our students and executives face counterparts who aren't interested in playing by those rules. So what happens when you encounter someone with a great deal of power, like Wal-Mart, who is also the ultimate non-negotiable partner?」 The case details how P&G executive Tom Muccio pioneers a new supplier-retailer partnership between P&G and Wal-Mart. Built on proximity (Muccio relocated to Wal-Mart's turf in Arkansas) and growing trust (both sides eventually eliminated elaborate legal contracts in favor of Letters of Intent), the new relationship focused on establishing a joint vision and problem-solving process, information sharing, and generally moving away from the 「lowest common denominator」 pricing issues that had defined their interactions previously. From 1987, when Muccio initiated the changes, to 2003, shortly before his retirement, P&G's sales to Wal-Mart grew from 350 million USD to 7.8 billion USD.

「There are obvious differences between P&G and a much smaller entity like Frey Farms,」 Sebenius notes. 「Wal-Mart could clearly live without Frey Farms, but it's pretty hard to live without Tide and Pampers.」

### Sarah Meets Goliath

Sarah Talley was 19 in 1997, when she first began negotiations to supply Wal-Mart with her family farm's pumpkins and watermelons. Like Muccio, Talley confronted some of the same hardball price challenges, and like Muccio, she acquired a deep understanding of the Wal-Mart culture while finding 「new money」 in the supply chain through innovative tactics.

For example, Frey Farms used school buses (1,500 USD each) instead of tractors (12,000 USD each) as a cheaper and faster way to transport melons to the warehouse.

Talley also was skillful at negotiating a coveted co-management supplier agreement with Wal-Mart, showing how Frey Farms could share the responsibility of managing inventory levels and sales and ultimately save customers, money while improving their own margins.

「Two sides in this sort of negotiation will always differ on price,」 Sebenius observes. 「However, if that conflict is the centerpiece of their interaction, then it's a bad situation. If they're trying to develop the customer, the relationship, and sales, the price piece will be one of many points, most of which they're aligned on.」

Research Associate Knebel points out that while Tom Muccio's approach to Wal-Mart was pioneering for its time, many othercompanies have since followed P&G's lead and enjoyed their own versions of success with the mega-retailer. Getting a ground-level view of how two companies achieved those positive outcomes illustrates the story-within-a-story of implementing corporate change.

⌈Achieving that is where macro concepts, micro imperatives, and managerial skill really come together,⌋ says Sebenius. And the payoffs—as Muccio and Talley discover—are well worth the effort.

### Sarah Talley's Key Negotiation Principles

When you have a problem, when there's something you engage in with Wal-Mart that requires agreement so that it becomes a negotiation, the first advice is to think in partnership terms, really focus on a common goal, of getting costs out, for example, and ask questions. Don't make demands or statements... you know, we can do this better and so forth. If the relationship with Wal-Mart is truly a partnership, negotiating to resolve differences should not endanger the tenor of the partnership.

Don't spend time griping. Be problem solvers instead. Approach Wal-Mart by saying, ⌈Let's work together and drive costs down and produce it so much cheaper you don't have to replace me, because if you work with me I could do it better.⌋

Learn from and lobby with people and their partners who have credibility, and with people having problems in the field.

Don't ignore small issues or let things fester.

Do not let Wal-Mart become more than 20% of your company's business.

It's hard to negotiate with a company that controls yours.

Never go into a meeting without a clear agenda. Make good use of the buyers' face time. Leave with answers. Don't make small talk. Get to the point; their time is valuable. Bring underlying issues to the surface. Attack them head on and find resolution face to face.

Trying to bluff Wal-Mart is never a good idea. There is always someone willing to do it cheaper to gain the business. You have to treat the relationship as a marriage. Communication and compromise is key.

Don't take for granted that just because the buyer is young they don't know what they are talking about or that it will be an easy sell. Most young buyers are very ambitious to move up within the company and can be some of the toughest, most educated buyers you will encounter know your product all the way from the production standpoint to the end use. Chances are your buyer does, and will expect you to be even more knowledgeable.

——Dr. Bob March's *The Chinese Negotiator*

Question: What can we learn from Sarah Talley's Key Negotiation Principles for negotiating with powerful negotiation partner?

## Exercises

(1) What are the definitions of negotiation and business negotiation?
(2) What are the characteristics of international business negotiation?
(3) What are the main forms of international business negotiation?
(4) What are horizontal negotiation and vertical negotiation?

# Chapter 2　Preparing for Negotiation

## 2.1　Establishing Objectives

Any negotiation should be oriented by its objectives. The objective is the prerequisite of a negotiation. Only under the guidance of clear, specific, impersonal and feasible objectives could the negotiation be in a positive position. If the objectives are vague with blindness, then it means an impossible successful negotiation. Negotiation is the art and science of reaching an agreement that meets your and your client's goals. Your strategic goals create the measure you judge yourself by at the end of the processes and need to be set before the negotiation begins. Your goals also will act as your guide during the negotiation, supporting everything you say, every move you make and every agreement you reach.

### 2.1.1　Decide on Priority Interests and Rank Them

Each party should determine the priorities of their interests. Negotiation is, after all, a matter of both parties conceding and reaching a solution. The key to interest-based concessions is to trade items of less importance in order to secure items of more importance.

To make the most of the negotiating sessions, each party should initially decide upon its goals for the session. What interests underlie the current demands that have been made? Is it only money? Is it a continuing relationship or an enhanced business relationship with the other side? Is it a resolution of this matter, which may be disrupting other business? Is it recognition of the validity of one's claims or status? Or is it the harm caused by the other side? The first important task to be done at preparatory stage is for negotiators to decide which interests to be fulfilled first and which to be obtained at the cost of others. Discussion in this regard facilitates negotiators to make their target decision.

When the interests of negotiating parties are of simple nature and related with single issue, the target decision can be easily made. Otherwise it will be difficult to decide. Here are two examples to illustrate the point: When the focus of negotiation is price, while for the seller he would try his best to make a deal at the highest possible price. When the issue concerns extending a loan, under the condition that there is no repayment risk, then at least two points will be considered by both borrower and lender, which are interest rate and length of time.

If the lender pursues higher interest rate he would have to make concession on maturity of the loan, and also take the risk of having his money being tied up for a longer time. On the contrary, the borrower has to make a choice between time and higher interest rate. The target decision in this regard is expected to be difficult since a balancing point has to be located among several things. The difficulty lies in how much of these interests will be attained at the cost of others. Very often, the result will be found out with the progress of negotiation.

### 2.1.2　Key Elements of Negotiation Objectives

The key elements of negotiation objectives are:
a. Who can contribute to and who will be affected by this negotiation?
b. What are the maximum and minimum targets we will seek?

By the minimum targets we mean the targets or benefits we would never give up, in other words there is no room to bargain. By the maximum targets we mean all the targets or benefits we could think of giving up under critical conditions.

c. When must we conclude this negotiation and when would we like to conclude?
d. Where is the best place for us to negotiate?
e. Why the buyer selected us to negotiate with? Does this suggest any bargaining strengths for our side?
f. How are we to make concessions and how will we seek counter-concession from the other party?

The objectives in different stages of negotiation are different. They might be summed up generally as meeting one or more needs of the participants involved. Making the objective of a negotiation rigid might cause the negotiation breakdown. An alternative method of formulating objectives might very well be keep them fluid in a process state so that the expectations can change with the circumstances of the negotiation. Learning to deal with the objectives of negotiation is like dealing with the conditions of the wind. The strongest tree often has to compromise with the wind. Also when kites use the force of the wind, they go higher.

### 2.1.3　Target Levels

The target point represents the best possible outcome that may reasonably be expected and could be an important anchor for negotiators. Setting the appropriate target is important.

In addition to interest preference decision, negotiators, in view of negotiation strategy, will set at least four objective levels, which are top target, desirable target, acceptable target and bottom target.

(1) The Highest Target, or the Maximum Expectation or Top Target

This is the best target that one party will seek to maximize its gains in the negotiation or the top limit that the other party can give up. This goal is very difficult to achieve because the maximization of one party's benefits means the minimization of the other party's benefits, especially in a zero-sum negotiation. It is the critical point at which the other party will retreat and cause the negotiation to break down. So it will be greatly appreciated if the negotiation personnel can achieve agreements at this critical point. However, the top target can be given up when it is quite impossible to achieve it.

(2) The Desirable Target

The desirable target is what negotiators wish to attain but in reality rarely reach. It serves two purposes in negotiations: setting a potential goal for negotiators to strive for and leaving room for bargaining in negotiations.

(3) The Acceptable Target

The acceptable target is what negotiators make all efforts to achieve. If negotiators take advantage of their power and strength, and manage the negotiations skillfully, the acceptable target is attainable and very often can be gained.

(4) The Bottom Target

The bottom target is what negotiators will defend and safeguard with all their might. Unless the bottom target is met, the negotiators would block further discussion and announce failure of negotiations.

Your bottom line is the absolute, last resort and final offer on each key issue. It's your walk away point. Setting a bottom line in advance of your negotiation is important because it makes it easier to resist the temptation of agreeing to an unprofitable deal. Setting a bottom line protects you from seller's remorse and it makes it easier for others to participate in the negotiation with you because you can provide a framework for them to negotiate in. There are some downsides though. The most not able is that having a bottom line can discourage creativity and may limit your ability to capitalize on new information revealed during the negotiation discussions. Be careful not to set your bottom line too high.

Objectives may change during negotiation. Your pre-negotiation objectives represent your best judgment based on the information available prior to negotiations. As more information becomes available, your objectives may change.

## 2.1.4 Setting Up an Appointment

Let's study the negotiation modes and their five related personal styles.

Competing style of persons tends to use high pressure such as deadline, ultimatum and sanctions. They show little concern to others' interests and force the other party to surrender to their demands.

As for collaborating kind of persons, as they are so named, cooperation is an outstanding feature in their negotiating activities. They show concerns and understanding to parties' interests, difficulties and satisfactions, which explains the reason why they can disclose information, trust others and offer help needed in negotiation.

Seeking middle ground is the representative feature of compromising style. They cooperate with others on some items but refuse to collaborate on other items. They treat assistance, information and trust as commodities, hence they look for trades with others.「I won't give you anything unless you can provide me with what I want」is the typical feeling of compromising style.

Avoiding style of persons is never willing to cooperate with others nor do they state their consent or objection openly. They resist passively often by finding excuses, or changing topics or leaving the matters to others.

People of accommodating style are the other extreme of competing style. They habitually accept others' desires and requests. Harmony is their motto. They avoid hurting feelings, damaging relationship and disturbing peaceful atmosphere, so they try to be very helpful and think a lot for others' ideas.

Competing style and accommodating style are at the high ends of assertiveness and cooperativeness.

And avoiding style is neither assertive nor cooperative, thus it is the least recommended style for negotiations.

Compromising style, corresponding its middle position, is inclined to take middle way and seeks balance between different people.

Collaborating style combines highest degree of both assertiveness and cooperativeness and should be recommended as the most suitable personal style for negotiations.

By cooperating with different kinds of counterparts, you can adopt different strategies accordingly.

## 2.2　Collecting and Analyzing Information Concerned

After the negotiating team and the negotiation target have been established, the next and the most important step in preparing for a specific negotiation is gathering information. In foreign trade activities, it is very important for negotiators to learn as much as possible about the market which they want to enter, the potential client or partner they will deal with before the negotiation. Various kinds of information are necessary, finance, market, technology, policy, even the background of a particular executive. In order to size up the probable goal and preferences of your counterpart, using his perspectives rather than yours as well as your own, the information gathered will have to be analyzed subsequently. Only when they have known them quite well can they have the initiative in business negotiations.

### 2.2.1　Collecting Information

(1) Market Research

In order to obtain the information concerned, market research should be made, using trade statistics published by most countries to narrow down the scope of their research. The following issues should be involved when making market research:

①Social and cultural background: they must bear in mind the cultural and social backgrounds of the target market, such as the language, religion and local people's aesthetical viewpoints, etc.

②The political and legal system: they must know the relevant laws and government policies. Such as, the extent of state control over business enterprises and its organization, the legal and judicial system, and their influence on business.

③Natural condition, infrastructure and logistics system: they should be familiar with the geographical conditions and features of different countries, because temperature, altitude and humidity extremes may affect the proper functioning of some equipment. As to infrastructure and logistics, it includes: the availability of labor and materials for construction in the territory, the local logistics problems relating to transportation.

④Product target market: They should know the target market conditions, such as commodities, the price, the competitors, alternative products, etc.

(2) The Counterpart Research

After market research, we have to focus our attention on something about the firm that we are about to do business with, especially a new one. There are various ways of obtaining such information concerning your counterpart. Instead of applying to a business friend, traders usually apply to banks, the chamber of commerce, the Chinese Commercial Counselor's office in foreign countries or other enquiry agencies, because the information obtained through the channels mentioned above is generally most reliable. However, bank will not give any information directly to an unknown trader, unless the enquiry from one of its fellow banks. Therefore, when taking up a bank reference, the trader must remember to do so through his own bank. The information needed usually includes:

- the financial position
- the credit
- the reputation
- the business methods

Besides what have been mentioned, the negotiators should get the knowledge of particular executive's background, family status, their strengths and weaknesses, their idiosyncrasies and even eccentricities, their blind spots and their areas of special expertise. You need to do as much of that as you can before you meet them, before you sit across the negotiating table from them, because all these will be a great advantage to you in negotiation. Every skillful negotiator knows that knowing who you will be bargaining with is far more important than most average people can assume.

Some of the information that you must now find out about these people will be fact-find, for example, what percentage of their negotiations had been successful or what discounts they gave last year. But some of it will be far less certain. This will be the sort of information that is based on opinions or views. But despite of this, it is useful information. It will tell you things like what other people's opinions of the other side are, or what is rumored about their financial position. But whatever the sources, nature of certainty of this information, it will tell you:

  • What the other side has done in the past.
  • What they might do in their negotiations with you in the future.

The connection between these is both strong and obvious. If you can see what they've done in their past negotiations, you can guess what they might do in your negotiation. These guesses about their future actions will also reach out to touch the present—a present that contains the decisions that you will soon make about the ways and means of your future negotiation.

Some people regard history as junk. But it is not true. The past can provide us with the foundations of our future successes. For example, when you face a negotiator who has a record of being a successful negotiator, then you can either take this to mean that:

  • You'll have little chance of 「winning」.
  • The opponent conducts his negotiations in an effective and professional manner.

In reality, having a record like that means that the latter of these conclusions is probably nearer the truth. You can then have a sigh of relief, for dealing with someone who negotiates in that way is a lot easier than dealing with an amateur. Similarly, you can either view the past as a heavy load of obligations, or you can view the past as a series of completed lessons—something that provides a data base for you to use when you decide how you're going to do it now. If you are going to do this, then there's some questions that you need to ask—questions that should be targeted at getting the information that you need so that you can be sure that you know everything that you need to know about the other side.

### 2.2.2  Analyzing Information

With so much information at hand, it is advisable and necessary to do a feasibility study before negotiation, because a feasibility study provides economic, commercial and technical base for decision making. It should define and analyze the critical elements with alternative approaches. A satisfactory feasibility study must analyze all the basic components and implications. Any shortfall will limit the utility of the study. A feasibility study is not an end in itself, but a means to arrive at a decision whether to go for business or not. It should arrive at definitive conclusion on all the basic issues a consideration of various alternatives such as those listed below using a project negotiation as an example.

(1) Political and social background: to ensure the success of the feasibility study, it must be clearly understood how the project idea fits into the framework of the economic conditions and the development of the country. It should include the description of the project idea, its historical development, studies and investigations already performed.

(2) Detailed analysis: it is to show whether it is possible to work on the project, describing the technology and the equipment that will be used in the project and the benefit obtained after its operation. For an instance, analysis should be made concerning the relationship between the

market demand and the plant capacity together with its production program and its marketing strategy, the basis for the selection of materials and inputs required for the manufacturing as well as its supply system.

(3) Location and site: a feasibility study has to define the location and site suitable for project under consideration. The choice of location should be made from a fairly wide geographical area. Sometimes, several alternative sites may have to be taken into consideration. Once the site has been selected, reasons for the selection and local conditions should be stated, and impact on the environment should be studied.

(4) Main costs: estimates should be made in the aspects of costs resulting from organization and management, the cost to operate the project, the overhead costs related to the operation, such as administrative overheads in industrial feasibility study.

(5) Manpower: a feasibility study should give the total manpower costs of the project starting at the department level. All labor and staff personnel should be included in the department, since it is a part of production costs. A comparison should be made of the required personnel with the structure of the labor force available in the project's geographic region. And the comparison will facilitate the assessment of training requirements and the need for foreign/domestic experts.

(6) Schedule implementation: it is an essential part of the feasibility study, as the implementation stages, such as negotiation, contracting, and project formulation, etc., in terms of requiring for each stage. It combines various stages into a consistent pattern of activities.

(7) Financial and economic evaluation: total investment costs, which include preproduction expenditures, fixed investments and the net working capital estimates, are calculated. Profitability analysis should be made to show the profit obtained from the project and the contribution it would make to the national or regional economy.

Having completed the status inquires, the trader should make a correct judgment according to the three cs of credit—character, capacity and capital, then he could make a final decision whether to do business with the firm concerned or not.

## 2.3　Forming the Negotiation Team

The organizational preparations for international business negotiations consist of deciding the size of the negotiation team, staffing the negotiation team and soliciting the coordination and support from the outside members.

### 2.3.1　Size of the Negotiation Team

The size of the negotiation team refers to the number of staff taking part in the negotiation. The following factors should be taken into consideration when we decide the size of a negotiation team:

(1) The Number of the Negotiation Team Members of Your Counterpart

The guideline is that both parties should have approximately the same number in order to reflect equality. When the negotiation is held at a host court, the host team can have more members than its counterpart due to the abundant mobile human resource, but large gap between the two parties is not suitable.

(2) The Complexity of the Negotiation

Generally speaking, the number of negotiation staff should be proportional to the complexity of the negotiation, for the more complicated the negotiating project is, the more knowledge and experience it'll be involved and the more team members will be needed.

(3) The Need for Technical Experts

The import and export trades usually don't need technical professionals, but the trades involving hi-tech products and patents require the participation of the experts in that field; trades involving laws in one's own country or in the counterpart's country, or relating to international or regional trade agreements have to include related legal experts in the negotiation.

(4) The Number of the Associates in the Project

If the negotiating project only concerns the benefits of one or two departments, we can have relatively fewer negotiators; if it concerns the benefits of more departments, it will need representatives from more departments.

## 2.3.2　The Staffing of the Negotiation Team

The composition of the negotiation team refers to the consideration about the professional backgrounds or credentials, expertise and the status of the team members, and the role they play in the negotiation.

(1) Principles for Team Building

While building a negotiation team, make sure the members are complementary in knowledge and characters and define their roles, responsibilities and tasks clearly.

①Complementary knowledge. Firstly, the negotiation personnel need to possess expertise and knowledge in their own areas respectively and be able to deal with different problems and form a united advantage by bringing out the best in each other in terms of knowledge. Secondly, their expertise and business experience should be complementary. Among all the negotiation members there should be knowledgeable experts as well as experienced and mature veterans so as to improve the force and power of the negotiation group.

②Complementary character. If the negotiation team members can make harmonious complementation among themselves in character and make good use of their strengths, then the greatest advantages of the whole group can be utilized. For instance, extrovert and outgoing members tend to be agile, eloquent, and decisive, but they are prone to be impetuous, not insightful enough or even careless and negligent. On the contrary, introvert members tend to be meticulous and precise in their work, perceptively insightful into the problems, and prudent in their words, stick to the principle, observant and thoughtful, but they are often hesitant, indecisive, ineloquent and not flexible. If the team members have different characters, and play different roles in a negotiation, one playing the hero and the other villain, which helps make up for each other's deficiencies, supplement and complement each other, the problem will be solved more satisfactorily.

③Clearly-defined roles. The negotiation team should have the first fiddler and the second fiddler; everyone has his or her position or role in the team. It is a table for anyone to be offside. Don't mix up the roles. It should also be avoided that all the members are eager to put in a word. Anyway, under the strict discipline, all the members should try to help and support each other, making a united effort to achieve the goal.

(2) Organizational Structure of the Team

The structure of the team must be taken into consideration for the negotiation group that consists of two or more than two members except for a one-to-one negotiation. A relatively 「standard」negotiation team should contain the following members:

①leading personnel

The negotiator in charge of a negotiation should be an authoritative person with relatively high rank and more power. The leading personnel should possess all-sided knowledge, the ability to make a resolute decision and an authoritative position. This person should be the core of the team and play a major role during the negotiation, in charge of constructing the negotiation group, controlling the process of the negotiation, adjusting the negotiation strategies and the plans in emergencies and making the final decisions on the concessions they are to make and the agreement they are to reach. The leading negotiator can be specially assigned for the negotiation or someone who held another concurrent post in the team.

②business/commercial personnel

Business/commercial personnel are usually the marketing personnel such as salespersons, sales managers, purchasing managers, project managers or other professional negotiation experts invited from the outside. They are usually very familiar with the international trade practice, highly-experienced in domestic and international marketing and negotiation, and well-informed in the situation of domestic and international markets of the project under the negotiation.

③professional and technical personnel

The engineers or the technical experts who are quite familiar with related technological and product standards and the status quo of the technical know-how are responsible for negotiating related production technology, products functions, quality standards, products check and accept, technological services as well as providing consultation and advice for making the decision concerning project prices bargain.

④financial personnel

The financial personnel who are familiar with accounting and finance professions and good at accounting are accountable for estimation of the prices, terms of payment, ways of payment, settlement currency and exchange rate for the project under negotiation.

⑤legal personnel

The specially invited lawyers or enterprise law consultants who know trade laws, commercial practice agreements and law enforcement well are mainly responsible for the validity, completeness and preciseness of the contract terms. They also take part in the negotiation related to laws.

⑥interpreters

Interpreters are usually full–time or part–time translators good at English and business whose task is to do written or oral translation. Interpreters in international business negotiations are required to express precisely and make good use of language skills. Their translation skills will directly affect the effectiveness of communication and negotiation.

⑦secretaries

As for large–scale and high–level business negotiations, special personnel should be arranged to record the process of the whole negotiation and the speeches made by all the parties so as to be reference for drafting an agreement.

In actual negotiation cases, the above-mentioned personnel can be increased or decreased in number according to the situation. Not all the personnel mentioned above will participate in the whole process of the negotiation but at least we need a person in charge and a professional member good at a foreign language or an interpreter. The interpreter and the secretary can be selected from the negotiation personnel.

## 2.3.3 Collaboration and Support from the Outside Members

Besides the negotiation personnel, some full–time or part–time personnel should be arranged to provide support and services for the negotiation activities.

These kinds of people include the following:

(1) Related Personnel in Other Functional Departments

These people may include department managers or the professionals from stock control and transport department, advertising department, public relations department and research and development department.

(2) Administrative Personnel

Administrative personnel such as company secretaries, librarians, office workers, drivers may be helpful in a negotiation as well.

The tasks of outside staff are to provide some accessory information support and services from behind, at the beginning or at the end of, or in the intervals of the negotiation. The guideline to choose this kind of staff is that they must be proper and indispensable people, highly efficient and be ready for providing service any time.

The basic principle of organizing a negotiation team for an international business negotiation is to keep the team as small and efficient as possible. Small: a principle that can demonstrate the high efficiency and authority of one part. Efficient: a principle that can show the high quality of the negotiation personnel and the power and management concept of a company. There is no doubt that 「small」 does not mean the fewer the team members are, the better the negotiation result can be. The key point here is to be practical. It is commendable to have enough members.

## 2.4 Planning for International Business Negotiation

### 2.4.1 Gist of a Negotiation Plan

The gist of negotiationplan refers to the basic requirements for developing a negotiation plan:

(1) Requirement Towards the Key Points of the Negotiation

The whole negotiation must focus on the key points.

(2) Requirement Towards the Thoughtfulness and Flexibility of the Plan

Thoughtfulness refers to appointing specific personnel responsible for every step of every project; flexibility means the negotiation plan should be adaptable or elastic allowing reasonable leeway.

(3) Requirement Towards the Predictability of the Plan

The negotiation plan should be able to foresee the various situations that may emerge in the course of negotiation, i.e. to forecast the different possible consequences in different cases and come up with the countermeasures that can be adopted in response.

(4) Requirement Towards the Negotiation Time

It should be decided that whether the intended negotiation should be immediately concluded, or be carried out like marathon race or be adapted to the actual situation.

(5) Requirements Towards the Negotiation Atmosphere

The negotiation plan should set the tone for the negotiation: whether the negotiators should be serious and tense, or friendly and relaxed; whether they should be flank and sincere, or alert and cautious.

### 2.4.2 Targets of a Negotiation Plan

Negotiation targets refer to the commercial goals that are expected to achieve through negotiation. Negotiation targets specified in a negotiation plan are what sort of problems are going to be solved through the negotiation. Targets of an international business negotiation can be generally divided into three categories:

(1) The Highest Target, or the Maximum Expectation or Target

This is the best target that one party will seek to maximize its gains in the negotiation or the top limit that the other party can give up. This goal is very difficult to achieve because the maximization of one party's benefits means the minimization of the other party's benefits, especially in a zero-sum negotiation. It is the critical point at which the other party will retreat and cause the negotiation to break down. So it will be greatly appreciated if the negotiation personnel can achieve agreements at this critical point. However, the top target can be given up when it is quite impossible to achieve it.

(2) Acceptable Target, or Expected Target

This is an intermediate expected goal for one party and still an acceptable one to the other as well, which is usually identified after the synthesis analysis about various related information, and scientific and thorough argumentation and reasoning, taking various concessions into consideration. This goal has shown the sincerity of both parties; however, it is still a flexible and faint area which can be set after several rounds of bargains.

(3) The Lowest Target, or Limited Target, Basic Target or Must-Be-Realized Target

It is the least requirement of the negotiation as well as the critical point where negotiation can break down. In other words, if the lowest goal can't be realized, the negotiation would rather be abandoned. The bottom line of the negotiation target must be strictly kept confidential. Generally, only the key personnel should be informed of it and other personnel do not need to know.

A complicated international business negotiation needs to attain many goals. In this case, we can divide the negotiating item into numerous sub-items which may be used as bases for making negotiation plans and set the negotiation targets. Then, the targets would be arranged in the order of importance or priority: as far as the overall situation is concerned, which terms or conditions, or clauses must reach the highest target, which can reach acceptable targets, which can be all right with the lowest target or which can be even given up.

### 2.4.3 Negotiation Strategies

Negotiation strategies refer to the tactics and techniques used in the actual process of a negotiation to meet the negotiation targets. International business negotiations are by no means simple bargaining. They are a synthesis competition in overall strength, capability, skills, culture, concepts and the like.

(1) Factors That Need to Be Considered in Designing Business Negotiation Strategies

①Will the negotiation take place at the host court, the guest court or a neutral ground?

②What are the advantages or strengths of each party?

③Which party will be affected more greatly by the outcome of the negotiation?

④What are the strengths (rank and composition) of the counterpart team and the character of their chief negotiator?

⑤Which party will be affected more greatly by the length of time the negotiation takes?

⑥Is it necessary to build up long-term cooperative relationship?

After comparing the overall strengths of all the participants and the above factors, negotiators can make a judgment about whether their ownparty has an advantageous position in the negotiation or not. Therefore, corresponding strategies can be established in turn for bidding, bargaining, sticking to a bid, making concession and breaking an impasse.

(2) Forms of Negotiation Strategies

①Thorough negotiation strategy, which is usually suitable for negotiations of medium-and large-sized projects. The information collected needs to be analyzed and discussed beforehand so as to develop a detailed negotiating plan which lists the issues including the negotiation gist and objectives, the advantages and disadvantages of each party, negotiation steps, staffing and the structure of the negotiation team, the chief negotiator, opening strategy, countermeasures in case of emergency, and bottom concessions. The plan should be submitted to the top level management for approval and used by key negotiating personnel as reference and implemented in negotiation.

②Sketchy negotiation strategy, which is usually suitable for usual business negotiations. The negotiation subject, personnel and structure of the negotiation team, the highest target, the lowest target, the acceptable target, key points worthy of attention and so forth are listed in written form and be used as reference by related personnel.

③Tacit-agreement negotiation strategy, which is suitable for routine business negotiations or 「one-to-one」 and 「two-to-one」 negotiation with regular clients. The negotiators of one side are quite familiar with the background and the targets of the other side, so they can make oral agreement on the negotiation targets and strategies with the senior managers and other negotiators from their own side.

No matter what forms of negotiation strategies are adopted, attention should be paid to keep it strictly confidential. The top manager and the negotiation team members should record the commonly-agreed targets and counteractions under special circumstances in written form respectively at the preparatory meeting for making negotiation strategies in order to be able to speak with the same voice. It is best advised not to ask the secretary or an outsider to print it and thus prevent the strategies from leaking out.

## 2.4.4 Negotiation Agenda

Negotiation agenda refers to the arrangement for the timing and site choice of the negotiation, and issues discussed. The agenda is usually prepared by the host party or discussed by both parties in advance, which can be segmented into open agenda and restricted agenda sometimes.

(1) Scheduling of the Negotiation

Negotiation agenda should list when the negotiation is conducted, how long it lasts and what issues are discussed in each session (such as at what time to begin and to end, morning, afternoon, what month, what date...). Whether the scheduling is proper and reasonable is also a part of negotiation strategies. Let us suppose that a company headquartered in Shanghai receives the negotiation representatives who arrive in Shanghai from Britain. The representatives from Shanghai could be calm, free from haste, and wait at their ease for the exhausted partners; while the British representatives would be affected in reasoning and judgment ability due to the jet lag. In addition, if the negotiation schedule is arranged too tightly, visiting representatives would have to get starting the negotiation in their haste without preparation and thus throw themselves into confusion, having difficulty carrying out various strategies; if the negotiation schedule is arranged too loosely, it would not only result in the waste of too much time, energy and money, but also possible loss of important opportunities with the changing situation.

(2) Negotiation Site

Negotiation sites are usually chosen by the hosting party and then informed to the visiting team, or one party proposes several plans for the other team or teams to choose. They are usually a negotiation hall, meeting room, manager's office of the host company. A meeting room or an office of a third party can also be rented for use; the negotiation can also be arranged in a reception room or a bar in a hotel, a restaurant, a gym or an entertainment center. Negotiation sites can be a fixed place or changed in order to adjust negotiation atmosphere. When the negotiation site is a meeting room of the host party, the host team can take advantage of the host court, assembling and utilizing data and resources conveniently. In case of a deadlock in the negotiation, alternative activities like a dinner party, sightseeing, swimming and playing golf can make some breakthrough, which is difficult to realize on the negotiation tables.

(3) Negotiation Issues

Negotiation issues refer to the various problems that each side has proposed and planned to confer in the negotiation. Both sides can have communications beforehand to identify negotiation issues; or each side proposes different issues and then has a discussion together. When issues are identified, they should be listed in terms of priority and logical order.

(4) Open Agenda and Restricted Agenda

①Open agenda, or general rule agenda, means the schedules of the negotiation that all the parties concerned observe and follow. The open agenda consists of issues to be discussed, time, place, staffing and reception arrangement, which is usually typed and printed as documents after the consensus was reached, used as negotiation reference and implemented by all the parties.

②Restricted agenda, or detailed rule agenda, refers to the detailed arrangement of negotiation strategies of one's own party, which is only to know the top executives and negotiation staff of the company because it is confidential information. Restricted agenda mainly consists of coordinated action and speech in the negotiation, counteractions under special circumstances, speech strategies (when to question, what kind of questions, who raises the questions, who complements, who answers certain kinds of questions from the partner, how to argue, when to adjourn the negotiation and so on), the exchange of negotiation team members and the negotiation scheduling strategies.

(5) Key Points That Need Attention When Making the Negotiation Agenda for One's Own Side

①Make good use of the factors of climate, favorable geographical conditions and the support from other people under the prerequisite of not baffling the partner.

②Design negotiation strategies to go along with the process of the negotiation. For example, under what circumstances should the trump card used to surprise the other side? How to drop a hint foreshadowing a counterattack on the other side? In what difficult situation is a concession made? And what concession to make?

③Avoid showing all the cards in one's hand.

(6) Points That Need Attention When the Other Side Designs the Negotiation Agenda

①Don't accept the agenda too easily without reading it carefully.

②Be careful to find out the issue that has been omitted on purpose or unintentionally and propose to make it up promptly, or leave it to be discuss, later to gain mastery by striking only after the other side has struck and forced one into difficulty, pointing out unexpectedly the oversight in the agenda.

③Point out anything unsatisfactory in the agenda immediately and provide revision instead of indulging the other party.

④Find out the weakness or negotiation intention from the other party's agenda and make the counteractions so as to attack the other party at the necessary moment.

Though business negotiation agenda is only a plan designed beforehand, somewhat like idle theorizing of an armchair strategist, a good negotiation agenda can indeed set and control the pace and direction of the negotiation. If a negotiation agenda can put every step and every change under its control, it can be called a very thorough and smart strategy.

## 2.4.5 The Choice of Negotiation Places

The choice of negotiation courts includes the choices of the country or region and the specific negotiation site.

(1) Negotiation Location

The second chapter of this book has offered an analysis about the advantages and disadvantages of the place choices at the 「host court」 (host country), the 「guest court」 (visiting country) and a third place or country. Choosing different negotiation places will make a difference towards the negotiation to some extent. However, wherever the negotiation takes place, it will be both advantageous a disadvantageous to both negotiation parties.

(2) Negotiation Sites

The American psychologist Mr. Taylor had conducted an experiment: most people can obtain the ability to persuade others in their own living room than in the living room of others'. Because human beings with animal nature have a common state of mind, that is, they can release more powerful energy within their own 「domain」 so as to be successful more often. This is also the case for international business negotiations.

If the site of an international business negotiation is the reception room, office or meeting room of their own company, negotiators will have the following advantages:

①Familiar surroundings will bring the feeling of calmness and superiority, which will place psychological pressures to the other party;

②Save the host negotiator's expenses and time to go abroad;

③It's convenient to report, ask for advice and acquire supporting information.

If the negotiation site is chosen in the hotel where the guests stay or at the exhibition stand of the guests abroad, guests will feel at ease just like at home, which helps reduce their nervousness in another country more or less. For instance, a Japanese manager who always goes to Shanghai for business likes to invite the Chinese manager to the teahouse of the Garden Hotel he stays in so as to gain a feeling of being the host instead of the guest.

## 2.4.6  The Importance of Team Solidarity

Whenever possible, the chief negotiator should have full control over the selection of negotiation team members. There can be no disputes over the chief negotiator's authority.

However, if success is to be attained, unified effort should be made because of the rivalry nature of international negotiations. While team members will have varying levels of authority and responsibility, all directions must come from the chief negotiator.

Lastly, because of the need for centralized decision-making, it's wise to appoint a second in command (in case illness or calamity should befall the chief negotiator).

The ideal person to head up or to assume responsibility for negotiating efforts should:

· Be thoughtful and sensitive to the feeling of others.

· Understand human nature.

· Be adaptive in order to satisfy the psychological needs of others.

· Not having a strong compulsion to be liked by peers.

· Be able to listen creatively and patiently.

· Be respected by the other members of the negotiation team as well as the other party.

· Be goal-oriented.

· Be highly logical, with good probability estimating and decision making abilities in order to exercise the best business judgment possible during the heat of negotiation.

## 2.5　Choice of Negotiation Venues

Generally speaking, negotiation sites can be divided into three categories: host venue, guest venue and third party's venue.

### 2.5.1　Host Venue

Host venues can be one party's own country, own city or own office building or any other places where the party hosts the negotiation.

As the host party, it can enjoy several advantages that it may not otherwise:

(1) Waiting at ease for exhausted counterpart.

(2) Familiar surroundings with no novel and foreign attractions distracting its members' from their tasks.

(3) Assistance ready at hand.

(4) And feeling of security, comfort and relaxation.

(5) It saves you money and traveling time.

The host side may also create pressure or obstacles to its counterpart if there is the necessity by making use of the decoration of the meeting room, accommodation and other devices.

Comparatively speaking host venue enjoys more advantages than other choices because the host party can benefit from all those favorable conditions as they are described by an old Chinese saying: good timing, favorable geographical location and support at hand from people all around.

### 2.5.2　Guest Venue

When negotiations take place at counterpart's country, city or office buildings, they are conducted at guest venues. For the guest part, almost all advantages enjoyed are reversed to be barriers and difficulties. In such cases the guest party has to be more patient, steadfast and perseverant.

Going to your opposer's home territory also has advantages:

(1) You can devote your full time to the negotiation without the distractions and interruptions that your office may produce;

(2) You can withhold information, stating that it is not immediately available. The inconvenience to sufficient information for sound judgment and absence of authority for a decision can always be explored as acceptable excuses for asking for a halt or even withdrawal from the on-going negotiation.

(3) You might have the option of going over your opposer's head to someone in his higher management.

(4) The burden of preparation is on the opposer and he is not free from other duties.

There are also cases when one party can host negotiation but gives it up for obtaining some petty benefits chance to go abroad for a trip.

### 2.5.3 The Third Party's Venue

The negotiation is held neither in the host party's places nor in the guest party's locality, but rather in the third party's place which is directly or indirectly related with the two parties. The third party's site is preferred frequently out of the following concerns:

(1) Historic events and modern international affairs, numerous cases have illustrated the importance and necessity of choosing a third place when dialogue channel between two adversary parties is blocked. The famous long lasting Middle East Peace Talks between Israel and Palestine has almost been conducted in a third place, usually in the United States.

(2) When a negotiation goes into an impasse and there is no sign of rapprochement, it is apparent that it would be impossible to carry on such negotiation in either party's places. A third place has to be considered if the two sides wish to resolve their conflicts through peaceful means.

(3) A third place has to be chosen due to the dispute that both parties demand strongly to the negotiation. Therefore, a place of neutrality is the only choice for settling the disputes.

### 2.5.4 Decorations of the Negotiation Sites

There is an art in the decorations of the negotiation sites, which seems to be done in more exquisite taste than for domestic business negotiations, but it is not necessarily the case for all. Some formal negotiations for large projects do have some requirements about the choice of the negotiation tables and the seating of the negotiation staff.

In some relatively formal international business negotiations, the properness of the negotiation location decorations can reflect the management level of the host party to some extent. If the host party does not know the correct seating of the negotiation location according to the international practice, it is hard to say the host party is an expert in negotiation. Therefore, some veteran negotiators judge whether the counterpart has negotiation experience and how much attention the other party has paid based on the decorations and settings of the negotiation location.

(1) Setting of Rectangular Tables

Rectangular tables are usually used in business negotiations with both parties sitting on each side: the host party sits behind the door or on the left of the door; and the other members all sit on the fight or the left of the chief negotiator of each party according to their ranks so as to communicate and support each other more easily.

(2) Setting of Square Tables

The major negotiators sit face to face with the host party sitting behind the door or on the led of the door. All the members sit on the right or the left of their chief negotiator from each party. If there is not enough space, they can sit around the square table.

(3) Setting of Round Tables

The major negotiators sit face to face with the host party sitting behind the door or on the left of the door. All the staff sit on the fight or the left of the major negotiator of each party according to the ranks or they can sit in a circle.

Square tables and round tables are suitable for relatively small-sized negotiators.

In fact, some international business negotiations often adopt a casual way of seating, even without a negotiation table: only a coffee table in the middle, or both parties sit on the same couch. The above forms are fit for small scale and informal negotiations between regular clients.

(4) Other Facilities and Equipment

Chairs: chairs should match the negotiation table in style and color. They should be comfortable to sit in because too soft and sunken chairs will make people sleepy and distracted.

Demonstration boards: they can be used to demonstrate figures and explain cases directly. To be fastidious, the negotiation room may be furnished with an electronic inductor board with printing capacity. Or a black or white board with writing pens is equipped.

Projectors: they can be used to demonstrate figures, pictures or information. Usually a reflection projector or a computerized project will be used.

Other devices: ashtrays, pad, boshes or ball pens, paper folders, tea, coffee, boiled water, iced water and so on.

We'd better not use the tape recorder unless we have asked for the permssion.

## 2.6 Negotiators Check List

Let's look at a negotiators check list to see how we might better prepare for our negotiations. Issues we've discussed in this chapter, as well as some aspects added, will be reflected in following questions:

(1) What Kind of Negotiation is it?

There are basically 3 circumstances to consider:

①Is it a one-time negotiation, where we will unlikely interact with the person or company again?

②Is it a negotiation that we are going to repeat?

③Is it a negotiation where we are going to form some kind of long term relationship?

Most of our business negotiations are likely going to fall in the last two categories. We will be handling a lot of repeated negotiations, where we negotiate with regular suppliers, or engage in labor negotiations with the same union reps for example. Or, we will be seeking a long term negotiated agreement such as a joint venture, where we will be mutually entwined over a long period of time.

(2) What type of conflict will we face?

There are basically two types of conflict situations we may encounter in a negotiation. Conflicts can present themselves singularly, or may be a mixture of the two. It is vital that the negotiator carefully analyze the conflict issues, both individually and collectively, to fully appreciate the unique challenges they present.

The first form of conflict might simply be called agreement conflict, where one person's views or position are in conflict with another individual, or members of a group. This is a situation that takes into account their conflicting views relating to opinions, beliefs, values and ideology.

For example, two executives may have different views about whether a policy should be implemented. Another example may consist of a trade dispute between two countries, and entail ideological or religious based differences. Or, the conservative viewpoints of management might conflict with the left wing approach of union leaders.

The second form of conflict entails the allocation of resources like money, quantity, production or, simply put, things. Any physical commodity will fall into this category of conflict. Other issues might entail the allocation of resources, as a separate segment of the trade dispute. Resource issues though, are more tangible as they comprise knowable items, or particular products.

One blaring example occurs when subsidized farmers of one country, 「dump」 cheaper products onto the market of another country, at the expense of the indigenous farmers of that country.

By analyzing the types of conflict into categories, negotiators can have a better understanding of the real measure of the disputes, and frame or focus their strategies more effectively.

(3) What does this negotiation mean to us?

There are only two reasons why we enter into a negotiation.

The first reason occurs when out of necessity, we have to. This could be due to either some immediate need, such as urgency to find a particular supplier, or it could be that we face severe cutbacks in personnel, if we can't increase our business.

The second reason occurs when we are seeking out an opportunity. This situation may arise simply because an opportunity has sprung up, where we can increase our overall business at an opportune time.

The reason for entering into a negotiation will affect both our approach and strategy, and also our relative negotiating power in comparison to our counterpart.

(4) Are there any ripple effects?

We also need to ask ourselves whether the results of the negotiation we are conducting, will affect other negotiations or agreements later. Many companies today have international interests. An agreement with a company in one country, may affect how talks will impact or be influenced, with negotiations that will transpire later with other countries. It's vital that we, as negotiators, consider the impact or consequences of an agreement in developing our strategy.

(5) Do we need to make an agreement?

We either enter into negotiations because we have to, or because we want to. Part of our strategy will involve a careful analysis of our BATNA. If an agreement is absolutely essential, and we have few alternative options, in the event of talks collapsing, this will affect our strategy. Or, if the negotiated agreement is not essential because we have a strong option, and can walk away with confidence, this also influences the approach to our strategy.

(6) Do other parties need to formally approve the agreement?

Many agreements made during the negotiated process require formal approval, or ratification before an agreement is official. A board of directors, CEO, stakeholders, or other outside constituents, may need to review and ratify an agreement, before it comes into effect.

(7) Is the clock ticking?

Time has an impact on the course of negotiations from two perspectives. Firstly, there are deadlines that might be imposed, to either make or break an agreement. Offers with expiry dates may be tendered. Secondly, we all know that 「time is money」. Negotiations use up time, and if a plant is shut down while the clock is ticking because of a strike, then this is costing money. Or, it could be due to some other resource issue, such as waiting for badly needed components, in order to resume production. The point to remember is that if we drag the negotiations out too long, time will negatively affect the bottom line.

(8) Your place or mine?

In much the same way as sports teams enjoy a 「home advantage」, negotiators playing away from home need to adjust their game plan and strategies. There are 3 possibilities to consider when deciding where the talks will occur. We can either hold the talks in their offices, our offices, or at a neutral domain. We might choose the latter so no one has the psychological and resource advantage of holding the negotiations on their premises. Sometimes, deciding upon where the negotiations take place can open up a whole new can of worms, especially in the case of international disputes for example.

(9) Will we be under the public microscope?

Negotiations are often private affairs with little fanfare, until an agreement is signed. There are also agreements that are advertised afterwards, to maximize the mutual benefit both sides obtain. On other occasions, negotiations may be held in strict secrecy.

Then, there are the highly publicized occasions when the press becomes actively involved. It could be that one of the negotiating parties uses the powers of the press, to lever an advantage to sway and manipulate the outcome. We need only to scan the daily newspapers, to understand the importance of how public involvement can influence and add intense pressure to some negotiations. The press can be utilized as a public forum to embarrass our opponents into action, or to deflect their strategy. Press releases are another means to use as an effective strategy in the negotiation process.

(10) Will we need a third party?

Third parties have many different functions and roles to play in developing a negotiation strategy. They may act as agents, intermediaries, translators, consultants, or other specialists who have an expertise, that one or both parties require. There are occasions when a neutral third party will act as a facilitator or chairperson, to manage the negotiations such as in multi-party negotiations, inter organizational negotiations, or even international negotiations.

Then, there are the other occasions when we hit a road block, or impasse in our negotiation. During these times we may use a neutral third party to act as a mediator or an arbitrator, to either facilitate an agreement or to impose an agreement, such as in a labor dispute for example.

(11) Who is going to blink first?

There are situations when we have to decide how a proposal or offer is to be presented, or in deciding who is going to go first. Will we make an informal proposal before we start the negotiations, or wait until we meet face to face? Will we be prepared to make an offer after listening to their proposal, or do we need more information? Will we respond right away, or refer the matter to our constituencies? Will it be to our advantage to be first in making an offer or proposal, to set an anchor around which the talks revolve? Or will it be better to hold our cards tight to our chest and let the other side go first? Of course, this will all relate to the issues, positions, goals and objectives that will determine our approach. These are very serious questions that we need to intelligently address, before we begin our talks.

(12) Who are the decision makers?

Before we enter into the negotiations, we must establish who is going to make the decisions. What is our authority and who do we report to in our organization? Similarly, what are the authority levels of our counterparts? Finally, can we make an agreement in principle, or an unofficial agreement that will likely stand the test of scrutiny?

(13) How far will we push it?

Negotiations can be a one shot occurrence where one party comes right out and says: 「This is a one-time offer—take it or leave it.」There are some instances where haggling is not considered acceptable, and will not be tolerated by the other party. Other situations will drag out into the equivalent of a marathon ping-pong match, as each party bounces offers and counter offers, back and forth between them. We need to know who we are dealing with, before we get too cute and find ourselves cut out of the opportunity altogether. It also depends on the offer and proposal, in relation to the circumstances such as time considerations, need, and many other factors.

(14) Are we strong or weak?

Two or more parties who are about to engage in a negotiation, seldom operate from an equal power base. If one party has something that we desperately need, for our company's survival and we have no alternatives, then we may find ourselves negotiating at a disadvantage. This all relates to our BATNA and how we stack up against our potential counterpart. Size is not necessarily relevant, as we've all heard the old biblical account of 「David versus Goliath」, and how that conflict turned out.

Weakness can be countered by strengthening our BATNA, or even by finding allies to support our position and add to our strength. Also, we should seek ways to diminish the power base of the opposing party where possible, before we begin our negotiations, or even during the negotiation process itself.

## Case Study

A company in Suzhou hoped to tab into the market of South Africa. Out of consideration of cautiousness, they sent a mission to the country for field survey.

The meeting with the general manager was arranged in a well. Lighted and carefully furnished room in a superb office mansion. The mission was received at the gate of the elevator and immediately led to the meeting room by a smiling lady.

The general manger, having an expensive cigar between his fingers and wearing confident expression in his face, introduced his company and his way of management in a detailed and enthusiastic manner.

The introduction and the whole atmosphere convinced the mission of their partner's financial strength and so as soon as they back to China. they sent the first batch of goods worth more than 1 million USD to their 「rich」 partner, but they did not receive anything in return.

Only some time later did they find out what they saw in the room was a carefully arranged 「trap」:

The fatty general manager was an invited local actor and the receptionist lady was the real manager, and the furnished and decorated meeting room was leased for this special purpose.

## Exercises

(1) What kind of role does information play in international business negotiations?
(2) How do we collect the data and information of the negotiation counterpart?
(3) How do we establish the negotiation goals or targets?
(4) How do we design the agenda for business negotiations?
(5) What kinds of problems should we pay attention to when we arrange the negotiation sites?

# Chapter 3　　The Process of Negotiation

## 3.1　Negotiation Atmosphere and Opening Steps

  The international business atmosphere refers to the atmosphere and the surroundings that one or both parties create before the negotiation starts, which can reflect the frankness, national characteristics, cultural attributes, style choice and psychological implications of one party or both parties. Good negotiation atmosphere will help the negotiation proceed smoothly; on the contrary, bad negotiation atmosphere will affect the course of the negotiation or even destroy the whole negotiation.

### 3.1.1　The Function of Negotiation Atmosphere

  The main purpose of multi-national business negotiation is to make the biggest profit; therefore, the negotiation atmosphere is mostly positive, friendly and constructive. However, some negotiations are aimed to solve the intricate trade conflicts or hope to force the other party to make concessions to sacrifice their interests. Under these conflicting circumstances, the negotiation atmosphere tends to be tense and contradictory.

  The negotiators taking part in international business negotiations are people from different countries. They are people; thus they have different characters and personality traits; they follow their own norms; and they are exposed to different cultures, beliefs, national attributes, religions, political environments, experiences, and family and education backgrounds. The special atmosphere and surroundings always have an immediate effect on people's moods: on the contrary, the attitudes and moods of the negotiators, in turn, also influence the negotiation atmosphere and influence the course and result of the negotiation.

  Different negotiation atmospheres have different impacts on the negotiations. There are positive and friendly, tense and contradictory, brief and straightforward, dilatory and protracted, cold and perfunctory and sedate and reserved negotiation atmosphere and so on.

### 3.1.2　Administer the Meeting Agenda

  Since there are usually language barriers in the course of international business negotiations or though both parties can use the same language, in order to improve the efficiency and to demonstrate respect and equality, the host party often provides a negotiation agenda to every representative printed in the language chat both parties understand. The main contents of the agenda are the schedules of the meetings, the subjects of the meetings and the profiles of the representatives. This can assure the appropriate progress of the negotiation, save some recording time and make the representatives more concentrate on listening to the statements of the other party and have a clear picture of the details and key points of the negotiation.

### 3.1.3 Opening Statements

Before the substantive negotiation, both parties always have to make a formal opening statement to clarify the basic principle regarding the discussion issues at stake with an emphasis on the self-interests (gains and losses) of both parties from the negotiation. The function of opening statements is to clarify the viewpoints, create advantageous atmosphere for the party and explore the reaction of the other party. For example, IBM Company emphasized to the Leela Palace Hotel that it was quite important to make sure that all IBM executives and technicians to India on their business trip have rooms to stay at any time, for it was vital to the corporate operation as it would affect the development of IBM in Bangalore. The representatives from the hotel stated that they paid much attention to IBM company and hoped to develop a long-term relationship with it, but they could only use annual quota and price lever to allocate the quota of the rooms under the situation that not any new hotels had ever been built. In this way, they could assure their own benefits and meet the needs of their key clients at the same time as they could. Therefore, we can see that IBM wanted to assure the number of the rooms as well as get the preferential prices. The hotel thought IBM was a large powerful company, so as long as it paid proper prices, the number of the rooms could be guaranteed. After the statements by both parties, IBM company realized that the number of the rooms and the prices would be the key point of the negotiation in the following discussion. The hotel also realized that they could neither charge too much to offend the key client, nor could they be too obedient so as to lose the excess profits that originally belonged to them.

Three points ought to be paid attention to in the opening statements:

(1) Contents of Opening Statements

In the opening statements, the opinions of both parties should be clearly stated. When you make an opening statement on behalf of your side, the contents of your statement usually include the following aspects:

①your party's understanding of the problems that have been discussed in the opening phase;

②the interests and assurance that your own party hopes to obtain in the negotiation (including the problem of principles that your party will not compromise, concede or yield);

③the parts that your party is willing to discuss with the other party (releasing signals for the potential concession);

④the benefits your party have brought to the other party in the previous cooperation (implying that the other party ought to have the gratitude and make compromises and concessions in turn);

⑤the possible opportunities and obstacle that will arise in the future negotiation and cooperation.

(2) Methods for Delivering Opening Statements

Negotiators usually choose different methods to present their opening statements in response to the different issues for discussion and different negotiating counterparts. A varied choice of statement methods can create a varied atmosphere for the negotiation.

(3) Proper Reactions When One Party Listens to the Statements of the Other Party

When the other party makes statements, our party should do the following things:

①Form a clear picture of the rival's opinion and ask them questions to clarify every point that we are not clear;

②Try to take notes while listening to them, and write down their arguments but do not argue, attack or question them immediately;

③We should be good at summarizing the points of the other party and make the key points of the negotiation stand out;

④Don't ask any aggressive questions when they are making the statement;

⑤Give a summing-up speech at the end to review and show your concern for the interests of all the relevant parties; propose a highly feasible and thorough solution to make the negotiation prospect expectant.

## 3.2　Opening Strategies

Opening strategies are the measures that negotiators take to gain an upper hand in the opening phase so as to in turn secure their control over the negotiation elements.

Various strategies are utilized in international business negotiations from the beginning to the end. If we can give free play to our strategies at the very outset of the negotiation, it will help us enhance the atmosphere beneficial to our side, enabling us to take the initiative in the negotiation so as to control the pace and direction of the negotiation as well as affect the ultimate results of the negotiation.

(1) Resonant Opening

Resonant opening is also known as one-paragraph opening strategy. At the beginning of a negotiation, this tactic allows negotiators to use an「assertive」tone to build up a kind of「resonance」so that under this friendly and harmonious environment both parties can work together to push the negotiation forward.

Psychological studies show that people tend to favor those who share the same opinion with them and are willing to adapt their opinions to those of the people who have「resonance」or identify with them. This is the psychological basis for 「resonance」 opening strategies.

Resonant opening can be used with the aim of creating conditions for the other party to agree with us. The commonly-used ways of resonant opening are conferring approach, inquiring approach and complementing approach.

①Conferring approach suggests that we ask for the opinions of the other party with a kind tone to boost discussion toward our goals (in fact, we have a clear picture in mind), then we approve of their proposals and are willing to follow their proposals (as it is the same with ours) to proceed with our work. But we need to pay attention: when we agree with the other party, we should not make the other party feel flattered, but let them feel we agree with them because we identify with them and we understand and share their ideas.

②Inquiring approach is to design your answer in the form of a question to induce your counterpart to movetoward the goal that you have set. For example, you may ask them questions like 「How do you think about the idea that we put the price terms aside and come to them at the end of the negotiation?」

③Complementing approach encourages you to avail yourself of the opportunity to add your own opinions to that of the other party and talk them around to your way of thinking and let them speak in your voice, much like what is advocated in *The Arts of War* by Sun Tzu—replace the beams and change the pillars—let your words penetrate his skull so that he would say what you want to say. We'd better use resonance opening in natural atmosphere or high-spirit atmosphere. Good use of resonance opening can turn the natural atmosphere to high – spirit atmosphere. But the use of resonance opening under low-spirit atmosphere tends to make ourselves embarrassed and passive.

(2) Frank Opening

Frank Opening refers to the way in which we convey our opinions to the other party frankly so as to make a breakthrough in the negotiations.

This kind of strategy is usually used between regular clients because it can save lots of courtesies and time, and we can put forward our opinions and requirements directly, which may also make our partners trust us more.

Frank opening also applies to the party with weak negotiation Power. When we are quite clear about each other's strengths and weaknesses, frankly revealing our weaknesses to the other party can help us gain the understanding and leave a good impression on the other party if we demonstrate our sincerity in this way.

(3) Evasive Opening

Evasive opening strategy, also referred to as reserved opening strategy, means that at the beginning of the negotiation, we do not answer some key questions raised by the other party definitely, directly or explicitly, but try to avoid or reserve the information too much and too soon, so that the other party will generate a feeling of mystery, then as they are wondering what we intend to do, they will follow our plan, driving the negotiation advance to the direction we desire and target.

There are some prerequisites for us to use evasive opening strategy: Firstly, we are quite confident about our competitiveness. Secondly, we should be good at deploying resources. Additionally, we should not disobey the game principles of international business negotiations, i.e. we should be trustworthy and should not convey false information, otherwise once revealed, not only will we be trapped in embarrassment, but also we will possibly lose our good reputation and business as well.

Evasive opening is usually used in the negotiations which begin with a natural and low-spirit atmosphere rather than high-spirit atmosphere. But it can turn the atmosphere of other negotiations to low-spirit ones.

(4) Nitpicking Opening

Nitpicking opening refers to the way in which at the very early beginning of the negotiation, we blame the other party for their bad manners, diplomatic and cultural mistakes severely so as to bring a sense of guilt to them and to create tension, to confuse them, to suppress their requests and to force the other party to make compromises and concessions.

However, nitpicking opening should not be used too casually, and it should be used according to the real situation. For example, our power is weak and we need the support from the other party. In this case, we should deal with the problem with a little tolerance. No tolerance, no happiness. Another example is when the other party encounters suicide bombing by terrorists and comes late due to the blockade made by the police. Under this situation, then, we should give them understanding rather than unreasonable blaming.

(5) Offensive Opening

Quite different from the tactics that we use to attack our counterpart when we chance upon their faults or weaknesses occasionally, offensive opening refers to the way in which we express our firm attitude through well prepared speech or behavior so as to gain the awe from the rival and force them to start the negotiation in accordance with our intention.

As offensive opening will get the negotiation trapped in a competitive, nervous and tense atmosphere from the beginning, hurt the other party easily and affect the ongoing of the negotiation, it should not be used casually and carelessly. Usually when we find the other party intentionally create low-spirit atmosphere to hinder the bargaining of our side and undermine our benefits or interests, offensive opening can be considered as a tool to put an end to the adverse opening situation for the better.

One thing that should be pointed out is that business negotiations of different types, with different rivals, and in different countries or areas need different opening strategies. We should thoroughly consider the relationships between each other and the strength of the other party. If we have repeat business and are in harmony with our partners for many years, flank opening ought to be applied; if we have general relationships with our partners, resonance opening can be used to create a friendly and harmonious atmosphere; if the previous cooperation was not smooth, then faultfinding opening can be applied; for the first meeting, resonance opening is applicable to eliminate the strangeness between each other and create a sincere and friendly atmosphere.

The choice of opening strategies is derived from the comparison of the powers between the two parties. Generally speaking, there are three situations: if two sides are evenly matched in power or strength, resonance opening can be used to eliminate the alertness or vigilance of the other party and discourage them to issue a challenge to a verbal duel; if we are powerful and in a strong position, offensive opening with a combination of flexibility and yielding can be attempted to play down the high expectation of the other party while efforts should be made not to scare the other party away if we are relatively weak and not powerful, flank opening is applicable which may help invoke the other party's understanding of our situation or at least make them not look down upon us.

## 3.3 Bidding and Bargaining

This stage covers a broad period of bargaining in which concessions are made and advantages are gained, so that the gap between the two sides is narrowed to a point.

Disagreement and conflict are commonplace in negotiations. If you're wise, you'll learn from these; they reveal something about the interests of the other side. Consequently, you should expect and welcome this phase of negotiations. Handling conflict effectively will bring the parties together; handling it poorly will divide them.

When presenting issues, most negotiators will tell you what they 「want」. It is your job to find out what they 「need」 or will settle for. Few negotiators get everything they want. It might be in your best interest to occasionally compromise or modify your goals as you learn more. In fact, it's best to remain flexible throughout the negotiating process.

In reality, negotiations rarely follow a neat, linear progression. For instance, 「getting to know each other」 is not confined to the opening of the process; the savvy negotiator continues to learn more about the other side until the very end. Likewise, disagreement and conflict are liable to occur at any time. Nevertheless, we should also admit that bargaining is like a ritual that generally proceeds through an ordered set of steps:

(1) Design and offer options;
(2) Introduce criteria to evaluate options;
(3) Estimate reservation points;
(4) Explore alternatives to agreement;
(5) Making concession or compromising.

◎ Design and Offer Options

Once both sides' interests are designated, it is time for negotiators to set forth suggestions and options for how to address the issues. Options reflect negotiators' consideration, suggestions and conditions for a solution. For example, in business negotiation, your offer, counter offer and firm offer are part of your option. It's crucial for negotiators to work out a well-prepared option, especially for complicated negotiations. Negotiation options may include the objectives of negotiation, terms and schedules. It is understandable that before exchange of each other's perceptions and views the options express basically each side's own views and understanding of how to carry on the negotiation.

◎ Introduce Criteria to Evaluate Options

Suggested options will be examined and evaluated by different criterion by each side. Every negotiator has their own criterion for evaluating the options based on their own value system. As in a daily transaction of buying a shirt, the seller, who is in a favorable position, gives his first offer order to test the market knowledge of the buyer, who in turn has to trust her common knowledge on products like this to make her decision if she is lack of sufficient knowledge of the products. The buyer can improve her bargaining power after she has visited several sellers.

The disparity of the criterion by the two parties is due to the fact that both parties wish to maximize their own interests; therefore it is on this stage that conflicts of interests of two sides will confront and clash with each other, which will surely incite argument and contradiction.

◎ Estimate Reservation Points

What negotiating parties do next is to gauge how big the gap is between their demand and the counter party's demand. When the gap of discrepancy cannot be bridged at all, or in other words, if the bottom lines of negotiator's requests cannot be satisfied, then it is time to walk away and leave negotiation table and announce break of the negotiation.

The reservation point means the target that negotiators have to achieve for assurance of their basic interests. In the long process of negotiating into the WTO, China set a few principles, one of which was to join the WTO as a developing country. China would rather stay outside the WTO if these basic principles were not met. However, bottom line should not be viewed as fixed and will mislead negotiators to get closer to the minimum of their interests. The reservation point only sets out one's own basic interests, and to maximize one's interests is the final target of all negotiators.

This reminds us of the concept that we mentioned in the previous chapter: BATNA.

◎ Explore Alternatives Agreement

Sometimes, when the disparity between the two negotiating parties seems too large to be mentioned, the negotiation is on the verge of breaking down. However, some negotiators do not want to give up easily because the failure of the negotiation means neither party can have their interests realized. There can be another way out: negotiating parties make efforts an explore alternatives to the options put forward before. A capable negotiator can always exhibit great initiatives and high ability by coming up with new options and constructive suggestions which show the concern to the interests of both parties. Quite often the final agreement of negotiations is reached based on several options.

Sometimes an opportunity for other better results can also be of great significance. An example can help to understand better. When you feel dissatisfied with your present salary and want to ask your boss to raise it, what do you hope to put in your pocket? Is it a gun or a job offer from another company that is a strong competitor to your present company?

◎ **Making Concession or Compromising**

As a result of the bargaining between the two sides, it is probable that each side will modify its original objective, reassess the potential outcomes and the time taken to achieve each of these. These will enable each side to determine the conditional value for each outcome and to estimate the probability of success. And then negotiating strategy will be selected to maximize the expected value.

In making the next move each party's concern is with the degree of commitment he attaches to any issue. On very minor points, there may be almost immediate agreement. On more significant points, both sides will reiterate and expand on their previous proposals with varying degrees of commitment, but without closing the door totally on the possibility of finding some way in which their respective viewpoints may be reconciled. The gap is gradually narrowed, and the outlines of the compromise may be clear. They are ready to move to the phase of making concessions.

At some point in the negotiations, one party may signal its willingness to compromise. If you hear statements that begin with 「Suppose that…?」 or 「What if…?」 or 「How would you feel about…?」, listen closely; the other side may be hinting at a move closer to your position. Don't try to pin the other side down quickly, because this could cause him or her to withdraw. Instead, play along and say, 「Well, there are several possibilities.」

When responding to statements of goals, positions, and offers, it's a good idea to use the reflective listening technique described earlier.

The final concession should be made at the right time, not too early or too late. For the purpose of timing it can be divided into two parts. The major part should be made at a time allowing the other party to review and consider before the deadline. One minor concession should be held as a final 「benefit」 and offered at the very last moment if it is absolutely necessary. The final concessions put emphasis on their finality.

# Case Study

When Toyota Company from Japan first came into the American markets, it wanted to find an American agency to promote the sales of its products because of its ignorance of the American markets. When the Japanese representatives went to the negotiation place appointed by an

American car dealer, they met with traffic jam and were delayed. The American representatives flew into fury and wanted to obtain more commission and other benefits. The Japanese representatives had no way to go and one stood up and said coldly (taking an offensive posture), 「Sorry to waste your time because of our lateness. However, we did not do it intentionally. We had thought the transportation in America would have been better than that in Japan, but it is really beyond our imagination (playing down the other party's posture). So it caused the unpleasantness. And we do not want to waste your valuable time any more. If you doubt our frankness for this, all we can do is to end this negotiation (launching an attack at the other party). Any way, as the terms and conditions we offer are very favorable, it will not be difficult for us to find other partners in the US (threatening the other party).」

The American representatives were shocked at what the Japanese representative said. In fact, they did not want to lose this opportunity to make money, and they only intended to threaten the Japanese party, but they failed. Then, they pulled in their horns, their anger dispersed, and they began to have the negotiation with the Japanese party at once, even-tempered and good-humored.

## Exercises

(1) What kind of impact do different negotiation atmospheres have on international business negotiation? Please cite some examples.

(2) What issues should the two sides exchange ideas about in the opening phase of a negotiation?

(3) What should we pay attention to when we make an opening statement?

(4) What factors should we consider when we design the opening strategies?

# Chapter 4　Closing the Negotiation

## 4.1　Identification and Means of Negotiation Closing

As the bargaining moves on, the parties involved are gradually agreeing on more issues. At this point, business negotiation enters the phase of making the deal, also known as the phase of closing the negotiation. How to determine if it is time for closure is a key point in this phase. If the negotiation is closed too soon, issues concerned will not be thoroughly discussed, leaving endless trouble for the future; if the best chance to close the negotiation is missed, things will change in the prolonged negotiation, resulting in the loss of the deal.

### 4.1.1　Identifying Closing Signals and Selecting Closing Approaches

Whether an international business negotiation can be concluded or not is usually decided by four factors: transaction terms and conditions, negotiation strategies, closing signals and the scheduled time period.

(1) By Transaction Terms and Conditions

This case indicates that whether a business negotiation has moved to the closing phase can be analyzed and recognized from the settlement of the terms and conditions involved in the negotiation. The following criteria will be helpful:

①one's own closing price range vs. the counterpart's proposed terms and conditions

One's closing price range refers to the terms arid conditions the least acceptable to one's party, which is the bottom line for closing a deal that one party has set beforehand. If the counterpart's terms and conditions fall within one's own range, it means the two sides are likely to conclude a deal at the lowest extent of interest. At this point, one should take the opportunity to improve this trend carefully. It would be better if one can gain more favorable terms and conditions. However, a variety of factors need to be thoroughly considered in order to avoid falling into a deadlock, resulting from one's strong desire for the best results, and thus losing a good chance to close a deal.

②the qualitative and quantitative analysis of the differing terms and conditions

Sort out the unsettled terms in proportion to the ones that both sides have agreed upon in terms of quantity. If most terms and conditions are agreed upon and only a small portion is left unsettled, it can be decided that the negotiation has basically moved to the final stage. Nevertheless, quantitative analysis is not always reliable. It is important to take qualitative factors into consideration as well. If the key issues in the transaction have been settled with only a few non-substantial ones unsettled, it can be decided that the negotiation has come to a closure. In the case above, the intended total closing prices of the two sides were already quite close to each other and the disagreement in other terms was too trivial to mention.

(2) By Negotiation Strategies

The strategies used to conclude a negotiation are called closing strategies. There are two common closing strategies:

①compromising strategy

Usually, two sides may use the strategy of meeting each other half way to continue the negotiation or make a compromise. For example, in the above case, the arms dealer from Country A reduced the total price of the riot gear to $77 million while the purchaser from Country B was only willing to pay $76 million. To close the negotiation as soon as possible, the purchaser proposed that they meet each other half way and each side give up $500 thousand; if the counterpart accepts it, it becomes clear that the negotiation has come to an end. This strategy is a quick way to settle differences when the negotiating parties insist on their own terms and conditions. However, it should be used only after several rounds of bargaining and when the difference between their demands has been reduced to certain extent. Using it too early or when there is a big difference tends to encourage the counterpart to ask for more concessions. As a result, the party using this strategy may land itself in a passive position or may have to sacrifice more interests.

②the ultimatum strategy

When two sides still cannot reach an agreement after many rounds of negotiation, one side shows its hand: either close the deal at the conditions granted in their compromise or declare the failure of negotiation. This ultimatum obviously can be viewed as a signal to close the negotiation. It is very risky to use this strategy. The key is to seize the right time. Only after both sides have made adequate bargaining offers can one side use this strategy, and then only if they have made a considerably great compromise and are sure that the other side does not want to see the negotiation break down. Otherwise, one side may disclose its own bottom line too early, losing any room for leeway; on the other hand, if the other side does not want to accept it, the result is that one ruins the negotiation oneself. Thus, one cannot be too cautions in employing this strategy. In other words, it should be used with great caution.

(3) By Closing Signals

Distinct from the foregoing closing approaches, as the negotiation moves on in a high-spirited or natural atmosphere, each side has made due concessions in all aspects possible with only last details to be settled, one side then gives suggestive closing signals to induce the counterpart's acceptance. Here are some common examples used in practice:

①The negotiator tidies away the papers in his hand. This indicates: we have said all that we want to say and now it is the time to conclude the negotiation.

②The negotiator assumes a gesture of making a final decision by winding up his talk in a film tone, putting away his papers, leaning back against his armchair with arms crossed on chest and fixing his eyes on the counterpart.

③The negotiator conveys a hint of final commitment. He clarifies his party's position with some phrases indicative of commitment, such as, 「This is our final proposal. How do you like it?」

④Negotiator answers question briefly with short phrases but few arguments. He tries to answer the questions as concisely as possible, often just a simple 「yes」or 「no」, indicating there is no room for making any compromise.

⑤The negotiator informs the other party of good reasons to bring the negotiation to an end. For example, he may reassure the other side that to close the negotiation at this point is the wise choice, and also gives some good reasons.

⑥The negotiator presents a complete proposal made in absolute terms without any loose ends. However, it takes a lot of talking to convince the counterpart and everything should be clearly expressed, free from any ambiguity. Anyway, it is much gentler than the 「ultimatum」 strategy, leading to the same result: the counterpart should accept the proposal and sign the contract, or refuses it to terminate the negotiation.

(4) By Negotiation Time

①by negotiation time mutually set beforehand

Before or at the outset of the negotiation, all the parties concerned confer to decide together how long the negotiation should take. Then the negotiation proceeds as agreed. When the bargaining approaches the time limit, the negotiation enters a natural phase of closing. The advantages of closing the negotiation at the agreed time are higher negotiation efficiency and avoidance of prolonging the negotiation without any results. Its disadvantage is that if the negotiator yields to the pressure of time, he may be unable to make a thorough consideration, leaving a hidden peril. It is advisable not to force oneself to reach an agreement within the scheduled time period. The negotiator can bring the negotiation to a temporary close and arrange time for additional negotiation or declare that the negotiation has broken down.

②by negotiation time set beforehand by one side

Usually, it is the powerful side or the one whose interests require that the negotiation be closed within a certain time limit that first puts forward an idea about the negotiation time. This side will tell or request the counterpart in consultation the time when they hope to conclude the negotiation. Obviously, one side setting the negotiation schedule apparently imposes some pressure on the counterpart. Of course, the counterpart can accept it, or raise conditions for 「exchange」, to gain more favorable conditions in exchange for their cooperation in setting the negotiation dine limit. If one party sets the negotiation time limit in order to put pressure on the counterpart, it may arouse strong resentment in the counterpart, destroy the negotiation atmosphere and make the negotiation break down.

③by the time when sudden change occurs

During the course of negotiation, something might prop up, for example, a sudden change of market price, an unforeseen event inside the company, natural or man-made calamities and the like, and so one side or both sides have to conclude the negotiation before the due time. This change of negotiation time caused by sudden change of outside factors is not one side's subjective desire. There are three methods available to handle it: one is to cut the Gordian knot and establish a quick agreement if the present terms and conditions are acceptable; the other is to terminate the negotiation and restart it at another time, or to totally give it up.

## 4.1.2　Three Approaches to Concluding the Negotiation

There are three approaches available to close an international business negotiation: closing the deal, suspending the negotiation and breaking off the negotiation.

(1) Closing the Deal

When the negotiating parties have reached an agreement on all the terms and conditions for the deal or had no substantial disagreement about most teens and conditions, it can be declared that they have closed the deal. This is symbolized by a highly binding and operational contract that all the parties participating in the negotiation have signed. Methods of closing the deal vary in international business negotiation since it takes place in different countries and at different times, and concerns different subjects and contents. In some counties or regions, an oral agreement can serve as a binding contract in accordance with their business practices, depending on how well the negotiating parties know each other. No matter what forms of agreement have been reached, they all provide principles and guidelines under which all the parties will carry out the deal.

(2) Suspending the Negotiation

When the negotiating parties fail to settle an agreement over all terms or issues, one party may announce that they will suspend the negotiation or all the parties may agree to suspend the negotiation for a while. The negotiation can be suspended until a fixed date or indefinitely.

Suspension with a fixed resumption date refers to setting a fixed date for all parties to resume the negotiation when they suspend the negotiation. This suspension happens when the parties involved have the intention to close the deal, but due to the limited authorities, they have to consult their respective higher authorities for further instructions. Doing so can create necessary conditions for restarting the negotiation.

Suspension without a fixed resumption date means that when they decide to suspend the negotiation, the parties do not set a specific date for reopening the negotiation. This suspension is clearly aimed to「freeze」the negotiation. It occurs when the negotiating parties have conflicting options, or their national strategies or market prices are undergoing dramatic changes, but even so they do not want to give up the negotiation completely. The first kind of suspension is a proactive 「cold treatment」, but the second one is a reluctant course, taken due to outside pressure. As to when to restart the negotiation, it can only be described as 「as soon as the market price is acceptable...」, 「as soon as the policy allows...」 or 「to resume the negotiation when we find an opportunity in the future.」 Note that since it is a suspended negotiation it should not take too long to resume it and the parties concerned should keep contact with each other.

(3) Breaking Off the Negotiation

After chains of bargaining, the negotiating parties still cannot reach all agreement about the major terms and conditions for their business transaction. It becomes meaningless to continue the negotiation. Nothing can be done but to declare that the negotiation has broken down. Based on the attitude each party has taken toward the breakdown, it can terminate in a friendly or antagonistic atmosphere.

In a friendly breakdown of negotiation, the negotiating parties understand each other's difficulties and thus conclude the negotiation in a friendly manner. This breakdown does not hurt their relationship and leaves an opportunity for future cooperation. To conclude the negotiation in such a friendly way demonstrates the negotiation spirit of 「keeping amiable and genteel even when you fail to strike a contract」.

Antagonistic breakdown of negotiation takes place when one party or all parties become angry and declare the closure of negotiation in a hostile manner without any agreement. Causes of such a breakdown include improper attitude, language and behavior of one side, the counterpart's refusal of one's highball tactics, or accusing each other of lack of sincerity. Concluding the negotiation in this way tends to destroy the relationship and makes it difficult to cooperate again in the future. Therefore, this kind of situation should be avoided in international business negotiation. Here is a helpful approach: keep one's head, do not use extreme language to attack the counterpart and close the negotiation gracefully and politely.

## 4.2　Tactics Towards Agreement

### 4.2.1　Recessing

By recessing we mean taking a short break during which each party moves out of the negotiation forum to reconsider the progress of the negotiation, and to reconsider its own position; or breaking off until a later session. Recessing is such an important device that the method of using it deserves to be examined. When do we use it? How do we arrange it? How do we restart?

At what time should we use our recess?

(1) At the end of a phase in the negotiations. That is:

(2) Before issue identification. It is strongly advocated to open negotiations in a manner designed to breed cooperation to mutual advantage. But this strategy needs to be checked before becoming too deeply embroiled. If in doubt, take a recess.

(3) When nearing an impasse. As long as we aim towards agreement, such a recess can be used to look for means together to tackle the problem that is facing the parties in their negotiation.

Under these conditions, great advantages can be gained from using the recess not for the parties to separate but for the parties to mix. Sub-groups of technical people, commercial people and financial people from either side are aiming to obtain some constructive move for the negotiations as a whole.

(4) Team maintenance needs. When the members of the party need to review their effectiveness as a team.

(5) Breaking a Rough. When concentration has lapsed and needs regenerating.

What is the recommended procedure to get a recess?

(1) State the need for a recess.「I think it would help our joint progress if we took a short recess now.」

(2) Summarize and look forward.「We're seeking to find ways to agree on the price/discount issues, and I suggest that we both look to see if we can see new ways to cope with the issue.」

(3) Agree on the duration of the recess.「… Would fifteen minutes be agreeable?」

(4) Avoid fresh issues. If others want to insert anything further, ask them to wait until after the recess.

During the recess, the main items for consideration by a party will be obvious discussions about how to handle the next stage, calculations on matters that have been discussed, reviews of the team's performance, or fresh plans for the rest of the negotiation.

After the recess, the meeting is re-opened with a miniature version of the steps that are taken to open a negotiation.

· A few moments of ice-breaking, as we again attune our wavelengths.

· Re-state the progress made on agreed plan.

· Confirm rest of agreed plan or suggest/agree changes to it.

· Re-opening statement, defining positions and interests as they are now perceived and paving the way to further creative development.

Recessing is potentially a very influential device. Disciplined use can make it a device that helps us towards profitable co-operation.

### 4.2.2 Setting Deadlines

Defining the time by which a negotiation meeting must have finished. (「I am booked on the 11:40 plane」); or the deadline for a series of negotiations (「I'm instructed to offer this to ABC Company if we cannot agree before 14 March」). These are seen as threats. They can cause resentment and counter-aggression.

However, if the deadline is agreed upon by the two parties (not simply imposed by one of them) then the atmosphere becomes more collaborative. Contrast the first quotation above and the following:

「It would be a great help to me if we were able to conclude this meeting in time to catch the 11:40 plane. Would it be all right with you if we aim to move at that speed?」

There are positive implications for setting a deadline for the negotiations. The setting of a deadline helps to concentrate the mind, the energy, the effort, and the speed of achievement.

There is, however, a negative influence if either party feels a deadline has been imposed too early.

### 4.2.3 Full Disclosure/The Straightforward Statement

Literally, this means complete readiness to give to the other party all one's information. In practice, there will always be some elements people are unwilling to disclose and some other elements they are unable to disclose. We therefore have to interpret 「full disclosure」 as meaning the disclosure of 90 percent of what we perceive.

There are some negotiators whose character is strongly inclined towards openness and frankness. This pattern of behavior can be highly productive, inducing the other party to respond and to cooperate. 「Full disclosure」 then becomes an advantage, providing that it is used in conjunction with all the skills of negotiation towards agreement. It is, of course, a fatal disadvantage when 「full disclosure」 is offered to others whose sole interest lies in their own advantage.

The straightforward statement that one cannot offer the full price asked, or cannot afford to wait the full delivery time, if true, is constructive. It is an element of full disclosure and it enables the parties together to concentrate on the problem and to search for solutions.

The same tactic, 「All I've got is 60 percent...」 can of course be differently used by one party to get independent advantage.

### 4.2.4 Lubrication/The Golf Club

Lubrication is an art. It may be more or less subtle. It is not necessarily the same as bribery. There are plenty of different ways of offering inducements to negotiators. In form and extent, the pattern varies from one region to another and it needs local expertise to manage the process. In some cultures lubrication is an essential ingredient from negotiating towards agreement. It is an ingredient a skilled negotiator must provide for, even when he himself is not the right person to handle it.

The Golf Club is a tactic to be used at times when the teams are reaching stalemate and progress is interrupted. The tactic is for the team leaders to agree to meet informally in some environment that encourages mutual trust and openness.

For many people that atmosphere of mutual trust and respect is found in the Golf Club. For Englishmen, it is found in the Gentlemen's Club. For Finns, it is in the sauna. For Japanese, it is found in the bathhouse.

This tactic has positive advantages in refreshing the cooperative spirit between the parties, in enabling them to recognize issues in common, and in providing time and opportunity for new initiatives to develop.

One disadvantage is that the team leaders are seen to be operating independently of their respective teams. But if used sparingly, it is a productive tactic.

### 4.2.5  The Study Group

When the negotiations between teams get bogged down, it is then helpful to set up a subgroup. For example, when matters are reaching an impasse over delivery, then the production people from the suppliers can form a sub-group with one or two members of the purchasers to find means of resolving the delivery problem to their mutual advantage.

At the same time the main parties are freed to concentrate on other aspects of the negotiations or to give time to their other duties.

## 4.3  Tips on Contract Signing

When both sides have reached an agreement on the main items, it should have a written form of a contract or all agreement.

A contract is a written agreement between the two trading sides in order to itemize the right and obligations of both parties. Once signed, it has legal force. Therefore we should pay close attention to the signing of contract, discuss every item quite seriously and in a very detailed way. The following are some tips on signing a contract.

### 4.3.1  The Draft of the Contract

Once the seller and the buyer reach an agreement, it is time to draw up the contract. There is the problem of who will take the task of making the draft. Generally speaking, the side that makes the draft will be in a positive position of the whole deal, so the focus should be more on the side who makes the draft. If one side can't control making draft, they should at least be involved with the other side for this process.

Typically one party prepares the contract listing the agreed upon clauses. The other party makes amendments to the wordings to make them more closely reflect the agreement. In most countries, legal systems are not depended upon to resolve disputes. It is advisable that each should be concerned about the mutual benefits of the relationship, and consider the interest of the other. What form a contract should take may have to be negotiated depending on the situation. It depends somewhat on the size and importance of the agreement as well as the size and experiences of the firms involved. Generally, larger deals justify the extra expense of including a review by the parties' lawyers.

### 4.3.2 Examination of the Qualification of the Contract Signer and Its Trading Items, Scope and Process

A disqualified contract signer is surely a problem to the negotiation. It means the contract he signed is invalid. Therefore a thorough examination should be done to the contract signer. Find out whether the other side is eligible to do this deal, see his business license, know his business operating range and check his capabilities of undertaking business activities.

The trading items, scope and its process should be within the law and the allowance of the government policy.

The signing of the contract should also answer for the law. To ensure the validity of the contract it must go through legitimate format and perfect procedures. All the contracts that need specific procedures or the approval of a government body must be reported for approval and the corresponding procedures need to be carried out for the contract to get signed.

Since different terminology, choices of words and differences in language contribute to misunderstandings, the two sides should ensure an identical understanding of the terms to which they agree when the bargain is struck. It is difficult to make general recommendations regarding contracts. But one point that should be emphasized is that the negotiating team should push for the kind of contract most essential and suitable for the company and for legal things to be consulted on the issue.

### 4.3.3 Characteristics of an International Business Contract

(1) It is all agreement between parties from different countries or regions.

As they are from different countries or regions, the parties involved in signing the contract have to be governed or regulated by the laws prevailing in their counterpart country or region. In addition, since the contracted items are shipped across a border and are subject to customs regulations, more complicated issues are inevitably concerned, including formalities of coming into or going out of customs; import or export licenses; payment settlement; cross-border arbitration; and international protection of industrial property rights.

(2) The laws of all the parties involved are binding.

The stakeholders in an international business contract are individuals, legal entities (corporations) or institutions from different countries or region. According to the principle of national jurisdiction, the behaviors of the parties to the contract and the clauses in the contract signed by them must conform with the laws of the countries or regions they are from. Additionally, the location of the contract signing is important. The reason is that the signing site of the contract usually determines which country's laws are adopted to settle any disputes and to establish how arbitration is carried out. According to international convention, the court or arbitration organization may make the adjudication or arbitration based on the law of the country where the contract is signed should any dispute arise. To avoid unnecessary trouble, it is wise to stipulate in which country or region disputes should be settled and which laws or arbitration authority should be adopted.

(3) Contract articles must be rigid and thorough.

For the sake of effective implementation of the contract, it is a must to give thorough stipulation of the main articles concerning the trading process or damages are very likely to occur. The main articles are items about the product quality, quantity, time and place of delivery, method of delivery, time limit of delivery and the liabilities against the contract or agreement.

In real practice there are many such cases of the damages caused by ambiguous contract article. For example, a restaurant signed a contract with a vegetable company. The contract includes only a few words, specifically,「cabbages of 20,000 kilograms」. Finally at the time of delivery, it turned out that half of the cabbages rotted during transportation. In this case, the buyer has to suffer all the damages because there is not a single word mentioned concerning the quality of goods in the contract.

(4) It is affected by international political relationships.

An international business contract involves economic interactions between different countries. Therefore, the political relationship between these countries or regions as well as subtle geographic political factors may have positive or negative impacts on the implementation of the contract.

## 4.3.4　Types of International Business Contracts

(1) Classified by the Contract Signatories

①Contract between the governments of different countries or regions: for example, multilateral or bilateral agreement, etc.

②Contract between legal entities from different countries or regions: for example, the sales contract between corporations from two countries.

③Contract between the government and legal entities of different countries or regions: for example, a purchasing agreement between the government of Country A and a corporation of Country B.

④Contract between an individual and a legal entity from different countries or regions: a housing rental agreement between the owner of an apartment or house in Country A and a tenant from Country B.

⑤Contract between individuals from different countries or regions: a housing rental agreement between the owner of an apartment or house in Country A and a tenant from Country B.

(2) By the Trading Items

①sales or purchase contract

②technological trade contract

③joint venture contract and contract for cooperation

④processing trade contract

⑤finance and loan contract

⑥equity transfer contract

⑦project construction contract

⑧labor exportation contract

⑨international lease contract

⑩international contracted operation contract

(3) By the Forms of the Contract

①oral contract

An oral contract or agreement is an arrangement or promise made by the parties concerned through verbal means such as conversation in person or via telephone. Article 10 of the Contract Law of the People's Republic of China and Article Ⅱ of the United Nations Convention on Contracts for the International Sale of Goods (UNCCISG) both recognize the legal status of an oral contract. Verbal contracts are convenient and quick, but can not provide necessary evidence in case of disputes and this makes it difficult to identify where the responsibility lies. Therefore, a verbal contract is usually suitable only in cases where the contracting parties know each other well and have regular business transactions within a short time span and maintain a simple business relationship.

②written contract

A written contract is an arrangement made between the contracting parties in written form. A written contract is the major form for international business contracts. It is evidenced in writing and thus it is easy to tell which party is responsible in case of any dispute. Therefore, written contracts are usually used in deals which involve a large amount of money, complicated contents and a long time span of implementation and payment.

Common forms of written contracts are listed below:

a. Formal contract, also known as agreement: this contains full terms and conditions and complete clauses.

b. Simplified contract, also called a letter of confirmation, memorandum and order, etc. After the negotiating parties have reached an agreement through correspondence or face-to-face bargaining, one party writes down the terms and conditions of transaction briefly, making two copies, which are signed and sent to the other party for confirmation. After the other party receives and signs them, they will send one copy back, keeping one themselves, and then the contract goes into effect.

c. Electronic contract: an electronic contract is the ratification in software or by means of electronic communication, such as fax and email, of a statement of intent that regulates behavior among the contracting parties. Though it is not a formal document with signature or seal, this form of contract is in conformity with the United Nations Convention on Contracts for the International Sale of Goods and carries legal force.

(4) By the Relationship Between the Contracting Parties

①Direct contract: the contracting parties all have direct interests in the deal and they sign the contract themselves.

②Agency contract: also referred to as contract for intermediation, this form is signed by a third party on behalf of one of the parties with direct interests in the deal.

### 4.3.5　Modification and Termination of the Contract

(1) Modification of the Contract

A contract may be modified if the parties reach a consensus through consultation. If the circumstances under which the contract is performed undergo changes, the parties to the contract shall modify certain clauses or provide supplements to the contract. Modification of a contract shall be partial, involving alteration of only a few individual clauses, while the principal contract remains unchanged.

(2) Termination of the Contract

A contract may be terminated if the parties to the contract reach a consensus through consultation before they begin to perform their obligations or before the contract has been fulfilled. Sometimes, changing circumstances make it impossible or unnecessary to perform the contract. In such cases, the parties to the contract may decide to rescind the contract, before the contract expires, through legal procedures or under the conditions or procedures stipulated in the contract itself.

If a contract or part of a contract has not yet been performed, its performance shall be terminated after the rescission. If it has been performed, a party to the contract may, in light of the performance and the character of the contract, request that the performance be completed, that the original status be restored or that other remedial measures be taken, as well as that proper compensation be made to offset the losses.

However, the rescission of a contract does not mean the termination of all rights and obligations of the contract. In reality, mutual legal obligations terminate only after the party responsible pays the required penalty fee, or compensates for any losses the other party may have suffered.

### 4.3.6　Circumstances That Allow Altering and Rescinding a Contract

(1) A contract may be altered or terminated if all the parties to the contract agree.

Since the contract is established as the outcome of the parties' agreement, any alteration to it or rescission should also be made after the parties reach a consensus through consultation.

Neither party may unilaterally modify or rescind the contract. To do so is an illegal act. In addition, if the modification or rescission is made in a way that it may damage the interests of the state or the public citizenry of one party, the government agencies or citizens concerned in the relevant countries may take legitimate action to stop the modification or rescinding of the contract.

(2) It is impossible to perform the contract because of a force majeure.

A force majeure or act of god refers to an irresistible force, that is, natural circumstances or events that are unpredictable or unexpected and inevitable that prevents someone from doing what they have officially planned or agreed to do. A force majeure usually manifests itself in the form of natural disasters, such as flood, earthquake, or tsunami, or social chaos, such as war, government instability, and strikes. Because a force majeure is totally beyond the expectations of the parties to the contract, they may alter or rescind the contract when they are thus prevented from performing the contract.

(3) One party to the contract fails to perform the contract within the agreed time period.

Three major circumstances exist:

①One party expresses explicitly or indicates through its acts, before the expiry of the performance period, that it will not perform the principal debt obligations.

②One party to the contract fails to perform the contract at the due date, thus affecting severely the projected interests of the other party, making it unnecessary for the affected party to have the first party implement the contract.

③One party to the contract delays in performing its principal debt obligations and fails, after being urged, to perform them within a reasonable time period.

Under these circumstances, one party has the rights to modify or rescind the contract in accordance with legal procedures and to ask the party in breach of the contract to pay a penalty or take other remedial measures to compensate losses incurred due to the breach of contract.

### 4.3.7 The Contract Signing Ceremony

As a symbol of the success of negotiation, signing ceremony is of great importance and a good preparation is necessary like:

①determine the signer

②documentation preparation

③the arrangement of the signing hall

The procedure of signing ceremony:

(1) Participants from both parties enter the signing hall at the same time.

(2) The signers take their seats and others stand behind their signer.

(3) The signers sign their own copy first.

(4) The assistants of both sides pass on the signed copy to the signer of the other party for signature.

(5) After signing it, the signers exchange the signed copy and shake hand.

(6) Champagne is served to celebrate the signing of the agreement.

For some important negotiation, especially international business negotiation, the location of the contract signing is important. The reason is that the signing site of the contract can normally decide which country's laws are adopted to settle the disputes. According to international convention, the courthouse or arbitration organization could make the adjudication or arbitration based on the law of the country where the contract is signed should any dispute arise.

# Case Study

In 2003, Airline S Company signed a contract with European Air Bus Corporation (Airbus) for the purchase of its newly developed A380 Super Jumbo Jetliners. The contract stipulated that Airbus should start to deliver the jetliners in early 2006, but for one reason or another, Airbus failed to make delivery at the due date. Airbus proposed altering the contract to read that the delivery time was postponed for half a year and Airbus should bear the losses arising thereafter and pay a certain amount of penalty. The two parties reached an agreement on the alteration of the delivery date, with the delivery of the first A380 Aircraft reset to June, 2006. However, as June 2006 approached, Airbus was yet unable to effect delivery at the newly agreed time. After the president of Airbus was forced to resign and Airbus paid the additional penalty to Airline s Company, the two companies restarted the negotiation, postponing the delivery date for the A380s stipulated in the contract for another half year. However, Airline S Company proposed that because the repeatedly delayed delivery had already affected the development of Airline S Company severely, Airline S Company had to terminate in part their contract with Airbus, reducing the number of A380s from the original order.

An airline company in the Middle-east was overjoyed to learn this news. They wanted to take over the two A380 jetliners that Airline S Company had given up. Because similar aircraft they had ordered from Airbus were to be delivered in four years, if Airline S Company agreed to assign the contract of these two A 380 jets to them, they could get the jets much earlier even though the delivery was delayed one or two years. Thus, the Middle-eastern airline company started negotiations with Airbus and Airline S Company on the assignment of this portion of the contract.

When Airbus failed to deliver the ordered aircraft to S Company the second time, S Company had to give up the second batch of A380 jets, that is, to rescind the contract. The reason why S Company wanted to rescind the contract was mainly to reduce the loss incurred when they could not update their fleet as a result of the 「delayed performance of the contract-waiting for the delivery」.

# Exercises

What functions does the contract play in this case?

# Chapter 5　Negotiation Principles

## 5.1　Win-Win Concept

### 5.1.1　Introduction of Win-win Concept—A Revolution in Negotiation Field

In the second half of the twentieth century, the rapid development of economic globalization and integration, by promises of great benefits from free flow of people, goods, services and capital, have mingled all countries and areas into one interdependent and interrelated body. Resolving political, especially economic disputes and conflicts by peaceful means based on equality and mutual benefit has prevailed in international affairs and also domestic affairs since countries started to view each other as partners and cooperators rather than adversaries and antagonists. Some scholars and social workers began advocating a brand new idea, which is win-win concept. Among those outstanding figures are American scholars Roger Fisher, William Ury, and British negotiator Bill Scott, to name a few.

The core of their thinking is mutual Success and convergence of interests. By mutual success, they mean under the condition that one party tries to gain his utmost interests or at least takes action not detrimental to one's own interests, each party may find one way or another to satisfy more or less the counterpart's interests as well. Seeking convergence of parties' interests is to conduct negotiations by exploring mutual benefits so that a better and bigger cake of common interests will be made jointly for mutual sharing. In the meantime, an American attorney, Gerard Nierenberg, created his educational nonprofit negotiation institute in New York, where he promoted his negotiation philosophy of 「Everybody wins」. Because of his success and popularity of his philosophy, he was recognized by Forbes magazine as 「the Father of Negotiating Training」.

Based on the concept, a win-win negotiation model has been developed. Practices have demonstrated their high effectiveness in dealing with disagreement and conflicts in negotiations; therefore it has become the most widely accepted negotiation principle.

Win-win model is expressed as:

(1) Determine each party's interests and needs;
(2) Find out the other party's interests and demands;
(3) Offer constructive options and solutions;
(4) Announce success of negotiations;

(5) Declare failure of negotiations or negotiations in impasse.

A significant point that win-win model differs from win-lose model is that both parties will not only seek means to fulfill their own interests but also hope the interests of the other party may be realized more or less. Negotiations guided by such concept are to be conducted in an atmosphere of mutual understanding and sincere cooperation and will be concluded with mutually accepted agreement to the satisfaction of both parties.

Win-win theory has proved to be successful and effective in many tough negotiations because it takes into full consideration of both sides' interests, which contribute greatly to the mutual understanding of negotiating parties, therefore, it can produce twice the result with half the effort. However effective win-win model can be, not all people in all situations will be guided by win-win concept by virtue of deep rooted one dimensional concept of win-lose, therefore, there is still a long way to go since it is a formidable task for people to establish a new concept.

### 5.1.2 How Can Both Sides Win

Win-win concept has been widely accepted as a philosophy, but how comes that both sides of negotiating parties can win remains a problem. British scholars George Holmes and Stan Glaser suggest that the win-win assertion is practically possible because every negotiator has his own priorities during negotiation.

To explain the matter properly, the concept of the hidden agenda has to be reconsidered. In fact the issues of importance to one party are seldom of equal importance to the other. In other words, the priorities attached to the various issues that are presented by both sides will always be different. Figure 5-1 sets out one example. It can be seen that the hidden agendas for a buyer and a seller have been placed within the framework of two inverted triangles. The most important issues have been placed at the top, and the remaining issues are then ranked in descending order to the least important at the bottom. The fact that the same issues appear in each list indicates that both parties are negotiating to the same overall agenda; it is only the relative importance of each that differs.

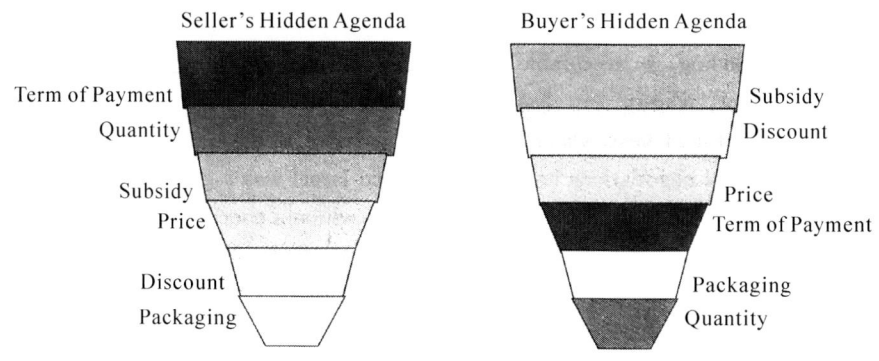

| Seller's Hidden Agenda | Buyer's Hidden Agenda |
|---|---|
| Term of Payment | Subsidy |
| Quantity | Discount |
| Subsidy | Price |
| Price | Term of Payment |
| Discount | Packaging |
| Packaging | Quantity |

**Figure 5-1   Concession Trading**

The crucial role that the conditional offer has in negotiation is now fairly apparent. It is the means by which a win-win situation is achieved. For example, suppose the buyer is anxious to obtain a subsidy of some kind from the seller and puts this forward as a demand. It can be immediately seen that while this issue is of paramount importance to the buyer, it ranks only third in importance in terms of the seller's perspective. So the seller is able to concede the subsidy, but makes it conditional on better payment terms. One is traded for the other and both parties are better off as a result. The buyer may then make a second demand and ask for a volume incentive discount. The seller may well be willing to grant this in exchange for a larger order quantity. If the buyer agrees, then they trade once more, and again both the buyer and the seller are better off. The larger order quantity could well reduce the seller's fixed costs, so in effect he may not be accepting any reduction in profit.

While this is clearly a contrived example, it undoubtedly reflects in a very real sense the different emphasis that is placed on individual issues by a buyer and a seller. And because each gives something of less importance for something of greater importance, the bargaining process becomes possible and both sides can win. The win-win outcome is a function of the fact that the buyer's and seller's agendas are different. In many third-party negotiations, it has never been found competing agendas to be the same. Yet the most common fallacy that exists among business people is the belief that what is important for one negotiator must be of equal importance to the other.

It would appear that individuals have a strong tendency to imagine that other people see the world from their perspective. They then go on to assume that their own concerns and priorities must also be shared by others. It is quite wrong for any business person to make this assumption because it is incorrect. In general, one side will win at the expense of the other, given two conditions only. The first is in the unlikely situation where the hidden agenda is precisely the same for both parties. If this should occur then one party can only win at the expense of the other. The second is where one party simply uses overwhelming bargaining strength to massacre the other on price. If this should happen, then it is likely that the injured party will retaliate at the first possible opportunity.

### Questions for Discussion and Consideration

(1) Do you think the establishment of win-win concept is a formidable task?

(2) Have you ever considered the other party's interests when you are in a negotiation with others?

(3) What is your feeling when you have lost your argument with someone? Do you have a strong incentive to do something later?

(4) Analyze one or two negotiation cases you have participated in and tell why you won or lost.

## 5.2　Collaborative Principled Negotiation

### 5.2.1　Collaborative Principled Negotiation and Its Four Components

　　Increasing acceptance of win-win concept has brought forth development of totally new negotiation theories. A representative one is collaborative principled negotiation, also commonly known as Harvard principled negotiation established by Roger Fisher and William Ury, professors from Harvard University. The two professors developed their theoretical system and concept in their works, especially the famous book *Getting to Yes*: *Negotiating Agreement Without Giving in*. The book is regarded by a lot of scholars and negotiators as the「Bible」of negotiations and its viewpoints are widely quoted and practiced.

　　The core of collaborative principled negotiation is to reach a solution beneficial to both parties by way of stressing interests and value but not by way of haggling. The method of collaborative principled negotiation developed at the Harvard Negotiation Project is to decide issues on their merits rather than through a haggling process focused on what each side says it will and will not do. It suggests that you look for mutual gains whenever possible, and that when your interests conflict, you should insist that the result be based on some fair standards independent of the will of either side. The method of collaborative principled negotiation is hard on the merits, soft on the people. It employs no tricks and no posturing. It shows you how to obtain what you are entitled to and still be decent. It enables you to be fair while protecting you against those who would take advantage of your fairness. When the interests of the two parties are contradictory, an objective criterion should be applied.

　　Collaborative principled negotiation consists of four basic components:
　　(1) People: separate the people from the problem;
　　(2) Interests: focus on interests but not positions;
　　(3) Gaining: invent options for mutual gain;
　　(4) Criteria: introduce objective criteria.
　　The four components are interrelated with each other and should be applied to the whole course of the negotiations. The four components are explained in the following.

### 5.2.2　Separate the People from the Problem

　　It is generally understood that in negotiations problems will be discussed and resolved if talks are going on in a friendly and sincere atmosphere. Unfortunately more often than not high tension is built up due to negotiators' prejudice against the other party or poor impression on each other or misled interpretation of the other party's intention. It is conceivable that negotiations would be directed to personal disputes and both sides say something hurting each other when such prejudice or misunderstanding exists. As a result negotiators' personal feeling is mingled with interests and events to be discussed. For example, you may feel very uncomfortable when your counterpart appears arrogant and superior, so you probably throw out something to knock off his arrogance, which may further irritate him and make him take retaliation action. The focus of negotiation is shifted from interests and issues of both parties to personal dignity and self-respect, thus the attacks and quarrels end up with nothing. In other cases your counterpart may misunderstand your intention and openly show his emotion when you make comments on his opinion and events he has described.

A basic fact about negotiation, easy to forget in corporate and international transactions, is that you are not dealing with abstract representatives of the other side, but with human beings. They have emotions, deeply held values, and different backgrounds and viewpoints; and they are unpredictable. So are you.

This human aspect of negotiation can be either helpful or disastrous. The process of working out an agreement may produce a psychological commitment to a mutually satisfactory outcome. A working relationship where trust, understanding, respect and friendship are built up over time can make each new negotiation smoother and more efficient. And people's desire to feel good about themselves, and their concern for what others will think of them, can often make them more sensitive to another negotiator's interests.

To find your way through the jungle of people problems, it is useful to think in terms of three basic categories: perception, emotion and communication. The various people problems all fall into one of these three baskets.

(1) Perception

Understanding the other side's thinking is not simply a useful activity that will help you solve your problem. Their thinking is the problem. Whether you are making a deal or settling a dispute, differences are defined by the difference between your thinking and theirs. Conflict lies not in objective reality, but in people's heads.

**Put Yourself in Their Shoes**   How you see the world depends on where you sit. People tend to see what they want to see. Out of a mass of detailed information, they tend to pick out and focus on those facts that confirm their prior perceptions and to disregard or misinterpret those that call their perceptions into question. Each side in a negotiation may see only the merits of its case, and only the faults of the other side's.

The ability to see the situation as the other side sees it, as difficult as it may be, is one of the most important skills a negotiator can possess. Understanding their point of view is not the same as agreeing with it. It is true that a better understanding of their thinking may lead you to revise your own views about the merits of a situation. But that is not a cost of understanding their point of view, it is a benefit. It allows you to reduce the area of conflict, and it also helps you advance your newly enlightened self-interest.

**Do Not Blame Them for Your Problem**   It is tempting to hold the other side responsible for your problem. Blaming is an easy mode to fall into, particularly when you feel that the other side is indeed responsible. But even if blaming is justified, it is usually counterproductive. When under attack, the other side will become defensive and will resist what you have to say. They will cease to listen, or they will strike back with an attack of their own.

One way to deal with differing perceptions is to make them explicit and discuss them with the other side. As long as you do this in a frank, honest manner without either side blaming the other for the problem as each sees it, such a discussion may provide the understanding they need to take what you say seriously, and vice versa.

**Give the Other Side a Stake in the Outcome by Making Sure They Participate in the Process** It is a simple reason that if the other party is not involved in the process, they are hardly likely to approve the product. If you want the other side to accept a disagreeable conclusion, it is crucial that you involve them in the process of reaching that conclusion. Apart from the substantive merits, the feeling of participation in the process is perhaps the most important factor in determining whether a negotiator accepts a proposal. In a sense, the process is the product.

(2) Emotion

In a negotiation, particularly in a bitter dispute, feelings may be more important than talk. The parties may be more ready for battle than for cooperatively working out a solution to a common problem. People often come to a negotiation realizing that the stakes are high and feeling threatened. Emotions on one side will generate emotions on the other. Emotions may quickly bring a negotiation to an impasse or an end.

**Allow the Other Side to Let off Steam** Often, one effective way to deal with people's anger, frustration, and other negative emotions is to help them release those feelings. People obtain psychological release through the simple process of recounting their grievances. Letting off steam may make it easier to talk rationally later. Perhaps the best strategy to adopt while the other side lets off steam is to listen quietly without responding to their attacks, and occasionally to ask the speaker to continue until he has spoken his last word.

**Do Not React to Emotional Outbursts** Releasing emotions can prove risky if it leads to an emotional reaction. If not controlled, it can result in a violent quarrel. One unusual and effective technique to contain the impact of emotions was used in the 1950s by the Human Relations Committee, a labor management group set up in the steel industry to handle emerging conflicts before they became serious problems. The members of the committee adopted the rule that only one person could get angry at a time. This made it legitimate for others not to respond stormily to an angry outburst. It also made letting off emotional steam easier by making an outburst itself more legitimate:「That's OK. It's his turn.」The rule has the further advantage of helping people control their emotions. Breaking the rule implies that you have lost self-control, so you lose some face.

(3) Communication

Communication is never an easy thing, even between people who have an enormous background of shared values and experience. There are three big problems in communication. First, negotiators may not be talking to each other, or at least not in such a way as to be understood. Even if you are talking directly and clearly to them, they may not be hearing you. This constitutes the second problem in communication. Note how often people do not seem to pay enough attention to what you say. Probably equally often, you would be unable to repeat what they had said. In a negotiation, you may be so busy thinking about what you are going to say next, how you are going to respond to that last point or how you are going to frame your next argument, that you forget to listen to what the other side is saying now. The third communication problem is misunderstanding. What can you do about these three problems of communication?

**Listen Actively and Acknowledge What Is Being Said**　　Listening enables you to understand their perceptions, feel their emotions, and hear what they are trying to say. If you pay attention and interrupt occasionally to say, 「Did I understand correctly that you are saying that...?」 the other side will realize that they are not just killing time, not just going through a routine. They will also feel a satisfaction of being heard and understood. It has been said that the cheapest concession you can make to the other side is to let them know they have been heard.

**Speak About Yourself, Not About Them**　　In many negotiations, each side explains and condemns at great length the motivations and intentions of the other side. It is more persuasive, however, to describe a problem in terms of its impact on you than in terms of what they did or why, like you can use 「I feel let down」 instead of 「You are a racist」. If you make a statement about them that they believe is untrue, they will ignore you or get angry; they will not focus on your concern. But statement about how you feel is difficult to challenge.

**Avoid Trying to Score Points and Debating Them as Opponents**　　Some negotiators often take a negotiation as a debate or treat it as trial. Negotiating parties are equal. It is unpersuasive to blame the other party for the problem, to engage in name-calling, or to raise your voice.

The techniques just described for dealing with problems of perception, emotion, and communication usually work well. However, the best time for handling people problems is before they become people problems. This means building a personal and organizational relationship with the other side that can cushion the people on each side against the knocks of negotiation. It also means structuring the negotiation game in ways that separate the substantive problem from the relationship and protect people's egos from getting involved in substantive discussions.

In general, to separate people from problems, the crucial point is to understand the other-party, control one's own emotion and strengthen communication. We look for chances to correct our counterparts afterwards if their opinion is not right; we allow them to express their dissatisfaction if they feel upset and we find more chances to exchange our opinions if misunderstanding happens. By doing so, we treat our counterpart as a cooperator sitting on the same boat sinking and floating together, and the course of negotiation as a process of achieving mutual success hand in hand.

### 5.2.3 Focus on Interests But Not Positions

Fisher and Ury distinguish the difference between interest and position in the story of two men quarreling in a library. One wants the window open and the other wants it closed. They argue back and forth about how much to leave it open: a crack, halfway, three quarters of the way. No solution satisfies them both. At this time a librarian enters. She asks one why he wants the window open: 「To get some fresh air.」 She asks the other why he wants it closed: 「To avoid the draft.」 After thinking for a minute, she opens wide a window in the next room, bringing in fresh air without a draft. This story is typical of many negotiations. Since the parties' problem appears to be a conflict of positions, and since their goal is to agree on a position, they naturally tend to think and talk about positions and in the process often reach an impasse.

Successful negotiations are the result of mutual giving and taking of interests rather than keeping firm on one's own positions. The librarian could not have invented the solution she did if she focused only on the two men's stated positions of wanting the window open or closed. Instead she looked to their underlying interests of fresh air and no draft. This difference between positions and interests is crucial. The method of focusing on the common interests of negotiating parties works well because firstly, there is always more than one way of fulfilling each other's interests, and secondly, both sides can always find out certain common interests, otherwise they will not sit together discussing and talking.

Negotiating parties can try the following methods in order to concentrate on interests but not positions.

(1) Identify Interests

**Explore Their Interests Which Stood in Our Way** The benefit of looking behind positions for interest is clear, but how to go about it is less clear. A position is likely to be concrete and explicit; the interests underlying it may well be unexpressed, intangible, and perhaps inconsistent. How do you go about understanding the interests involved in a negotiation, remembering that figuring out their interest will be at least as important as figuring out yours?

One basic technique is to put yourself in their shoes. Examine each position they take, and ask yourself 「Why」. Your purpose of finding out the reasons is not for justification of this position, but for an understanding of the needs, hopes, fear, or desires that it serves. One of the most useful ways to uncover interests is first to identify the basic decision that the other side perceives that you may want them to make, and then to ask yourself why they have not made that decision. What interests of theirs stand in the way? If you are trying to change their minds, the starting point is to figure out where their minds are now.

**Examine the Different Interests of Different People on Their Side** In almost every negotiation each side will have many interests, not just one. A common error in diagnosing a negotiating situation is to assume that each person on the other side has the same interests. This is almost never the case. In fact everyone of each side has multiple interests. If negotiators realize these and analyze their different interests, they will find out the most important interests behind their position.

**Look at Their Human Needs Underlying Their Positions**   In searching for the basic interests behind declared position, look particularly for those bedrock concerns which motivate all people. If you can take care of such basic needs, you will increase the chance both of reaching agreement and, if an agreement is reached, of the other side's keeping to it. Fundamental as they are, basic human needs are easy to overlook. In many negotiations, we tend to think that the only interest involved is money.

What is true for individuals remains equally true for groups and nations. Negotiations are not likely to make much progress as long as one side believes that the fulfillment of their basic needs is being threatened by the other. In an acquiring negotiation of a Chinese oil company over an American oil company, the Chinese company increased its purchasing price to a level much higher than its American competitor, but the Chinese company did not succeed because the American government did not ratify the acquisition for security and political concern.

(2) Talk About Interests

The purpose of negotiating is to serve your interests. The chance of that happening increases when you communicate them. The other side may not know what your interests are, and you may not know theirs. How do you discuss interests constructively without getting out of rigid positions? If you want the other side to take your interests into account, explain to them what those interests are. If you want the other side to appreciate your interests, begin by demonstrating that you appreciate theirs. In addition to demonstrating that you have understood their interests, it helps to acknowledge that their interests are part of the overall problem you are trying to solve. This is especially easy to do if you have shared interests.

Be hard on the problem, soft on the people. It may not be wise to commit yourself to your position, but it is wise to commit yourself to your interests. This is the place in a negotiation to spend your aggressive energies. The other side, being concerned with their own interests, will tend to have overly optimistic expectations of the range of possible agreements. Often the wisest solutions, which produce the maximum gain for you at the minimum cost to the other side, are produced only by strongly advocating your interests.

If the other party feels personally threatened by an attack on the problem, he may grow defensive and may cease to listen. This is why it is important to separate the people from the problem. Fighting hard on the substantive issues increases the pressure for an effective solution; giving support to the human beings on the other side tends to improve your relationship and to increase the likelihood of reaching an agreement. It is the combination of support and attack that works; either alone is likely to be insufficient.

## 5.2.4  Invent Options for Mutual Gain

The first two components look at the relation between people and problems, and interests and positions, which are conducive for negotiators to establish an objective view on those important factors in negotiations. The third component of inventing options for mutual gain provides an approach to the fulfillment of the two parties' demands.

Why are negotiators easily trapped by their own positions? The explanation is that many negotiations simply focus on a single event and the solution to the event is either win or lose, for example, price of a car, size of commission, or time limit of a loan. The distributive[①]nature of interest gaining limits people's scope of thinking and causes people to insist on their own stance. In such case, there is one way out, which is to jointly make the cake of interest as large as possible before cutting it apart so that both sides may get what they desire for. To this end, negotiators should be able to provide creative options and alternatives to unaccepted solutions. There are always alternative solutions to those problems, a point often not realized unfortunately.

Generally speaking, there are three factors hindering people from seeking for alternative solutions.

The first is the fixed plan. Both sides perceive the size of the cake is fixed, thus your gain is my loss and my gain is your loss. A negotiation often appears to be a 「fixed-sum」 game; $100 more for you on the price of a car means $100 less for me. Why bother to invent if all the options are obvious and I can satisfy you only at my own expense? The rigid distributive concept retards creative thinking and options and hence results in failure of negotiations.

The second is seeking for only one solution. Negotiators are inclined to rest on their laurel they have achieved and hope to arrive at the final solution without other nuisances. They are not aware of the fact that creative thinking and options are an indispensable part of a successful negotiation.

The third is considering only one's own options suiting one's own needs. A successful negotiation is a process of giving and taking which means options provided should be a consolidated body of both sides' interests. When keeping in mind not only one's own party's interests but also the other side's interests, stimulated creativeness will bring about alternative options conducive to success of negotiations.

To get rid of the above mentioned barriers and offer creative options, the following steps can be considered.

(1) Invent Creative Options

**Separate Inventing Options from Evaluating Them**　　Since judgment hinders imagination, separate the creative act from the critical one; separate the process of thinking up possible decisions from the process of selecting among them. Invent first, decide later. As a negotiator, you

---

① 兩分法，或輸或贏的分配法。

will of necessity to do much inventing by yourself. It is not easy. By definition, inventing new ideas requires you to think about things that are not already in your mind. You should therefore consider the desirability of arranging an inventing or brainstorming session with a few colleagues or friends. Such a session can effectively separate inventing from deciding. A brainstorming session is designed to produce as many ideas as possible to solve the problem at hand. The key ground rule is to postpone all criticism and evaluation of ideas. The group simply invents ideas without pausing to consider whether they are good or bad, realistic or unrealistic. With those inhibitions removed, one idea should stimulate another, like firecrackers setting off one another.

**Develop Several Options Before Looking for a Solution**　　A brainstorming session frees people to think creatively. Once freed, they need ways to think about their problems and to generate constructive solutions. The key to wise decision-making lies in selecting from a great number and variety of options. The sources of options can come from considerations on both general and specific thinking, for example, finding out the problems first, analyzing the problems second, considering what to do done next and finally coming up with some specific and feasible suggestions for action. Another way to generate multiple options is to examine your problem from the perspective of different professions and disciplines. In thinking up possible options over the mounting housing price, for example, look at the problem as it might be seen by a salary earner, a contractor, a banker, a minister, a speculator in real estate, an economist, or a sociologist.

(2) Look for Mutual Gain

A major block to creative problem-solving lies in the assumption of a fixed pie: the less for you, the more for me. Actually, there almost always exists the possibility of joint gain. This may take the form of developing a mutually advantageous relationship, or of satisfying the interests of each side with a creative solution.

**Identify Shared Interests**　　In theory it is obvious that shared interests help produce agreement. By definition, inventing an idea which meets shared interests is good for you and good for them. In practice, however, the picture seems less clear. In the middle of a negotiation over price or a piece of land, shared interests may not appear obvious or relevant.

Three points about shared interests are worth remembering. First, shared interests lie latent in every negotiation. They may not be immediately obvious. Second, shared interests are opportunities, not godsends. It helps to make a shared interest explicit and to formulate it as a shared goal. In other words, make it concrete and future-oriented. Third, stressing your shared interests can make the negotiation smoother and more amicable. Passengers in a lifeboat afloat in the middle of the ocean with limited rations will subordinate their differences over food in pursuit of their shared interest in getting to shore.

**Look for Options That Would Make the Decision Easier for Them**　　Since success for you in a negotiation depends upon the other side's making a decision you want, you should do what you can to make that decision an easy one. Rather than make things difficult for the other side, you want to confront them with a choice that is as painless as possible. Impressed with the merits of their own case, people usually pay too little attention to ways of advancing their case by taking care of interest on the other side. To overcome the shortsightedness that results from looking too narrowly at one's immediate self-interest, you will need to put yourself in their shoes. Without some option that appeals to them, there is likely to be no agreement at all.

### 5.2.5 Introduce Objective Criteria

The first three components advocate the benefits of considering both parties' interests and designing a constructive pattern that would satisfy both sides' demands. However, conflicts and disputes of the two parties over interest gaining will not disappear no matter how considerable the two sides try to be and how creative in providing options. When the two sides can not decide which option is reasonable and rational, looking for an objective criterion will be a way out.

Once at an international ocean law conference, India and US were arguing about whether ocean mineral exploring companies should pay an initial fee when exploring in the deep seabed. India, representing developing countries, insisted on a sum of $ 60 million per site while US rejected firmly the proposal, suggesting there be no initial fee. The two sides haggled over the issue and could not reach an agreement. Later a representative found out a model for the economics of deep-seabed mining by Massachusetts Institute of Technology (MIT), which could calculate all payment proposals and their impacts on economic return of ocean exploration. The model was accepted as an objective criterion of economic analysis on deep-seabed mining by all sides. The model showed that India's proposal of the initial fee did have an impact on the exploration, i.e., a company's normal operation might be interrupted since the company had to pay the fee five years before the mine would generate any revenue, which would make it virtually impossible for a company to mine. The Indian representative thus agreed to reconsider his proposal. The model also told US that initial fee of reasonable sum was possible economically and as a result US gave up its position.

(1) Developing Objective Criteria

**Look for Fair Standards**  The case demonstrates that an objective criterion should be fair, effective and rational if it is regarded as objective. The following points will be considered when telling if a criterion is objective or not.

①An objective criterion should be independent of wills of all parties and thus be free from sentimental influence of any one.

②An objective criterion should be legitimate and practical. In a boundary dispute, for example, you may find it easier to agree on a physically outstanding feature such as a river than on a line three yards to the east of the riverbank.

③An objective criterion should be at least theoretically accepted by both sides, as in the case of MIT model.

One point is clear that different issues have different objective criteria. For example, criteria of price talking will include factors of cost, market situation, depreciation, price competition and other necessary factors. In other negotiations, experts' opinions, international conventions and norms and legal documents will all serve as objective criteria.

In the Sino-US negotiation on China's accession into WTO, the two parties disputed over China's developing country status. US took the position that China should be treated as a developed country. To back US stance. American negotiators cited China's growing exports and large foreign reserve holdings. They argued that in developing countries China's sophisticated technology in launching and retrieving satellites had no parallel. One American negotiator even compared the situation in China with that in India and some African countries. He said when he opened the door of a family in a poorest area randomly chosen by the Chinese government and asked the people if they had their breakfast, he was told they did, and he went on asking if lunch and supper were guaranteed, the answer was yes. However, he had a very different story in some African countries and even in some areas in India. People there had little food for breakfast, not to mention lunch and supper.

The two countries insisted on their own standard and it was hard to bridge the discrepancy. Here the focus is which criterion to apply to for resolving thedispute. In fact there is a ready criterion provided by the World Bank, which is measured by per capita countries whose per capita GNP. According to the World Bank's standard, countries whose per capita GNP below $ 785 (1996) are the poorest countries. China's per capita GNP in 1997 was $ 750, which is among the poorest countries.

**Look for Fair Procedures** To produce an outcome independent of wills, you can use either fair standards for the substantive question or fair procedures for resolving the conflicting interests. One example of fair procedure is when one party cuts a cake, ask the other party to choose first. Other procedures which may be called fair can be 「doing it in turns」, 「drawing lots」. Drawing lots, flipping a coin and other forms of chance have an inherent fairness. The results may be unequal, but each side had an equal opportunity.

(2) Standards for Successful Negotiations

In Fisher and Ury's view, the three standards described below can be applied to judging success or failure of a negotiation approach:

①If an agreement is possibly reached, it should satisfy the legitimate interest of both parties to the maximum and resolve their conflicts, meanwhile protecting public interests;

②The agreement should be highly efficient;

③The agreement will improve, or at least not hurt the relationship of the two parties.

CPN provides us with a way to reach a wise agreement for tough negotiations. CPN has proved to be suitable to almost all situations from international negotiations to domestic and private negotiations, from simple events to complex situations and from routine talks to urgent meetings. Principled negotiation can be used by diplomats of countries in nonproliferation of nuclear weapon talks with each other, by Wall Street lawyers representing Fortune 500 companies in antitrust cases, and by couples in deciding everything from where to go for vacation to how to divide their property if they get divorced. Anyone can use this method.

Every negotiation is different, but the basic elements do not change. Principled negotiation can be used whether there is one issue or several; two parties or many; whether there is a prescribed ritual, as in collective bargaining, as in talking with hijackers. The method applies whether the other side is more experienced or less, a hard bargainer or a friendly one. Principled negotiation is an all-purpose strategy. Unlike almost all other strategies, if the other side learns this one, it does not become more difficult to use; it becomes easier. The success of CPN does not relay on playing tricks or negotiators' resourcefulness but on fairness, objectiveness and mutual understanding.

## 5.3 Law of Interest Distribution

### 5.3.1 Needs Theory

The satisfaction of needs motivates virtually every type of human behavior and has a direct impact on negotiations.

Professor Abraham H. Maslow of Brandeis University, in this valuable book *Motivation and Personality* (1954), presents seven categories of needs as basic factors in human behavior. These provide a useful framework for studying needs in relation to negotiations.

Here is Maslow's list:
①Physiological (homeostatic) needs;
②Safety and security needs;
③Love and belonging needs;
④Esteem needs;
⑤Needs for self-actualization (inner motivation, to become what one is capable of becoming);
⑥Needs to know and understand;
⑦Aesthetic needs.

(1) Physiological (Homeostatic) Needs

Physiological needs are common to all human beings. Their goal is satisfaction of biological drives and urges such as hunger, fatigue, sex, and many more. The recently developed concept of homeostasis[①]refers to the automatic efforts of the body to maintain itself in a normal, balanced state. Homeostatic needs are undoubtedly the most dominant of all needs. A

---

① 體內平衡。

person may lack many things such as love, safety, or esteem; but if at the same time he is really thirsty or hungry, he will pay no attention to any other need until his thirst or hunger is at least partially satisfied. A starving man has no desire or drive to paint a picture or write a poem. For him no other interest exists except food. All of his capacities are devoted to getting food, and until he gets it, other needs are practically nonexistent.

It should be noted that the entire organism is involved in the gratification of a need. No one says「My stomach is hungry」, but rather「I'm hungry」. When a person is hungry, his whole being is involved, his perceptions change, his memory is affected, and his emotions are aroused by tensions and nervous irritability. All of these changes subside after he has satisfied the hunger need. When one group of needs has been somewhat gratified, however, another set becomes the motivating force.

(2) Safety and Security Needs

After the physiological needs are taken care of, the organism is primarily concerned with safety. It becomes a safety-seeking mechanism. As with the hungry man, so it is with the individual in quest of safety. His whole outlook on lire is affected by a lack of safety. Everything looks less desirable to him than the achieving of the goal of safety. Safety needs are more easily observed in children, because adults in our culture have been taught to inhibit any overt reaction to danger. But anything unexpected and threatening makes the child feel unsafe, and changes its world from bright stability to a dark place where anything can happen. A child feels safe in a predictable, orderly world; he prefers an undisrupted routine. He tends to feel safer in an organized, orderly world that he can count on and in which he has his parents to protect him against harm.

Adults in our society seldom come face to face with violence, except in war. They are safe enough from such perils as wild animals, extreme climate, slaughter or massacres. However, the need for safety expresses itself in seeking the protection and stability afforded by such things as money in the bank, job security, and retirement programs. Though human beings no longer live in the jungle, they need protection against the dangers that confront them in the ominous 「jungle」of economic competition.

(3) Love and Belonging Needs

After the physiological and the safety needs have been reasonably gratified, the next dominant need to emerge is the craving for love and affection. This longing for friends, or a sweetheart, or family, can take complete possession of a lonely individual. When he was starving or threatened by danger, he could only think of food or safety; but now that these needs have been taken care of, he wants, more than anything else in the world, to be loved. He hungers for affectionate relations with people in general, for a place in his group. This need for love must not be equated with sex. Admittedly it is a component of the sexual drive, but sexual behavior has many facets and is primarily a physiological urge.

(4) Esteem Needs

Next in the hierarchy of basic needs is the need for esteem. Actually it is a plurality of needs, all of the same general character. These needs can be divided into two categories. First and foremost is the desire for freedom and independence. Coupled with this is the need for strength, competence, and confidence in the face of the world. The second division comprises the desire for reputation or prestige, the striving for status, domination, and the esteem of the other people. Satisfaction of esteem needs helps a person feel useful and necessary in the world. The healthiest self-esteem is based on respect from others that is deserved, not on unwarranted adulation.

Research and experience continually demonstrate the power of esteem in motivating human beings. Studies of individuals at various levels of the business structure have attempted to find out what makes people feel good about their jobs. The strongest and most lasting 「good」 feelings come from learning and growing on the job, expanding one's competence, increasing one's mastery, becoming recognized as an expert.

(5) Needs for Self-Actualization (Inner Motivation, to Become What One Is Capable of Becoming)

Even assuming that all the foregoing needs have been adequately satisfied, the individual may still be discontented and restless. What need does he now seek? Most people are not happy unless they are working at something that they feel they are fitted for. A musician wants to make music, an artist wants to paint, everyone would like to do the kind of work that he can do and enjoys doing. Unfortunately this is not always his lot, but insofar as he attains this goal he is at peace with himself. This almost universal need has been termed by Maslow self-actualization. Broadly speaking, self-actualization braces the desires and strivings to become everything that one is capable of becoming. This striving takes various forms and will differ from individual to individual.

(6) Needs to Know and Understand

In the normalperson there exists a basic drive to seek out knowledge about his environment, to explore, to understand. We are all motivated by an active curiosity that impels us to experiment and attracts us to the mysterious and the unknown. The need to investigate and explain the unknown is a fundamental factor in human behavior. This need to know and understand a condition of freedom and safety in which this curiosity can be exercised.

(7) Aesthetic Needs

Lastly, human behavior is actuated by certain cravings that might be called the aesthetic need. Some individuals actually get sick in ugly surroundings and are cured by removal to a beautiful setting. Naturally this longing for beauty is strongest among artists. Some of them cannot tolerate ugliness. But Maslow includes in the category of aesthetic needs the action of a man who 「feels a strong conscious impulse to straighten the crookedly hung picture on the wall」. Indeed, the need for order and balance is a basic part of all aesthetic expression.

These seven basic needs have been presented in a descending scale of importance. For most people and for most human behavior this fixed order holds true. However, it must not be regarded as rigid and it certainly does not apply to all people. (All set of generalizations has its limitations.) Undoubtedly there are many individuals to whom self-esteem is much more important than love, just as there are creative people for whom the aesthetic need fulfillment is just as important as a more basic need.

To sum up, an individual's existence is a constant struggle to satisfy needs; behavior is the reaction of the organism to achieve a reduction of need pressures; and behavior is directed to some desired goal. Our objective is to employ these facts about human needs in successful cooperative negotiation.

### 5.3.2　Application of the Needs Theory in Negotiation

Needs and their satisfaction are the common denominator in negotiation. If people had no unsatisfied needs, they would never negotiate. Negotiation presupposes that both the negotiator and his opponent want something; otherwise they would turn a deaf ear to each other's demands and there would be no bargaining. This is true even if the need is merely to maintain the status quo. It requires two parties, motivated by needs, to start a negotiation. Individuals haggling over the purchase and sale of a piece of real estate, a labor union and management bargaining for a new contract, or the directors of two corporations discussing the terms of a proposed merger are all seeking to gratify needs.

The knowledge of the needs theory permits us to find out what needs are involved on both sides of the bargaining table. The theory goes further, it guides our attention to the needs and varieties of application that actuate the opposition and shows how to adopt alternative methods to work with, or counter-act, or modify our opponent's motivations. These needs, as we have explained, arrange themselves in a definite order of importance. The needs theory enables us to determine the relative effectiveness of each negotiating technique. Moreover, the needs theory gives us a wide variety of choice for our affirmative or defensive use. Knowing the relative strength and power of each need, we can decide on the best method of dealing more basic need in each case, which will probably be more effective.

The needs theory provides such a structure in the following sections.

### 5.3.3　Three Levels of Interests at the Domestic Level

Any negotiations occurred at home involve two levels of interests and sometimes three levels of interests: personal, organizational and national interests. Personal interests are represented by individual negotiators who act in negotiations on behalf of organizations and states, whose interests depend on individual negotiators' efforts to be fulfilled. Organizations are defined as private or state-owned enterprises, institutions, collective bodies or other kinds of entities. States here refer to all sovereignty countries and independent states. To what extent these interests can be coordinated, integrated and balanced determines largely by the progress and outcomes of negotiations. Based on the divisions of individuals, organizations and states, the three-leveled interests will be analyzed.

(1) Interests of Individual Negotiators vs. Interests of Organizations

In spite of different levels of human needs, a negotiator's personal interests, which are closely related with his basic material and spiritual needs, can be easily brought into line with that of organizations since the realization of his needs, no matter what levels of needs, are linked closely with his performance and achievements done for the organizations. Therefore, there is an interior connection between personal and organizational interests, so realization of organizational interests means fulfillment of personal interests and vice versa. By virtue of this linkage, negotiators will make his utmost efforts to achieve interests of organizations he represents in the negotiation.

However, personal interests are not always in convergence with that of organizations particularly when individuals place their own interests before that of the organizations or when their own interests are in conflict with that of the organizations, which are often of monetary nature. Once desires for gaining personal interests prevail, the outcome of negotiation would be foreseeable, i.e., fulfilling petty interests of individuals and suffering of grand interests of organizations. Investigations show that there are much more cases of bribery and corruption in state-owned enterprises because their leaders sacrificed the organizational interests for their own gaining. The corruption cases have caused great losses to the organizations as well as the country. A case released by Qianjiang Evening News (on 29, June 2000) in equipment procurement for the Three Gorges construction provides a lesson to point.

In 1993, a group of 3, the formal general manager of Gezhouba Three Gorges Industrial Company, the general engineer of the company and the manager from Hong Kong Minda Company, set out for a business tour to US looking for a seller who could provide secondhand equipment suitable for GeZhouba's construction. In the negotiation, Chinese engineer put forward three conditions for the equipment: a. all the equipment being manufactured after 1985; b. technical conditions of the secondhand equipment equal to 80% of new equipment; c. price of secondhand equipment not exceeding 40% of that of new equipment. American agent basically had no difference for the terms. In addition, it was willing to offer a seller's credit in three years' term, which meas Chinese company can make the final payment three years after purchasing the equipment.

After the first round of negotiation, the engineer was sent away to Sweden for a business inspection, meanwhile, the Chinese general manager and Hong Kong Minda Company signed the final contract with the American company. The signed agreement gave up the favorable term of seller's credit and changed into buyer's credit instead. Besides, the manufacture date and technical conditions of the equipment fell far behind the initial requirement, but the price was raised considerable. What is worse, some vehicles could not even drive into the cargo liner at American port, so they were dragged into the ship's hold. The procured equipment at the cost of several hundred million RMB yuan turned out to be a junk of discarded iron. Later at the strong request of the company management and employees the contract was terminated. The payment for more than one hundred million RMB yuan equipment is unable to be retrieved and the Three Gorges Industry Company suffered a loss of 430 million yuan and was having a debt of 1.12 billion yuan. It was found out later that the general manager had a private deal out of the counter with Minda Company at the sacrifice of Gezhouba Company's interests.

(2) Interests of Individual Negotiators vs. Interests of Organizations and States

Personal interests for found easier to be brought in line with that of organizations by reason of close linkage between the two, but may be frequently in conflict with interests of the state. For individuals, national interests appear to be quite remote and indirectly connected with individuals' and thus they are often looked upon as a general guideline. However, when an individual represents his country in binational negotiations, he will definitely defend the interests of the country and make every effort to gain state interests, since on such occasion state interests are so overwhelmingly important that any suffering of state interests will bring heavy losses not only to the state but to organizations and individuals as well. Long Yongtu, China's chief negotiator for WTO negotiation, says he is filled with strong patriotism when representing China talking with other nations. Nothing, not to mention money and other personal interests, can be compared with the pride as the spokesman of 1.3 billion Chinese. Nevertheless such possibilities can not be ruled out that a few negotiators manipulate his right in negotiation for his personal gains even at the cost of state interest, particularly in some business talks.

Interests of organization and the state should be in convergence and well coordinated since state interests represent that of organizations in all. However, it is inevitable that some organizations pursue only collective interests while ignoring or even undermining state interests. For example, a few enterprises imported from developed countries industrial garbage only in view of their own economic interests. Some other enterprises are manufacturing heavily polluted chemical products transferred from industrialized countries jointly with foreign firms at the expense of long term interests of the country and people for their immediate interests.

However, when it comes to issues involving bilateral relation of two countries, organizations will have to turn to the government for backing and ask the government as their representative. Bilateral or multilateral relations of countries are mixed up with many complicated factors, which are beyond organizations' abilities and authorities to manage, such as international politics, diplomacy, national security and other factors. For those issues, only the government has the power to make a forceful decision. However, a request for the state support does not suggest that organizations count for little in government decision making. As a matter of fact, organizations can exert strong influence in government decision making process, eminently when organizational interests are in line with the government policy. In almost no exception the government will give its full support to the realization of the common interests of both the state and the organizations.

## 5.3.4　Law of Two-Level Game

When the focus of interest is shifted from domestic arena onto international scene, outcomes of bilateral and multilateral negotiations have demonstrated that consequences of such negotiations depend on interaction of both domestic interests (Level II) and international interests (Level I), i.e., variables at two levels. American scholar Robert D. Putnam expounds, in his *Diplomacy and Domestic Politics: Law of Two-Level Game* (1988), how both domestic and international variables interact with each other and jointly influence the result of binational negotiations and thus reveals the law of two-level games. Ellis S. Krauss further illustrates two - level game model by close examination on negotiation cases and provides empirical implication of the law.

Variables at Level II may be represented by such actors as government, government institutions, interest groups and coalitions. Krauss' research demonstrates that the more common interests the related parties share, the easier all parties reach a consolidated resolution, thus their negotiating power and bargaining leverage as a whole will be enforced and the possibility of success will be increased in negotiation with another country (at Level I). This is because a specific and narrowly ranged acceptability-set at domestic level will fundamentally shape conditions, strategies and dynamics of international negotiations; no agreement will be ratified by the key actors at home without these—and all these—requirements included. Vise versa, the larger the divergence of interests among all parties involved, the harder all parties reach a consensus at domestic level, a result weakening their bargaining power and thus reducing possible gain of interests at negotiating table. The diverged acceptability—sets which have to cover all interests of all parties will allow negotiators with little flexibility since they are closely constrained and any minor modification will break the weak balance of interests of the parties.

Acceptability-sets or win-sets arrived at home will be brought onto international negotiation table for comparing and bargaining. The success or failure of the negotiation is subject to the condition that if there is any, after carefully examining respective interests, common ground for further discussion, i.e., how much one party's interests overlap that of the other party. The chance of success will increase when the overlapping parts are large or cause to make larger. If there is no common ground at all, negotiations will be impossible.

The change of overlapping parts is subject to such variables as mutual efforts of both parties, increasing or decreasing of domestic and international power affected by political, economic and diplomatic situations, security, trade, or change of negotiation team members. The outcome of negotiation is the result of all those variables at both domestic and international levels interacting and checking one another. The US-Japan negotiation on semiconductors provides an excellent example to illustrate the law of two-level games (read the case after the chapter).

One important finding from the case study is that when the win-sets (acceptability-sets) of Party A is more specifically shaped and narrowly ranged than the other party's, the chance of success for Party A will increase greatly. To achieve a narrowly ranged win-set, all the major actors at domestic level should tackle the internal diversification first so that they may appear at negotiating table as one consolidated body.

In the semiconductor case, a united US side with a fixed and specific win-set faced a divided Japan whose win-set was incompatible, because of resistance of some Japanese manufacturers. American demands fit with the Ministry of International Trade and Industry (MITI)'s domestic political interests to enhance its control over the industry—essentially both US and MITI implicitly agreed on the need for MITI to organize a government—led solution to resolve the dispute. These paralleled interest, combined with pressure the Americans could place on Japan because of the unusual combination of anti-dumping and Section 301 leverage induced the Japanese government to enter an agreement against the wishes of some of its own industry. The result was defection, since MITI could not initially force its industry to adhere to the agreement outside its own borders, nor could it push the pace of Japan's markets opening that Americans expected. A pure domestic politics (Level II) explanation cannot account for the results of the negotiation. For example, why would MITI pressure a powerful industry like semiconductor manufacturers to enter an international agreement that they did not want and that could undermine the continued growth of their global market share? MITI's concern for the US-Japan relationship must be taken into account. An international unitary-actor (Level I) analysis alone also does not work. The US forcefulness on semiconductors, even onto retaliation, has a great deal to do with the effective lobbying of the American's semiconductor industry and the consequent US cohesion behind the negotiators.

From the perspective of extending two-level game theory, the case is more interesting in terms of what it suggests about domestic interest groups and the international table. First, domestic interest groups need not be merely「ratifiers or nonratifiers」, a static element in the win-set equation that the government manipulates to gain a stable agreement. Second, we must not assume that politically powerful interest groups can always exercise veto power over government and the outcomes of negotiations. Finally, we must not think that only governments play at both levels. With the increasing inter-dependence of economies, major interest groups often have international interests, and may also make moves at an international table. In the semiconductor case, the international interests of the Japanese firms were so strong as to lead them to undermine their own government's bilaterally negotiated agreement.

The case also reveals an identical negotiating strategy on both American and Japanese sides. On the Japanese side were tough negotiating stances, often much narrower than the domestic win-set; the attempts of the government actors to settle the dispute without American retaliation, despite resistance from disobedient bureaucratic or industry actors; and last-minute concessions to gain an agreement. On the US side were constant threats of executive retaliation; the use of the「bad cop」Congress and the trade law as negotiating levers; and the ultimatums and deadlines to bring about agreement. In part these commonalties reflect the differing international positions of the two countries with Japan economically dependent on the US market and politically and strategically an ally of the more hegemonic American power, giving the US threats of sanctions, ultimatums, and summit embarrassment a great deal of leverage.

## 5.4 Law of Trust

### 5.4.1 Trust and Its Interpretation

When questioned what 「trust」 is, many people say 「trust」 means belief, faith, reliability, a good understanding of a person, or a feeling of affection. These explanations are quite different from each other and failure to appreciate the difference causes much difficulty. American professor Dale E. Z and elaborates the meaning of trust in his publication and points out that trust means increasing your vulnerability to another person whose behavior is not under your control in a situation in which the penalty, loss or deprivation you would suffer if the other person abuses or fails to protect your vulnerability is substantially greater than the benefit, reward or satisfaction you would gain if the other person fulfills or protects your vulnerability.

A simple example explains the meaning of the definition. Parents show trust when they hire a baby-sitter to take care of their baby so they do not have to quit their job or they may leave home to pay a visit to a friend or go for an entertainment. Leaving their baby to someone they do not know very well or have no affection increases their vulnerability significantly because they can not control the baby-sitter's behavior after leaving home. If the baby-sitter abuses their vulnerability and hijacks the baby, the tragedy will surely adversely affect the rest of their lives. But if the baby-sitter protects their vulnerability and takes good care of the baby, then the parents can keep their mind on their work or enjoy their meeting with their friend or a party.

### 5.4.2 How to Decide a Person Trusts or Is Trusted?

There are three fundamental elements: information, influence and control. A person shows trust when he reveals information he need not disclose. He increases his vulnerability by telling others his goals, purpose, plans, alternativesor his problems, others may make use of the information to impede or undermine his efforts. A designer struck on a brilliant idea which he told a colleague working in the same office. The colleague used the idea to advance his own interests and was promoted soon. So a person who does not trust others will conceal or distort relevant information. He will withhold facts, disguise his purpose and hide his feelings.

A person shows trust when he allows others to influence his decisions since he increases his vulnerabilities by asking for others' advice which may deliberately mislead him. As a China's famous story of Fighting in Chibi in the Tale of the Three States depicts that Caocao (premier of East Han Dynasty) asked for Pangtong's (a counsellor secretly working for Dongwu, Caocao's enemy) advice for defeating Dongwu. Pangtong offered him a seemingly clever advice, which turned out to be a part of fatal plot inducing him and his troops into a trap. Therefore, a person who shows mistrust will resist other's influence, deny and reject their suggestions and advice.

A person shows trust when he delegates and permits others to act on their own on his behalf. By this way he increases his vulnerability because he has to rely on others to make a judgment and to implement his plan and others may commit serious errors, delay implementation and undermine his plan. So if a person does not trust, he will try to impose control over others and minimize his dependence on others. As an example, the principal of a middle school had peepholes installed in all the doors of classrooms in order for the administrator to have a tighter control over students. However, the device produced skeptical atmosphere among staff members as well because anyone teaching or staying in the classroom feels he is being watched over and he is not trusted.

The three elements—information, influence and control act on each other, feed back on each other and together influence the level of trust (see Figure 5-2).

Trust and Negotiation

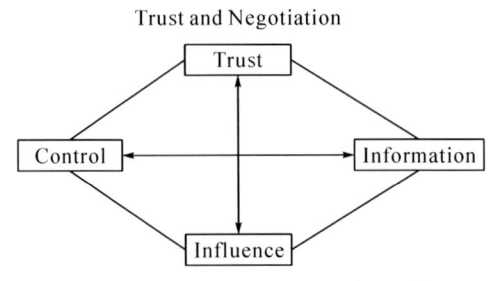

**Figure 5-2   Trust is Enacted Through Information, Influence and Control**

### 5.4.3   Determinants Affecting a Person's Trustful or Mistrustful Behavior

In negotiation or in people's daily life, elements affecting a person's trustful or mistrustful behavior can be divided into two categories: unchangeable elements and changeable elements. Unchangeable elements come from two main sources: childhood education and professional or special training. Changeable elements come basically from people's experiences and perceptions.

(1) Unchangeable Elements

**Childhood Education**   Studies on childhood education on trust began in the 1950s, with the publication of Erik Erikon's Childhood and Society. Since then many developmental psychologists have viewed trust and mistrust as the cornerstones of human development. Erikson divides the human life cycle into eight stages and suggests that each period is a time for a major developmental dilemma or crisis. The first of these crises is the trust versus mistrust crisis, which faces the human infant on entering a world of confusing and complexity. The determining relationship is, of course, with the infant's mother. If the tentative balance of trust and mistrust tilts in the direction of trust, Erikson suggests that the infant gains a basis for expecting the virtue of hope in the future, which in turn lays the groundwork for giving-and-receiving behavior.

A child's understanding of trust is from his own experiences and the environment he is brought up. When a child's desires and reliability are fulfilled in most cases, he tends to conclude that people are trustful; otherwise, he may draw the lesson from his unfulfillment that people are not trustful. A child will tend to trust others if he is brought up in a simple, warm and friendly environment, and he is told the stories of mutual help and trust. However in other context, a child's parents and other people intentionally inform him of examples of mistrust to drive home the lesson that 「You can't trust people」. Understandably, such child inclines not to trust others when he grows up.

**Professional or Special Training**　A person's professional or special training can incline him a different orientation to trust. For instance, accountants and financial workers are oriented to be skeptical of financial statements full of identical numbers and how much they may differ from the real data. People working in human resources department appear to question more the accuracy of a person's description of his educational and working background, and it is an important reason that the application documents should be, at the request, endorsed by official certificates.

In contrast, soldiers and policemen are trained to trust their comrade-in-arms orpartners by reason that they have to rely on each other to carry out a dangerous mission under covering fire, a moment when one solder's life is in the hand of the other. Teaching orients people to trust others due to two reasons: the first is teachers believe what they tell students are knowledge, facts and truth. There is no point to question accuracy of knowledge. The second is out of moral consideration that mutual trust is a good virtue and therefore it is teachers' responsibility to advocate concept of trust first by their own examples.

In addition to the above-mentioned two elements which are enduring and difficult to change, there are also some other important elements which affect trust. Those elements are changeable and accessible.

(2) Changeable Elements

**Past Credit Record**　A person's willingness to trust another person depends on his knowledge of the other's past credit record. We will not trust someone who fails to perform his duty or is unable to complete a task or fails to keep his promise. The reason for the failure may differ from time to time; however, if there is repeated record of the person's failures, mistrust is the natural result. Surely, a person can do better to improve his future record and thus win other's trust.

**Competence of Others to Perform a Task**　A person's willingness to trust another person depends on his estimation of the other's ability to complete a task successfully. At this point, there should be a distinction between capability and affection. Our feeling toward a person is different from trust, which means affection does not grow with trust. You may feel fond of a person very much, but it is highly possible that he is not capable of doing the job he is assigned. For instance, you will not trust a teenager to send a large sum of money to a far away place although you love him very much. When affection is confused with capability in one's interpretation of other's intention and motives can be different from time to time depending on their understanding of others.

**Reward System**  In a win-lose reward system, when competition is rewarded, i.e., our gain is the other's loss and our loss is the other's gain, trusting the other is clearly not in our self-interest companies selling the same products are rivals in business and understandably they will conceal or distort information, withhold facts and disguise their ideas. Things will be different in a joint-reward system in which cooperation is encouraged because in such reward system things won't be done without joint efforts, so it is all natural that the two sides will trust each other, share information, ask each other for advice and reach common conclusions. Of course, in today's world there are neither permanent competitors nor cooperators. Where things will be directed depends on our efforts. It is hoped that trustful relationship among people should be established on account of positive effects of trust.

### 5.4.4 Effects of Trust

Trust is a decisive element in people's relationship. We need trust between peers, superiors and subordinates, between producers and consumers, teachers and students. Studies show that trust stimulates intellectual development and originality, and leads to greater emotional stability and self-control. Trust facilitates acceptance and openness of expression. Trust encourages cooperation and mutual understanding, and it is fundamental for establishing sound relationship among negotiating team members as well as between negotiating parties. People working in a team with high level of trust send signal of trust to each other and receive trust from each other, which will increase level of trust among the members (see Figure 5-3). Negotiations based on high level of trust can increase chances of double win results.

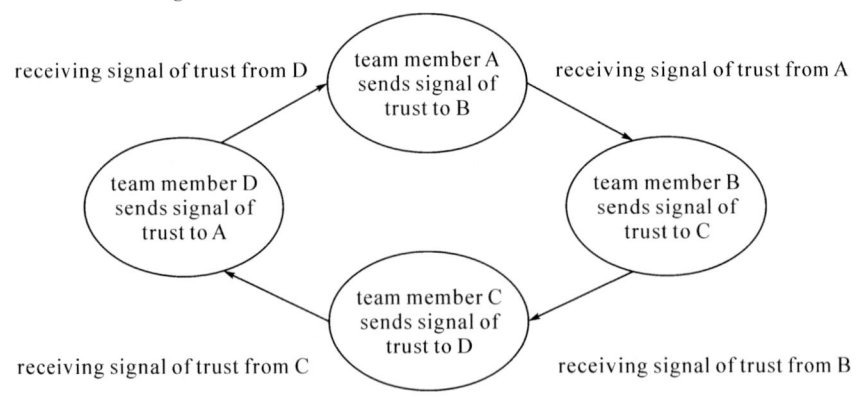

**Figure 5-3  Mutual Trust Results in Higher Lever of Trust**

Conversely, mistrust provokes rejection and defensiveness, damages collaboration and relationship of team members and negotiating parties. When working in a group with high level of mistrust, members send signal of mistrust and expect mistrust from others, thus produce low level of trust. In such a team, members have difficulty in concentrating on their tasks, and misperceive the motives and values of others, and as a result they refuse or deny good suggestions (see Figure 5-4). Mistrust damages cooperation and mutual understanding. Suspiciousness caused by mistrust will finally lead negotiation into failure. Many cases have made clear the point that important negotiations were spoiled not because of lack of constructive options or efforts, but because of lack of mutual trust and sincerity. Paradoxically, high corrosive and destructive effects of mistrust may often drive out trust because there is always a strong desire for a better relationship among people and between negotiating parties.

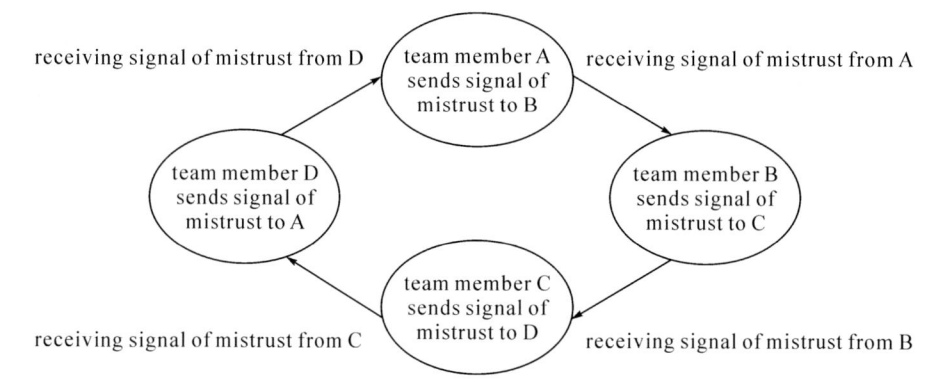

Figure 5-4  **Mistrust Results in Higher Level of Mistrust**

Middle East Peace Talk between Palestine and Israel has seen the serious setback in 2001, which has caused the death of more than 1,000 civilians in exchange of fire and clashes in one year time. Countries showing concern to the peace talk process, such as US, European countries and Arabian countries have come up with various suggestions or solutions, some of which were considered feasible by both parties. However, deep mistrust between the two sides has again and again prevented the implementation of the solutions. The future success of the peace talk rests with the two sides to establish mutual trust. There is the promise that the peace talk will turn to the better because mistrust between the two sides has brought about devastating results, loss of human lives and property, slowdown in economic development and drop of confidence in the government. If the conflicts develop further toward negative direction, the turning point for the better will emerge. As a Chinese proverb says, 「Things will develop in the opposite direction when they go to extreme.」

### 5.4.5　Suggestions of Enhancing Mutual Trust

In the complexity of negotiation, ambiguous and mixed interest situation leads negotiators either to convergent alignment of interest or divergent alignment of interest. Mutual trust among negotiating parties leads to emphasizing the convergent aspects of alignment. Trust encourages cooperation by increasing one's focus on common interest and joint benefits. On the contrary, mistrust emphasizes the divergent aspects of alignment and discourages cooperation. Mistrust focuses on differences and heightens the desire to protect one's interest. Mistrust polarizes thinking and undermines the search for creative options. It drives negotiators toward distributive solutions which maximize self-interests. The striking contrast of trust and mistrust between negotiating parties tells us that it is worthwhile that we take great pains to find out ways to enhance mutual trust.

Some tentative suggestions are made here for consideration.

(1) Encourage mutual trust by establishing trust-rewarded system in childhood education, in job training and in negotiation. It makes little sense to demand trust when the reward system is clearly and totally win-lose. Such a complete opposition of interests can only foster low trust. In a purely competitive market, low trust between organizations may be acceptable when it stimulates efficiency and innovation. Within an organization, however, the benefits of competitiveness and low trust among components of the organization must be carefully weighed against the costs. If negotiators wish to increase trust, the system would have to be changed toward mixed or joint rewards. This is a necessary step. Without it other steps will fail.

(2) Build up people's confidence in trust through giving information, influence, self-control and concessions, and seek reciprocation from the other. In this approach, the negotiator increases his exposure moderately, thereby signaling that he seeks a similar response from others. The increment should be moderate because other low-trust negotiators misunderstanding the behavior may initially exploit the new vulnerability rather than offer a matching increase in their exposure. The process of tendering small exposures may have to be repeated many times. A major shift from low trust to high trust rarely occurs after only one or two exposures. Increasing trust requires a period of offers and tests of sincerity.

(3) Discuss frankly with the other party what is generating mistrust in negotiation. Another more direct but more difficult approach is to analyze the sources of trust or mistrust in an open way. Such a discussion probes issues beneath immediate, tangible business problems. This may be difficult because some people become defensive, believing that trust is personal matter not to be revealed to others. Therefore, it is fundamental to be sincere and honest to your negotiating team members and your counterparts so that you will be able to talk about your mistrust frankly. The paradox is that people must have some trust to be able to talk about their mistrust.

(4) Build up people's confidence on mutual trust by rules and regulations. Some people

driven by selfishness opt for advancing their own interests by cheating or telling lies, which can greatly reduce people's confidence in mutual trust and produce corrosive effect on trustful social atmosphere. Rules and regulations can limit those who want to benefit from cheating by increasing their cost of doing so.

# Case Study

The case study explains the result of a negotiation simulation in management development seminars.

### Introduction of the Background Information

The Conrad Electronics, a medium-size company with headquarters and manufacturing facilities in the northeastern United States, designed and manufactured receivers, transmitters, amplifiers, and other specialized electronic equipment. It sold its products in several markets including the military, the government, original equipment manufacturers, and distributors who supplied retailers. The company had been profitable during World War II and into the middle 1950s with 55 percent of its annual sales on a cost-plus basis to the military and various prime contractors. Then military and government purchases declined, technology began to change, and the company faced increasingly strong competition.

In an effort to reverse its financial losses, top management cut the work force by 25percent. To sustain cash flow, capital expenditures were cut by 75 percent. One year after these drastic steps, the company broke even. Then the board of directors replaced the president and the vice presidents of manufacturing and industrial relations. The former controller was promoted to president. Other insiders were moved up to the vice presidential posts.

During the next two years, the new management operated the company at a small profit. It earned 4 percent on net worth. But manufacturing facilities were increasingly obsolete each year. Although marketing were making progress in developing sales in the nonmilitary market, manufacturing was having difficulty meeting delivery promises. There was high turnover in the labor force, many superior engineering and production people left to take jobs with nearby competitors.

The new top managers felt they were beginning to get control of the situation. They agreed that modernization and expansion of facilities was essential to the company's long-term success. But unknown to the vice presidents, the board of directors held a special meeting with the president in which it demanded improved profits next year. If this was not attained the board would ask for the president's resignation.

Under the circumstances the president tentatively concluded that modernization and expansion were not feasible in the short term. It would take more than one year to locate a new site, construct buildings, move equipment and people, and arrange the necessary financing. Also the board probably would not approve a heavy capital program, because these activities would interfere with productivity and decrease short-term profits. The president had to meet with his vice presidents to announce his decision and formulate appropriate plans.

**Negotiation Simulation**

This case background was given to executives of several majorcompanies. Then the groups of executives took the roles of the president and the vice presidents of the Conrad Electronics Company and conducted the president's meeting. Other executives in the seminars were nonparticipant observers.

The managerial problems facing the Conrad Electronics Company were critical and complex. Small improvements in the quality of management's decisions and small increases in the motivation of managers would have great impact on results. The central problems required developing a strategy that would increase short–term profits without undermining long–term growth. And this had to be done with management support for short-term actions despite the vice presidents' disappointment over delays in modernization and expansion.

All the executives simulating the managers of the Conrad Electronics Company were given identical financial and operating data. More than 80 different groups of executives worked on this case. Half of the groups, however, were briefed to expect that they tended to mistrust each other as a result of their past two years of working together. The other half were briefed to expect that they tended to trust each other. The decision outcomes of the different groups clearly and consistently supported the model of trust that has been presented previously.

**Results of Low Trust**

Low-trust groups resisted examining the situation in any depth. Instead, they blamed the president or the board of directors for short-sightedness. Usually, after much frustration, the president would forcefully issue edicts backed by implied threats of dismissal. The vice presidents would reluctantly agree to examine limited alternatives such as reducing the product line to further emphasize high-profit items or substantially reducing the labor force again.

Such behavioris common in low–trust groups under stress. They were defensive. They blamed others. They were unable to see the situation in its entirety. They were unwilling to accept responsibility for their part in the dilemma. They focused on the withheld goal of modernization and expansion. They had great difficulty in considering other aspects of the situation and inventing other options.

When two vice presidents found they agreed, they joined forces to attack the president or whoever disagreed. These attacks polarized relationships and drove people further apart. Although some workable ideas were proposed, they were not heard or were rejected for false reasons. Each manager concentrated on protecting his area and pursuing only his interests. There was little attention to their interdependence. After the meetings the majority of managers were frustrated and said they would seriously consider employment with another company.

### Results of High Trust

In contrast, high-trust groups analyzed the situation responsibly and creatively. They also recognized their disappointment over not being able to modernize and expand immediately.

They generated alternatives not requiring much capital in the short run but which could substantially improve profitability and aid their long-run interests. These included leasing nearby vacant manufacturing space and sourcing more semifinished or finished products. They would select promising new products and move them more rapidly from research into production. They agreed to revise their short-range and long-range plans and planned to present and discuss a new overall view with the board.

Their behavior provided evidence to that of high-trust groups under stress. They could deal creatively with new constraints and at the same time assist each other. They explored a range of goals, near-term and long-term. They could listen to many alternatives, select promising ones and shape them into workable courses of action.

They were supportive. They could use their differences to develop plans that integrated the functional areas—marketing, manufacturing, finance, and so on. They balanced short-term constraints with long-term needs and interests. After their meeting, the majority of managers said they would not consider employment with another company.

These results may sound unrealistic and overly optimistic. Actually the managers were realistic and hard-nosed. They were aware of the risks and the real possibility of failure but they said the situation was not hopeless and they were willing to dedicate themselves to surmounting the difficulties.

# Exercises

(1) Exchanging relevant ideas and feelings more openly.
(2) Defining goals and problems more clearly and realistically.
(3) Searching for alternatives more extensively.
(4) Having greater influence on solutions.
(5) More satisfied with their problem-solving efforts.
(6) Having greater motivation to implement conclusions.
(7) Becoming more of a team.
(8) Having greater loyalty and less desire to leave for another job.

# Chapter 6  Negotiation Strategies and Tactics

## 6.1  Developing Your Negotiation Strategies

Because of different culture, background, education and other elements, everyone has his or her own characteristic negotiation approach, or style, when it comes to managing conflict. For example, a particular person may be characterized as being more (or less) aggressive, dominating, inflexible, dishonest, constructive, compliant, co-operative, competitive and so on. According to Thomas and Kilmann (1974), these different approaches can be grouped into five distinct categories as follows.

The five main negotiation strategies are Competitive, Accommodating, Compromising, Collaborating and Avoidance. Competitive strategy involves an 「I win, you lose」 attitude. Accommodation is 「I will let you win in exchange for some other benefit I hope to gain now or later」. Compromising is 「I don't care who wins, I just want to get this over with quickly」. Collaboration is 「We can both win by expanding the pie before we cut it」. And avoidance is 「I don't really want to play at all」.

### 6.1.1  The Competitive Strategy

The competitive strategy of 「I win, you lose」 is the one most often used in settlement negotiations. It involves the use of intimidation, distraction, and diversion tactics to gain leverage.

You can choose a competitive strategy regardless of your bargaining position. If you have greater leverage, you can use competitive tactics to realize your advantage. But if your case is weaker, competitive tactics themselves can create value.

Most negotiations of every type begin with a competitive strategy. The parties need to test each other's wills before they begin bargaining seriously. The parties then continue their competitive bargaining or shift their approach to one of the four other strategies.

Following are examples of some competitive tactics:

(1) Alternatives to Settlement

Emphasize you have better choices than settlement. The side that cares more about settling is weaker. If you have the better BATNA (Best Alternative to a Negotiated Agreement), you have more「chips」. Make that clear to your adversary.

One example is the threat to「beat your adversary in the market place」.

This threatens the lawful use of market power to make a legal victory Pyrrhic. Properly used, this tactic is effective.

(2)「Anything But That」

Claim your adversary's offer is not enough, even when it is. Pick up other concessions before he「wrenches」your agreement from you.

(3) Bluffing

Bluffing is at negotiation's core because each side has limited information. A good bluff uses your adversary's uncertainty to create even more doubt. And doubt translates into risk, and risk into money. Look for signs of uncertainty on her face or in her body language. But a bluff is not a lie—never expressly mislead.

A standard「bluff」is「take it or leave it」. Meet this bluff (and most others) by calling it. You won't know your adversary's limit unless you push for it.

(4) Bringing In the Media

Threaten to report some action or behavior to the media to induce concessions. Plaintiffs will use this tactic in media-sensitive industries, such as the entertainment industry. Recognize that parties in such industries have fair resistance to this tactic and will combat your disclosure through press releases of their own.

(5) Creating Deadlock

Create deadlock to force your adversary into concessions to move the negotiations along. But distinguish this tactic, as a tactic, from a legitimate impasse. Even reasonable people can disagree.

(6) Diversion/Distraction

If you feel you are losing an important issue, shift the discussions to a different issue before you concede. Even change the subject altogether or use some other technique to distract your adversary from completing the current discussion.

(7) Done Deal

Take some unilateral action and present it to other side as a「done deal」. Your adversary is thus forced to acquiesce or walk out. An example is when a co-party shows up at the negotiation only to discover that the other co-party has already settled.

(8) Good Cop/Bad Cop

Team an aggressive negotiator with a friendly negotiator to win concessions. The aggressive negotiator uses competitive tactics to anger and distract your adversary. The friendly negotiator steps into smooth things over. The friendly negotiator becomes the mediator between your adversary and the aggressive negotiator, and you can strike a deal on the friendly negotiator's terms.

(9) Irrational Behavior

Sometimes act irrationally, not only to distract and unnerve, but also to undermine your adversary's confidence. Lawyers tend toward rational argument. The irrational can throw off even an experienced negotiator.

(10) Limited Authority

Claim to lack authority to settle at some amount and ask your adversary to reduce the offer to your authority limits. To prevent your adversary from using this tactic, determine her authority in advance. If she lacks full authority, do not proceed.

(11) Limited Time

Constrain the time limits of the negotiation. Counter this tactic by clarifying time constraints in advance.

(12) 「Poor Me」

Act like you have no background or training in negotiation and ask your adversary's help. He may sympathize with you and be more reasonable than he intended. This tactic can be especially effective for younger advocates.

(13) Silence

Very few people can endure silence. Silence can impel your adversary to give you more information or concede more than he intended.

If your adversary's silence discomforts you, say something like, 「I see you are thinking about my offer. I'm going to leave the room for a bit. Please let me know when you are ready to respond.」 And begin to leave. The silence will end before you reach the door.

(14) Straw Man

Demand agreement on Issue 1, which your adversary cares about most. Create deadlock and then 「reluctantly」 concede Issue 1 to gain agreement on Issue 2 (the one you care about most) —and maybe Issues 3 and 4 as well.

(15) Turnabout

After you have conceded an issue or otherwise acted defensively, 「gain space」 by coming out strong on the next issue. But choose that issuewisely. It must be important, and you must win it.

(16) Use of Power

Threaten to use your power and sometimes actually use it. But heed this chess axiom: 「The threat is more powerful than its execution.」 The threat creates doubt and, hence, concessions; but once implemented, you limit your adversary's choices, and she will do what she must respond to.

## 6.1.2 The Accommodation Strategy

An accommodating party will sublimate its concerns to satisfy the other party's, at least for the present. You choose an accommodation strategy if you have done wrong and want to get the matter over with quickly and less expensively (airplane crashes and oil spills are two examples where quick settlements will save money). And there are less dramatic examples where a desire to limit personal or business disruption will encourage you to end the matter quickly. Or maybe you wish to gain some goodwill or other benefit now or later through a quick resolution.

Some accommodating tactics:

(1) Face-Saving

Prioritize the other side's dignity. Use every opportunity to give 「face」 and respect to the other side. Allow the other side to make tactful retreats to avoid embarrassment.

(2) Identification

Align your interests with your adversary's, see the facts from her perspective, and agree with her arguments. But don't concede unnecessary issues.

(3) Take the Lead Oar

Move the negotiation forward regardless of who created the difficulty. Suggest solutions, offer to prepare the documents, and be flexible about timing.

(4) Take Reasonable Actions

Always be the party of reason, whether setting realistic deadlines or other conditions of the negotiation. Rarely if ever use a competitive tactic to move the other side.

## 6.1.3 The Compromising Strategy

Compromisers look for an expedient, partially satisfactory middle ground. Their primary interest is haste and 「rough justice」. Thus, compromisers are willing to trade concessions, sometimes despite the merits, simply to make a deal. One example is a dispute involving an ongoing business relationship. You may choose to give a little to preserve the relationship.

Following are the compromiser's tactics.

(1) Bit-By-Bit

Gain your concessions 「bit-by-bit」 rather than all at once. As the direction of the incremental movement becomes clear, suggest meeting at the mid-point.

(2) Conditional Proposals

Make a proposal conditioned upon your adversary's acceptance of issues you need favorably resolved.

(3) 「Log-Rolling」

Concede on an unimportant issue to you (but important to your adversary) in exchange for your adversary's concession on an issue that does matter to you.

(4) 「Splitting the Baby」

At some point offer to split the difference with the other side, whether through an exchange of remaining issues or halving the dollar amount still in issue.

(5) Tit-For-Tat

Never make a concession without obtaining one in return. This rule underlies all bargaining (「I won't negotiate against myself!」). But you must adhere to it when compromising or you will「compromise」away all your value simply for expediency's sake.

### 6.1.4　The Collaborative Strategy

The collaborative strategy (「Win-Win」) seeks to create value for both sides. Its focus is on each side's underlying interests and not their positions. You give the other side something it wants in exchange for something you want. You both gain in the process.

Business negotiators use the collaborative strategy. Business negotiations involve many different components of value and risk allocation, all of which can be traded against one another for an ultimately satisfactory outcome. The lesser opportunities for value and risk allocation in litigation settlement talks explain why most litigants begin with a competitive strategy.

Following are some collaborative tactics.

(1) Flexibility

Be flexible—the hallmark of a skilled collaborator. Know when to mount a tactical retreat and when to press for an important point. Be willing to reexamine decided issues, but don't feel obligated to make further concessions unless you also gain something.

(2) Focus on Process

Process often translates into improved substance. Rearrange the mechanical steps of the negotiation to overcome impasse and deadlock and enhance problem-solving prospects. Typical examples: take a break in the negotiation; change the physical setting of the negotiation; or return the negotiation to the fact-finding stage.

(3) Identify with Others in Similar Circumstances

This tactic might be termed the「transitive rule」of negotiation: argue that the other side has already treated similarly-situated X in a particular way, and they should treat you the same way. Defendants in multi-defendant suits often use this tactic when the plaintiff has settled favorably with one of them.

### 6.1.5　The Avoidance Strategy

Avoiders try to ignore the entire dispute, or some specific issues, for at least some period of time. The avoider uses tactics to sidestep or postpone an issue or withdraw altogether from what the avoider perceives as a threatening situation.

(1) Negotiate Money Issues First

If you prioritize money, insist that money be negotiated first. By fixing the money component of the settlement, you avoid discounts for the cash-worth of any non-money concessions.

(2) Negotiate Non-money Issues First

But if you wish to avoid paying money, address the non-money issues first. You can then value your non-monetary concessions and use those values to reduce the amount of money you will pay your adversary.

(3) Refuse to Combine Negotiation of Related Disputes

If you are litigating multiple related actions, refuse to negotiate the actions together if you determine that you are stronger in one case than another. You can thus avoid off setting your strong case with the other cases' weaknesses.

(4) Walk Out of the Negotiation

If you become engaged in negotiations you are not ready for, walk out. You may state dissatisfaction with your adversary's proposals, but your goal is to defer discussions to a later time.

(5) Withdraw an Issue

If you are not yet ready to address an issue, perhaps because it is too painful or simply not ripe for discussion, remove that issue from the negotiation, for at least some period of time.

(6) Switching Strategies

You may decide to switch strategies if you feel you are making insufficient progress. As negotiations move forward and you want to encourage continued progress, you may abandon a competitive strategy for one of the cooperative strategies (accommodation, compromising, or collaborative). Or you may instead move to a more competitive strategy in response to the other side's competitive behavior.

In a word, the game of negotiation requires specific strategies and the fight tactics to implement that strategy. Your case and bargaining position will determine which negotiation strategy will work best for you: competitive, when you must have what you want; accommodation, when you have done wrong and want to settle quickly; compromising, when expedience matters most; collaborative, when you want to create a bigger pie; and avoidance, when you are not yet ready to bargain.

## 6.2 Strategic Considerations

Besides of the strategic approach we discussed hereinbefore, there are quite a few background considerations which will influence the strategy: repeatability, strength of both parties, importance of the deal, time scale and negotiation resources.

### 6.2.1 The Repeatability of a Negotiation

Repeatability is an important influence on the styles and tactics that should be used. If it is a whole series of deals with one organization, then there needs to be goodwill and lasting relationships built with that organization; a personal relationship is essential, as in the case of PANASONIC. If on the other hand, the negotiation is for one time dealing with an organization not likely to be met again, then the situation is strategically different. It is not necessary to have the same concern to establish goodwill. Thus the first strategic consideration is the repeatability of the deal. If it is likely to be a repeat business, then the first strategy (cooperating) mentioned beforehand can be a good option in the negotiation.

### 6.2.2 The Strengths of Negotiating Parties

The second influence is each party's strength. If a party is the only people with whom a deal could be made, then the party is in a strong position. If there are many potential customers or suppliers, then the party is in a relatively weak position. Both the styles in which the party operates and the personalities of those who negotiate on their behalf will influence the choice of strategy by the opposing team.

The second party's strength is the converse of the first. The second party is strong if they dominate a market either as buyers or sellers, and weak if they are just one of many. The second party also has a style characteristic of the organization personalities and strengths on which they should capitalize.

### 6.2.3 The Importance of a Deal

Then there is the importance of a deal. If the negotiation is about a deal worth millions of dollars, then the strategy needs to be different from negotiations in thousands of dollars. Or if negotiating a deal for a well-established product in well-established market, there is less strategic concern than if at the dramatic point of launching a new product into a new market.

### 6.2.4 The Time Scale

In international business negotiation, the time scale for the deal may also influence the strategy. If it is imperative that the deal be concluded quickly, then the negotiation strategy may be different from what it would be if there is little urgency. In the former case, the powerful side might choose 「controlling」 strategy while the weak side might give up (if the agreement to be reached leads to loss on its side or the conditions are unacceptable) or use 「avoiding or accommodating」 strategy.

### 6.2.5 The Negotiation Resources

And the negotiation resources may also influence strategy. If there are few qualified negotiators and many projects to be negotiated, then the negotiators cannot be spared for long periods on any one deal.

These are not the only strategic considerations. It's not possible to generalize about the special situations. However, these general considerations will influence the choice of strategy.

## 6.3 Useful Negotiation Strategies

Usually, 「strategy」 is considered as something comprising the techniques used in actual process of negotiation, as well as the tactics used as devices to implement the strategy.

「Negotiation situations may be linked to the techniques used when dancing in a crowded ballroom.」(Quan Ying, 2003) When to move, where to go, how fast to go, all are determined by certain definite conditions: the tempo of the step, the partner, the other couples, the mental state of the team, the presumed mental state of the other people, subconscious adherence to traffic rules and regulations, and so on.

To accomplish the aims in negotiation, the inexperienced negotiator's strategy will be limited to a few simple and obvious devices. The expert negotiator, however, will employ a variety of means to accomplish his objectives. These means will involve 「when」 strategy or 「how and where」 strategy.

## 6.3.1 「When」Strategy

「When」 strategy essentially involves a proper sense of timing. It is easier to use in a negotiation when a new element enters the picture rather than when all elements are stated. But properly applied, it can change a static situation into a dynamic one. It can be separated into the following: forbearance, surprise, fait accompli, bland withdrawal, apparent withdrawal, reversal, limits, and feinting.

(1) Forbearance

When one puts off answering a question, or does not answer a question at all, or pauses to leave the site thinking outside about possible decisions, he or she is using the strategy often referred to as forbearance. Waiting so that the team members can think better about the case and letting the other side have time to think about it also come under this heading. Forbearance avoids a direct conflict and eventually achieves a settlement.

Another element of forbearance is to know when to stop. Just as the lawyer must know when he or she has sufficiently cross-examined the witness, the salesman must know when to stop barging, a qualified negotiator should know when to stop for a while, so it is often said that forbearance or patience in negotiation clearly pays dividends.

(2) Surprise

This strategy involves a sudden shift in attitude, requirement, method, argument, or approach. The change is usually drastic and dramatic, although it need not always be so. Surprise can be used as a tactic in negotiation when new information is introduced or a new approach is taken. For example, in the middle of a negotiation it is sometimes effective to substitute a new team leader. The substitution of the chief member follows the alteration of the negotiation terms and the content of the contract. If the other parties continue the negotiation, they will have to face some new faces and this will mean a new concession for them. Sometimes during a negotiation, when one party acts completely irrationally, it is very likely using the surprise tactic. The seemingly irrational person feels that this behavior will make it more difficult for the other side to cope with the situation.

(3) Fait Accompli

This is a risky strategy, but there is often a temptation to use it. It demands that one acts and achieves the goal against the opposition and then sees what the opposition will do about it. Those who employ this strategy must make an appraisal of the consequences in case it should prove to be a failure.

For example, if a contract is sent which contains a provision that is not agreed with, you cross out the portion that is not wanted, sign the contract, and send it back. Thus, your opponents are confronted with a fait accompli, which means it is now up to them. They can either return the contract and reopen the negotiation, or accept the deletion. Quite often they will accept the changed contract.

(4) Bland Withdrawal

Here the management is using a bland withdrawal strategy. And the union was satisfied that the problem was so easily solved; the company was more than happy to have put the most costly part of the construction work behind them at a considerable saving over the Texas. In the negotiation between Shanghai American School and the Golf Club mentioned at the beginning of this chapter, the American school just used this strategy.

(5) Reversal

In this strategy, the action is in opposition to what may be considered to be the popular trend or goal.

Bernard Baruch, a master in international speculation, once said that people who make money in the stock market are those who are the first in and the first out. By this he meant that one should buy in when everyone was pessimistic at the bear market and sell out when the prevailing atmosphere was optimistic at a bull market. This strategy may sound easy but be difficult to execute. When it is so, and it is as simple as it is theoretically said, everyone could immediately become rich and powerful.

Reversal strategy allows time to think of new alternatives. Double reversal has its advantages.

(6) Limits

This strategy means this is the absolute end or bottom line. Limits can be of many types. There are communication limits placed on each negotiating team as to what they may talk about and to whom they may talk; time limits set a deadline to conclude the negotiation, and geographical limits such as a proposal applying to only one section of the country or only to one company.

When a party sets a limit, there is no reason why one must be restricted by it unless it suits the ultimate goal to inform. In negotiation, if one chooses to ignore a limit, try to save face for the person who has set the limit. Humor can often be helpful in this regard. For example, once a limit was set at 4 o'clock, the other side drew a cartoon of a clock face without the number 4. This released the tension and the negotiations continued.

Limits of many sorts may be employed merely to test the strength of one's position. It is of importance to have other counterstrategies available.

## 6.3.2 「How」Strategy

(1) Feinting

It is somewhere looking to the right but going to the left. This strategy involves an apparent move in one direction to divert attention from the real project. It can also involve a situation in which one gives the opponent a false impression that they have more information or knowledge than they actually possessed. In the course of a negotiation, feinting can be useful when giving in on a point that is not especially important and can be used to cover up important elements, ignore the important things and stress the things that are not important. The purpose of doing this is to give enough time to make the coordination and decision for some key articles, to divert the others' attention on important matters. Satisfy the other side through concessions on matters of minor importance and this will create a positive atmosphere and pave a way for the settlement on items of vital importance.

(2) Release and Catch

Using this tactic means to let the counterparts have the impression that you are indifferent to the final contract.

As a skill and tactic, this one is widely used not only in military area, but also in negotiation area where competition and cooperation are highly united. One side of the negotiation is willing to cooperate with the other side and hopes to bring benefits to both sides. However, the other side usually uses strict condition to push the negotiation into the deadlock. Under this condition, the other side of the negotiation can use this tactic by firstly expressing the fake purpose of abandoning the negotiation. As the counterpart can not even get the least benefit, the counterpart will give up their own requirement in order to reach an agreement.

## 6.4 Useful Negotiation Tactics

The competent negotiator first ensures that he or she knows what the other party is bidding. On this basis, he or she must have an idea how to satisfy the other party in gaining their interests and at the same time have to figure out what are the interests that really belongs to them and what are the things they expect to get.

### 6.4.1 Offensive and Defensive Tactics

Offensive tactics are designed to take the initiative while defensive tactics are the counter to offensive ones, and they are the springboards from which a counter-offensive can be launched.

Negotiators cannot rely on defensive tactics only, because no defensive is ever perfect, a weak point will be found upon which the opponent can concentrate his attack.

◎ **Offensive Tactics**

(1) Asking Questions

There are four kinds of questions involved: probing, specific, attacking, and 「yes/no」 questions.

The probing questions are difficult to answer because they are phrased in general terms. They are intended to gain information for one party to make sure the weak point in the opponent's propositions before a major attack. For example, 「We have had a look at your quotation, but perhaps you could explain rather more fully the way in which you have arrived at the increase in price.」

The specific questions are designed to force an admission based on the information gained from the probing question and data already known. For instance, 「What is your program for manufacture arid testing?」 These questions are simple and short without disclosing all facts.

The 「yes/no」 questions should never be asked unless the questioner has prepared the ground in advance, and is satisfied that the answer he will obtain is the one he wants to hear. They are designed to set up a direct attack. The attacking questions are designed to force a concession based on the answers to the specific questions and other data, such as 「How can that be valid?」

(2) Making the Other Side Appear Unreasonable

It is a method of challenging the validity of a proposition. A case is found in which application of the propositions would be absurd, so the person who posed it is challenged to redefine it in more limited terms.

(3) Pulling the Pig's Tail

It is a colloquial term referring to the result of the activity that the animal pulls as hard as it can in the opposite direction. One party will over emphasize the apparent importance to his securing a particular point when his real objective is the direct opposite. Some negotiators are suspicious of any proposal made by their opposite partner.

(4) Use of Commitments

The use of commitments is needed to persuade the opponent of the truth of the statements the party is making. It is a major offensive negotiating tactic that both sides will use. When the commitments are of different rank, the higher will normally prevail.

(5) Discovering Interests

As negotiating about interests is a better way to conduct technology trade negotiations, discovering the other side's interests becomes a paramount necessity. This simply means asking questions: 「Could you tell us…?」 「Why do you need…?」 or 「So your real interest is…?」

To facilitate the search for options, both sides should not only try to find out the real interests of their counterparts but also state explicitly those of their own, giving reasons wherever necessary.

(6) Presenting Arguments

In negotiations, a party often feels the need to show to the other side that they know exactly where the other's real interests lie and will not compromise theirs. The valid reasons must be put into some kind of an order. Each point should be stronger than the one before until the argument.

(7) 「The Right Answer」 Tactic

When the two parties have conflicts of interests, which are pretty difficult to resolve, they may try 「the right answer」 tactic, which works in this way:

Agree that a state of deadlock exists;

Step out of the role of negotiators;

Study the problem objectively;

Seek the right answer;

Agree on the right answer;

Return to the role of negotiators and see if the right answer offers acceptable solutions.

This tactic is particularly useful to business people. Whenever the other side suggests something doubtful, ask about it until it is absolutely justifiable.

(8) 「The Best Alternative」 Tactic

This is often used in tender business. After a receiver receives a number of offers, he decides which company has made the most attractive offer and then negotiates with the other companies with a view to improve his 「best alternative」. Once he can improve it no further, he begins negotiation with his first choice, negotiating from a much-strengthened position.

◎Defensive Tactics

(1) Minimum Response and Pretended Misunderstanding

The most effective of defensive tactic in negotiation is to say just enough to compel the other side to go on talking. The more they will reveal, the more they feel compelled to reveal in order to be persuasive, and the nearer they will come to exposing their genuine motives and the real level of their minimum negotiating objective.

(2) Side-Stepping

If one party does not want to answer the opponent's question directly, he may seek to side-step the issue. So, in answering to a question 「Can you guarantee completion by a specified date?」 the party might reply, 「Here, have a look at the program, then I can show you how we have arrived at the end date and you can see for yourself the problems.」

(3) The 「Yes-But」 Technique

If the negotiator faces a question that he wishes to answer in the negative, but he does not want to give offence, he may use the technique of 「yes-but」. The affirmative part of the answer should appear to align the negotiator alongside his opponent, and so establish the negotiator as someone who is cooperative and appreciative of the viewpoint of the other side. The negative part is intended to identify some of the reasons that prevent the negotiator form doing what the other side would like him to do.

(4) The Counter Questions

If the opponent uses questions as offensive tactics, the party's correct response is the counter questions. The questions are designed to compel the opponent to limit the scope of his inquiry and to reveal more of his own position.

(5) Straw Issues

A straw issue is one that is of no value to one party in itself, but it is raised with the intention to be lost, thus provides the opportunity for the party to secure a genuine concession from the opponent in return. Securing a particular concession from the opponent must allow the opponent something in exchange. By including one or more straw issues in his initial demands, the party ensures that he has something in the bank to allow the opponent as compensation for the opponent abandoning or modifying his own initial demands. The party must view the problem through the opponent's eyes in deciding on what to select as a straw issue.

(6) Exposing Dirty Tricks

It is quite common in negotiations that the negotiators find their counterparts playing dirty tricks. First, they must recognize that what is happening is in fact signs of dirty tricks. Next they must show their counterparts that they understand the game by exposing it.

### 6.4.2 Tactics of Making Concessions

Making concessions is one of the most popular tactics used in the bargaining process to keep the negotiation ongoing. Making concessions however has a lot to do with many other factors. Every concession is very closely connected to a party's own interests. Although it depends mainly on the negotiator's flexible usage of the tactics of making concessions, it also is constrained by some basic principles. The following principles are often used:

(1) A concession by one party must be matched by a concession of the other party.

(2) It's better for the pace of concession to be as little as possible and the frequency of concession to be slow. What's more, the pace of concession must be similar as between the two parties.

(3) A party should trade their concession to their own advantage, doing their best to give the other party plenty of satisfaction even if the concessions are small.

(4) A party must help the other party to see each of their concessions as being significant.

(5) Move at a measured pace towards the projected settlement point.

(6) Reserve concessions until they are needed.

### 6.4.3 Towards Settlement

When the parties become aware that a settlement is approaching, they should make the final offer. Characteristics of this final offer are:

(1) It should not be made too soon. Otherwise it will be taken as just another concession—one of many still to be hoped for.

(2) It must be big enough to symbolize closure. Rounding off a bid sufficient yet not too generous would certainly have the required impact.

(3) Negotiating to our advantage demands the last halfpenny. If you do not squeeze the final 1/4 percent off his discount or the final two days off his delivery—he will not have the satisfaction of believing that he has taken you absolutely to the limit.

(4) Give him that satisfaction.

Finally, at the end of the negotiation:

(1) Summarize.

(2) Produce a written record.

(3) Identify action needs and responsibilities.

## Case Study

This case reveals how different negotiation tactics can be employed to negotiate and concludes a better international agreement.

The completion of the Panama Canal is one of the world's greatest engineering feats. The negotiations to complete and build this vital connector between two oceans spans decades. The cost in human lives, suffering, and capital staggers the imagination. It all began in 1847 when the United States entered in a treaty with New Granada (later to be known as Colombia), and which allowed the US a transit passage over the Isthmus of Panama. The treaty guaranteed Panama's neutrality and recognized that Colombia would have sovereignty over the region.

Nothing really occurred with this development and ultimately, a French company called the Compagnie Nouvelle du Canal de Panama acquired the contract to build the canal in 1881. By 1889, the Compagnie had gone bankrupt and had lost roughly around 287 million USD. It is also in 1889 that the US has become convinced that the canal passage was absolutely vital to their interests. They appointed Rear Admiral John Walker to head the Commission and to choose the most viable route.

Naturally, the US was interested in the Panama route already started by the French. The French company which had been heading for bankruptcy, and seeing the writing on the wall before their bankruptcy in 1889, had entered into negotiations with the US. The French company was eager to extricate themselves from the project. At the time, their holdings were extensive and included land, the Panama Railroad, 2,000 buildings, and an extensive amount of equipment. They felt their total holdings should be valued around 109 million USD, but Rear Admiral Walker estimated them to be not greater than about 40 million USD, a significant difference.

As negotiations progressed, the Americans began to hint that they were also interested in the possibility of building an alternative canal in Nicaragua. The French countered with the ploy by claiming that both Great Britain and Russia were looking at picking up the financing to complete the canal's construction. It was subsequently leaked to the US press, much to the French company's pique, that the Walker Commission concluded that the cost to buy out the French company was too excessive and recommended the Nicaraguan route.

A couple days later after this news, the president of Compagnie Nouvelle resigned. The resulting furore caused the stockholders to demand that the company be sold to the US at any price they could get. The Americans became aware that they could now pick up all the French holdings for 40 million dollars. However, the Walker Commission had not just been a ploy by the Americans because the Nicaraguan route was actually a serious proposal that had a lot of backing in the US Senate. President Roosevelt had to engage in some serious political manoeuvrings to get everybody on board of the Panama passage. The Walker Commission changed its recommendation to favour Panama as the canal route.

But the story doesn't end there. Next, the US signed a new treaty with Colombia's charged affairs which gave the US a six mile area across the Isthmus and agreed to financial remuneration that was to be paid to Colombia. The Colombian charged affairs had signed the treaty without communicating with his government. The treaty was rejected by Colombia. In the meantime, revolution against Colombian authority was afoot in Panama. Since they believed they had signed a legitimate treaty, Roosevelt sent warships to the area to negate the Colombians, and thus secured US interests, and offered aid to the Panamanians in their quest to separate from Colombia. Panama succeeded in their revolt and became a republic. In 1914, the Panama Canal was opened.

## Exercises

(1) What are the tactics used in negotiations?
(2) How do you develop your own characteristic negotiation approach according to different culture, background, education and other elements?
(3) Name some tactics, strategies, tricks or tips about what one should do during the negotiation process.

# Chapter 7 Professional Skills for International Business Negotiation

## 7.1 Skill of Talking

### 7.1.1 Negotiation Language

Negotiations are almost always conducted on three basic levels of communication: the subconscious level, the emotional level and the level of reason and logic. Consistently high achievement in negotiation can be obtained by mastering all three levels of negotiation so that the negotiator's position can be communicated in a manner that is simple, attractive, suggestive, enthusiastic, truthful, fair, logic and personal.

The most logical and sound reasoning will be of little value if it is not communicated in simple and precise terms. You should set forth only the points needed to encourage the action you desire. You should be informative with regard to supporting details only to the extent necessary to make your offer clear. Some of the most common and serious errors committed by negotiators involve their use of words and terms with broad or ambiguous meanings. Do not say anything is large if you can give exact measurements. Sentences should also be simple, with the subject first, the verb next, and the object last.

Your presentation should be executed in all attractive manner that is pleasing, not offensive. It should be fair and consider able of the pros and cons, not suspicious. It should be cooperative and friendly, not argumentative or hostile. It should emphasize the positive, not the negative, stress the familiar, not the unknown, and be democratic, not dictatorial. Your presentation should be understated, not exaggerated. It should progress by starting with easy issues, not the frustration and stalemate promoted by hard issues. It should be complimentary and encourage agreement, not offensive or demeaning, discouraging cooperation. It should reveal reward consequences, not punishment or a threatening outcome, and should entertain and be enthusiastic, keeping the other person glued to your thoughts.

### 7.1.2 How to Open and Close

The most important parts of your presentation are the opening and closing statements. The beginning is important because your listeners are fresh and easy to impress. The end is important because people remember best what they hear last. It is therefore advisable to give much thought to your introduction and conclusion. There are a number of approaches you can use to attract immediate attention.

(1) Arouse curiosity by asking a question related to your talk.

(2) Say something humorous.

(3) Start off with an interesting news item.

(4) Begin with a specific illustration or case, which tends to lend an air of seriousness and reality to your talk.

(5) Open with the impact of a profound quotation.

(6) Show a visual illustration of your main points, which can be either a chart, picture or item related to your talk.

(7) Open with a simple explanation of how your topic affects the common interests of the listeners.

(8) Start off with a shocking statement.

(9) Casually comment on something that has just happened or been said at the meeting if it ties into your presentation.

Your closing statement can be the same as one with which you would end a memorandum, summarizing and briefly outlining the main points you cover. You can appeal for action. You can pay the listeners a sincere compliment by making reference to their organization, state or other aspect of common interest. Do not throw out the standard compliment that sounds shallow and insincere, such as,「You've been a great audience.」You can also leave them laughing when appropriate.

### 7.1.3　Practical Tips for Making Statements

The following eight tips might be helpful in making statements:

(1) Be Clear and Concise

When you make a statement, you should avoid lengthy or redundant expressions. Use long and complicated sentences carefully. Obscurity, jargon or excessive technical terms should be avoided in order to be concise and effective.

(2) Differentiate Primary from Secondary Issues, and Achieve Unity and Coherence

Except by intentional arrangement, your statement should not confuse primary and secondary issues, and should not fail to follow logical order. It should not stray from the subject. Whether you progress from the concrete or specific to the general or from the general to the specific, you should go forward point by point, presenting your idea in a clear and logical way.

(3) Try to Be Accurate and Consistent

When you mention figures and numbers, you should make sure they are correct and avoid using the suggestive or indefinite words like「about」「possible」and so on. You should not restrict your price scale lest your counterpart find it easy to choose the upper or lower limit most favorable to them and take advantage of this opportunity to make their bargains. In addition, your statements should reflect identical views so as to avoid self-contradictory ideas.

(4) Give a Vivid and Visual Account

When you make your statements, do not speak in a dull, flat way. Boring and abstract styles should be avoided as well. Remember you are not delivering dogma or a sermon. You should try to use vivid, concrete and persuasive words.

(5) Try to Be Objective and Genuine

You should give your statement objectively and accurately, without overstatement or understatement. Otherwise, once your exaggeration or inaccuracy is recognized, your reputation will be seriously undermined. Of course this does not contradict the principle of emphasizing strong points and deemphasizing weaknesses.

(6) Have a Sense of Propriety in Speech or Action

Negotiators should use language appropriately: try to use neutral and polite language, i.e., even though sharp or modest words may be required to implement the negotiation strategy, they can not be overused. You should know what to say and what not to say. You should see to it that your statements reflect the proper degree of tension or relaxation by appropriate use of hard and soft tactics.

(7) Try to Be Self-Oriented

When you do your statement, you should just focus on presenting your party's proposal no matter what kind of response your counterpart has given. Try to avoid confronting your counterpart's ideas too early, i.e., during your statement. Do not mention whether you agree with your counterpart or not so as not to be drawn into argument or deadlock at this early stage.

(8) Correct Mistakes Quickly and Repeat Your Words If Necessary

If there are slips of the tongue or self-contradictory statements, you should correct them immediately. Never try to conceal faults and gloss over wrongs, leaving mistakes uncorrected and making the best of them. If you try to cover up with a lie, telling one lie will escalate into telling a train of lies. A negotiation full of lies is a disaster.

When your counterpart does not hear you clearly or catch your main idea, you may slow down your speed and repeat what you have said appropriately. In case of misunderstanding by your counterpart, you should point it out and help them to get what you mean as quickly as possible.

## 7.1.4 Several Aspects to Beware of

Listeners unconsciously judge you by how you talk. Your speaking voice is one of the first impressions people have of you, and that impression is often dominated by your voice quality.

A person may be characterized as friendly if his or her voice sounds warm and well modulated. Someone may be thought of as dull and uninteresting if the voice sounds monotonous. Someone who is too loud may appear bombastic. Someone who is too soft may be tagged as timid. Speaking too fast may convey impatience or anger. Speaking too slow may cause someone to be viewed as hesitant or fearful.

When you speak, your words convey your thoughts, and the tone conveys your mood. Speaking in a monotone is monotonous, fatigues the listeners, repels the listeners' initial attraction and hurts memory retention. Most people speak in too high a pitch, especially when they get excited. A high, shrill voice is irritating and unconvincing.

Measurements of superior speakers indicate that the ideal pitch for men is close to C below middle C, whereas for women is close to G sharp below middle G.

Your talking rhythm—that is, your speech speed and pauses—will depend on how complicated your message is and how clearly you articulate your words. In general, listeners find a person who speaks faster than average to be more knowledgeable, more persuasive and more enthusiastic. However, if you talk too fast, you may give the impression that you lack self-confidence and are nervous.

## 7.2 Skills of Asking and Answering

There are always questions and answers in international business negotiations. The ability to raise skills questions and offer effective answers is embedded in art of language. Apart from asking and answering questions skillfully, negotiators should also know how to be good listeners.

### 7.2.1 Techniques for Asking Questions

Asking questions is an important means for one party to acquire information from its counterpart. Negotiators always use questions to crystallize their understanding of the counterpart's needs, get to know their thoughts, and convey their emotions as well as direct the counterpart's thinking. Hence, we should have a clear picture about why to ask questions, what questions to ask, when to ask questions and how to ask questions. Generally, questions can be categorized into open-ended questions and closed questions.

(1) Closed Questions

Closed questions are the questions that can evoke given answers under given conditions, to which the only answer is「Yes」or「No」. Typical examples are「Could you provide an instruction manual for this product?」and「Will you ship the goods in September?」etc. This sort of questions can help the questioners to get certain and specific information, and meanwhile, answering these questions does not take too much effort. Yet asking closed questions may be perceived as threatening to some extent, and closed questions can be divided into the following specific types:

①selective questions

Selective questions offer several situations among which the counterpart is asked to make a choice. For example,「Is this machinery driven by lithium battery or photoelectric cell?」「Are your sample products usually mailed by common parcels, air mail or international express service to the clients?」and so on. That is, we give two or more choices among which the counterpart may choose. When selective questions are used, questioners should be careful to use a mild tone and an appropriate expression, so as to avoid giving a forceful or imposing impression. In addition, don't narrow down the choices within which the counterparts can choose, or they may find all the choices unacceptable.

②suggestive questions

The expected answer may be embedded in the question one has asked. For instance,「The quality of our products has always been good, hasn't it?」

「According to the CIF terms, once the cargo has crossed the ship's rail in the shipping port, the risk and the responsibility will be transferred to the insurance company compensate the damage?」and so on. These questions include the answers, and the questions themselves simply urge the counterparts to make a quick decision. In general, questioners should introduce the suggestions they hope will be adopted in order to reach a satisfactory result.

③clarifying questions

Clarifying questions refer to the questions through which urge our counterparts to restate or complement their previous answers, such as「Just now you said the products will be delivered in October. Can you guarantee it?」「Just now you mentioned our bilateral trade plans to adopt the payment by L/C this year, have you decided about that?」and so on. This kind of question is aimed at getting the counterparts to clarify their attitude again after they have expressed certain ideas, ensuring that both parties can get accurate feedback and enhancing mutual understanding.

④reference questions

Reference questions refer to the questions asked on the basis of the opinions given by a third party. For example,「Most of the international media reports that the price of the product will keep receding, what do you think about it?」「Dr. John said that the product had achieved the top level of precision internationally, do you agree?」This kind of question requires both parties to confirm the comments made by their well-known and mutually respected third party. It will always make a significant impact on the counterpart; but if one refers to an unfamiliar figure or institution, the outcome will just be the opposite.

(2) Open-Ended Questions

Open-ended questions don't limit the answer, and they can't be answered with the simple word「Yes」or「No」. For instance,「What do you think of the market prospects for the product?」「How many sets of this kind of equipment do you plan to purchase per year?」and so on. Questioners can always elicit more information, for there is no fixed range of answers for this kind of questions and they encourage the counterparty to talk freely.

Open-ended questions can be divided into the following types:

①probing questions

Probing questions are further questions based on information the counterparty has already given, such as 「You do not think there is any space for the price to be lowered. Are there other reasons apart from the two you have already cited?」「You hold that the export volume of crude oil has been limited by the shipping capacity. So if we send more ships to solve this problem, what else might influence the export volume?」and so on. Putting probing questions to the counterpart is like sending out scouts. They can be used not only to dig out more information, which is then used to make comparisons and analysis in order to find a better solution, but also show one's attention to, and interest in the problems that the counterpart is talking about, and tend to make the counterpart more willing to communicate with the party asking these questions.

②conferring questions

These questions ask counterparts for their opinions. For example, 「In March next year. The East China Export Commodities Trade Fair will be held in Shanghai. Do you think you will be able to be there then?」「Our company plans to purchase a petrol company in North Africa. Would you be willing to join in this profitable project?」and the like. These questions are usually related to the counterpart's benefits, and may be viewed as a constructive way to ask questions in order to solicit the counterpart's opinions.

③proof-seeking questions

These questions urge the counterpart to prove a point or explain the circumstances of a certain problem. Usually, a string of questions is asked.

The techniques for asking proof-seeking questions requires that the questioner have precise logical thinking and have accurate knowledge about the situations concerned. Finally, he should be able to use the facts and well-founded reasons accepted by the counterpart to overwhelm the counterpart's objections. Otherwise, the questioner will lose the negotiation because he cannot prove with further questioning or reasoning.

④heuristic questions

This is a method aimed to stimulate the counterpart to give opinions and suggestions. For example, 「The industry in general thinks the price of iron ore may possibly rise next year. What's your opinion?」「The liner costs less, but only one liner sails each month. This can't ensure punctual delivery. Can you suggest any better solutions?」and so on. The purpose of such questions is to evoke the opinions of the counterpart so as to solicit a new and more desirable suggestion, or one beneficial to both parties.

⑤leading questions

Different from heuristic questions, leading questions guide our counterpart into our own orbit of thinking by step-by-step reasoning under the prerequisite or initial common grounds, and finally make the counterpart give the answer we have been expecting. Leading questions can be answered in broad and various ways.

After this discussion, the French couple changed their mind and bought the yellow Ferrari sports car.

Leading questions were created by the Greek logician Socrates over 2,000 years ago. They are still accepted as 「the cleverest induction」. The principle when we have an argument with others, is to ignore the disputed points, and emphasize the common ground and the opinions on which both parties agree. After the common ground is reached, one can guide the other into the orbit of a single, desired opinion. In the above case, the Italian manager put himself into the shoes of the French couple, analyzed the problem and posed a series of questions that led to the agreement of the French couple. All these questions drew attention to common sense fact that both parties agreed upon. The questions were asked in a modest and mild tone with no hint of lecturing or irony. His manners as well as his leading questions finally persuaded the French couple to agree with him and facilitated closing the deal.

(3) Questions That Should Not Be Asked

①Questions about private life, job, income, family status, woman's age, religion and party beliefs.

②Hostile questions.

③Questions that indicate suspicions of the quality of the other party.

④Excessive questions irrelevant with the negotiation contents.

(4) Techniques for Asking Questions

①Ask questions sincerely.

②Ask questions in simple and short sentence patterns, or the counterpart will get impatient or feel fooled.

③Avoid raising doubts, or asking harsh questions like a judge in a trial, and do not speak with an overbearing air or aska succession of questions at one time.

④Ask different questions according to the age, position, personality, education level, and negotiation experience of the counterpart.

⑤Prepare some questions beforehand that will be difficult for the counterpart toanswer immediately.

⑥Ask questions at a fight moment; asking a question too early will reveal the intention of the questioner, and asking your question too late will hinder the negotiation process.

⑦Do not interrupt the topic of your counterpart at will, and avoid bringing up a new topic before your counterpart has discussed the old topic completely.

⑧Do not deliberately ask questions the other party has made painstaking efforts to avoid answering. If necessary, we can ask such a question from a different point of view to obtain the answer to our inquiry, or wait for the right opportunity, and ask indirectly.

⑨Avoid asking questions that may hinder the other party from making a concession.

⑩Test the honesty of your counterpart with a question to which you already know the answer.

Keep silent after asking a question to wait patiently for the counterparty to answer it, and do not give additional remarks over and over again, which will make it impossible for the other party to answer the question.

### 7.2.2 Techniques of Answering Questions

There is an old Chinese saying,「A kind word keeps you warm for three winters while a vicious remark makes you feel cold even in June.」The equivalent wisdom in English is this:「Honey catches more flies than vinegar.」There often are different possible answers to the same question; different answers will have different effects. In international business negotiations, the motivations of the questioners are so complicated that simple words「Yes」or「No」can not suffice. An improper answer will endanger the success of the negotiation. So to some extent, answering techniques are more important than questioning techniques in negotiations.

(1) Six Principles for Answering Questions

①In order to avoid the possibility of being trapped or revealing information that one's party does not want to disclose, do not answer a question rashly.

②Answer the question that is asked, and avoid ambiguity.

③Before answering a question, try to find some time to think about the question. One may「buy time」for thinking by such devices as drinking some water, lighting a cigarette, changing one's sitting posture, browsing through some materials and so on.

④Do not reveal too much information, leaving your party with no alternatives; it may be wise to keep back some information, not revealing everything at one time.

⑤Don't allow your counterpart to pose incessant questions. In this way you may prevent him from getting the information you do not want to disclose.

⑥Ask probing questions about some limiting conditions such as ordering quantity, co-operation time and the like.

(2) Six Approaches to Answering Questions

①direct approach

This is a method used to answer a question to which the counterpart has anticipated the answer. (Whose mind? I don't think you need the last three words at all, actually.) Before answering this kind of question, you should have a clear picture of the intention of the person asking it. Otherwise, your answer can hardly satisfy him, or, on the other hand, you may reveal your secrets. For instance, when you are asked about the materials you use to make mold machines, it's obvious that the counterpart already knows what they are. Hence, if you do not tell the truth, you will be shown to be dishonest; if you answer the question in too much detail, you will reveal the cost secrets of your party. You may well answer the question directly,「Are you trying to determine the cost of our product's materials? Sorry, the materials used in our products are our secret. What is more, material cost is not the deciding factor in setting product prices!」

②limiting approach

This is a method through which we narrow down the questions posed by the counterpart first and then answer the downsized questions. In business negotiations, when the counterpart poses a big question consisting of many small questions, we do not necessarily answer every small question in detail, but select the questions that will be favorable to our party to answer. For instance, when the counterpart asks questions about the features of a product, in response, just choose some special features to describe. This will enable you to impress the counterpart.

③equivocal approach

Equivocal answers not only avoid revealing the genuine intention of one's party to the counterpart, but also may make it difficult for the counterpart to reach a decision. As this kind of answer does not offer any specific explanations, there could be many different interpretations and it should in turn leave much space for follow-up negotiations. For example, 「Our clients have an urgent need for the goods. We're attempting to look for other sources of goods besides your company. Meanwhile, we will consult together about date of delivery, means of payment as well as prices, then we'll compare them to select the most favorable one.」

④questioning approach

Erotesis is a figure of speech by which a strong affirmation to the contrary is implied under the guise of an earnest interrogation. More simply put, one may phrase the answer as a question. One simply asks another question in order to answer the question posed by the counterpart, as in the following example. When your counterpart asks whether you will discount the price by 5%, you can answer, 「Well, can you send ships over to collect your order early next month?」As a matter of fact, you know very well that there is only one liner that ships to the counterpart's country in the middle of every month. This kind of answer not only allows us a breathing spell and an opportunity for preparation, but also uses the other party's weaknesses to help us answer a difficult-to-answer question.

⑤redirect/transferring approach

Redirect the topic when answering the questions posed by the counterpart, i.e., 「give an irrelevant answer to the question」. When we use this method, we should steer the discussion to a new topic naturally based on the previous one. For instance, when the counterpart asks about the sensitive question of commissions, you may give a reply such as this: 「I know you are concerned about this issue, but please trust me, the ratio of the commission is bound to satisfy you! However, before I answer this question, may we verify the means of delivery and the requirements for the delivery date?」In this way you can transfer the topic from the commission problem to issues of means of shipment as well as delivery date, and after the counterpart hears your statement, the binding of commission ratio and the safety of the delivered goods as well as the delivery date will be no doubt favorable to your own party.

⑥refusal approach

Try to find some excuses to justify your refusal to answer those tough and difficult questions. You might say,「It is too early to discuss that problem now」. Or, you could elaborate with comments like,「I really want to know your opinion, but I actually can not meet your request for a price decrease because of the quantity you plan to order.」Say「No」to your counterpart with sound and well-founded reasons in order to relieve the pressures on your party.

(3) Techniques for Answering Questions

①think first, and then answer

Leave some time for contemplation before you answer the questions posed by the counterpart. Your answer can be accurate and forceful as long as you have a clear picture about the motivation and intention behind your counterpart's questions. You may extend your thinking time through some accepted procedures, such as browsing some materials, drinking water, etc. Negotiators must abstain from racing to be the first to answer a question without careful thinking. Try to reply in a measured tone in order to avoid breaking this taboo in negotiation.

②answer selected questions

When the counterpart poses a string of questions with the hope of「sending out a scout to see if anybody is about」, it's unnecessary to answer all the questions—especially questions that are unfavorable for your party. You can narrow down the questions or steer away from the main topic or talk ambiguously. For example,「Could we please take this question in separate parts?」「I can hardly agree with some parts of your questions…」「We usually deal with such problems in this way…」and so on.

③delay answering questions

Some of the questions posed by the counterpart are not impossible to answer, but until conditions are mature and the opportunity you want arrives, it is better to adopt a delaying approach to deal with them. The first method is「delay first, then answer」. This includes such responses as,「Could you please repeat your question?」「I don't fully understand what you mean…」「Before I answer your question, may I hear your suggestions…」The second method is to「delay instead of answering the question」, meaning that you do not answer at all. As for questions that it is unnecessary to answer, or that appear to be nonsense, you might give a perfunctory answer or entirely avoid answering the questions.

④ask a question in reply

Rhetorical questions can be adopted when the counterpart poses some probing, leading or proof-seeking questions, and you do not want to reveal details but neither do you want to refuse the counterpart directly, lest you negatively influence the negotiation atmosphere. You may wish to limit the questions of your counterpart or to probe for details from your counterpart. For instance, the seller asks,「Why do you insist that international express services be used?」(They are afraid that it will be too expensive.) The buyer answers,「Do we have any quicker and safer means of delivery besides international express services?」(The buyer is trying to relate it to the deal, and to block the counterpart from seeking other cheaper but slower means.)

⑤give irrelevant answers

The method of giving irrelevant answers can be adopted when we are confronted with some harsh, sharp or complicated questions that are very difficult to answer in a positive manner. Apparently, we are answering the question, but in fact, we are answering another question related to the original question. This enables us to avoid a sharp question as well as escape the embarrassment of having no answers. For example, we can change the definition, transfer to a related topic, avoid the counterpart's strength and focus on his weakness.

⑥use ambiguous and general answers

Answer sharp or sensitive questions posed by your counterpart in ambiguous, general and flexible ways. This may relax the negotiation atmosphere as well as keeping the secret of one's party. Take this sentence as an example:「We will solve the problem as soon as possible.」「As soon as possible」in here is flexible and general because it does not state any specific time, and at the same time leaves large space for one's party.

⑦do not answer a question if you don't know the answer

Do not try to answer any question when you really do not know the answer. After all, no one is perfect. Remember: one's interests are far more important than face.

⑧refuse in a polite way

If you can't say「No」directly for fear of destroying the negotiation atmosphere, but you disagree with counterpart, you can conform their opinions first, then use a buffer to give them some comfort, and finally clarify your unchangeable attitude with polite negative words. For instance,「I completely agree with you, but...」「I understand your meaning and have the same thoughts as you on my mind, but...」「I know that it will cost less if you send the samples through common parcels, but...」

⑨cater to the willingness of the counterpart

When there are great differences between the conditions desired by both parties, in order to avoid a deadlock due to a face-to-face direct answer, you may propose following the wishes of your counterparts, guide them to see that this propose following the wishes of your counterparts, guide them to see that this would have an extremely absurd outcome, then demonstrate the fallacies in their opinion till they surrender.

⑩pretend to know nothing

Sometimes in order to urge the counterpart to give up sticking like a limpet to a question that we are unwilling to answer, we may well adopt the tactic of asking about something that we already know, and asking the counterpart to explain their questions over and over again until the counterpart gets bored and gives up the question and turns to other issues. For instance,「I can not fully understand your question. Could you please explain it again?」「I still can not understand what you mean. Could you please explain it once more.」「Well, I seem to understand it now. Do you mean that... (turn to another topic).」

Keep in mind, however, that this kind of strategy should not be adopted too frequently, or it will be seen through or you might be considered to be unintelligent and be looked down upon.

Silence can be adopted as a special 「answering」 strategy when there are some sensitive questions difficult or inconvenient to answer. Appropriate silence can work wonders. Your unexpected silence will make your counterpart feel uncomfortable: 「Did I ask the wrong questions or did they feel my question was not worth answering?」 This kind of self-doubt and reflection will create intangible pressure. In order to escape embarrassment, your counterpart may abandon the previous requirement, transfer their topic or put forward new proposals. Some Japanese businessmen like to adopt this kind of strategy to achieve their goals.

Remember silence can be used only occasionally, or the whole negotiation will be too low-toned and low spirited.

### 7.2.3 Listening Techniques

「Listen more, speak less」 is a basic policy and tactic a business negotiator should possess. Listening helps you acquire information, get to know your counterpart's intentions as well as predict their further movements. Listening in negotiations involves not only listening with our ears, but also observing facial expressions, reactions and gestures of our counterparts with our eyes, feeling the negotiation atmosphere with our heart as well as analyzing their words with our mind while we are listening.

(1) Three Listening Techniques

①listen attentively and patiently

When your counterpart states opinions, you should concentrate on them completely. Do not be absent-minded. Meanwhile, keep abundant patience and do not interrupt the speech of your counterpart.

②listen actively

In the course of listening, you should provide active feedback to the statements by your counterpart. For example, maintain eye contact with your counterparts, encourage your counterparts to give their opinions by nodding or smiling, or express your puzzlement by frowning or shrugging your shoulders.

Meanwhile, you should insert a word into his talk by asking relevant questions in order to understand your counterpart's statement better or to direct the negotiation.

③overcome preconceptions

The intonation, wording, tones and ways of expression can provide certain clues to the meanings behind words. But sometimes your counterpart may give false impressions, so you should overcome your preconceptions and make correct observations. Analyze the words and behavior of your counterpart objectively and reasonably.

(2) 「Five Tips」 for Good Listening

①Don't cut in or refute in haste. You can make your comments after your counterpart finishes the whole statement, or you will be likely to paint yourselves into a corner and find yourself trapped and helpless. Learn to be patient. Unpleasant or offending words deprive one of the ability to use rational reasoning.

②Don't be absent-minded. You should have a good grasp of key points and new information, and do not think about other problems while listening.

③Keep proper records. Putting down the key points, especially during a long and complicated negotiation, can help you maneuver through the process of negotiation as well as giving you a way to exert pressure on your counterparts to keep their word.

④Do not let your counterpart lead you by the nose. Sometimes, your counterpart may subtly attempt to change the topic or distract you by paying you a compliment. In these cases, you should keep clear-headed and direct the conversation back to the topic you have been talking about.

## 7.3  Skills of Body Language

### 7.3.1  Distance Between People Conversing

Different people have different ideas about the proper distance between people conversing. According to the studies, it seems there are four main distances in American social and business relations: intimate, personal, social and public. Intimate distance ranges from direct physical contact to a distance of about 45 centimeters; this is for people's most private relations and activities, between man and wife. For example, personal distance is about 45~80 centimeters and is most common when friends, acquaintances and relatives converse. Social distance may be anywhere from about 1.30 meters to 3 meters; people who work together, or people doing business, as well as most of those in conversation at social gatherings tend to keep a distance is farther than any of the above and is generally for speakers in public and for teachers in classrooms. The important thing to keep in mind is that most English-speaking people do not like people to be too close. In negotiations being too far apart, of course, may be awkward, but being too close makes people uncomfortable, unless there is a reason, such as showing affection or encouraging intimacy. But that is another matter.

### 7.3.2  Physical Appearance and Physical Contact

Physical appearance conveys messages. It plays a very important role in creating first impression. You need be aware of the effect that your physical appearance may have on nonverbal communication. Awareness may permit you to build on your natural advantages. However, awareness of any natural disadvantage may be even more important.

Research has found that: physical attractiveness affects the way you perceive yourself and the way others perceive you. Personal dress: the importance of how we dress is highlighted by the saying,「Dress for Success.」Clothing has been found to affect perceptions of credibility, likeability, attractiveness, and dominance, but researchers agree that clothing has the most potent affect on credibility.

Unfortunately, many otherwise good negotiators ignore the importance of personal dress during negotiations, and that ignorance negatively affects their ability to attain mutually satisfactory negotiation results. In English-speaking countries, physical contact is generally avoided in conversation among ordinary friends or acquaintances. Merely touching someone may cause an unpleasant reaction. If one touches another person accidentally, he/she usually utters an apology such as「Sorry, Oh, I'm sorry, Excuse me.」In China, a common complaint of western mothers is that Chinese often fondle their babies and very small children.

Such behavior—whether touching, patting, hugging or kissing—can be quite embarrassing and awkward for the mothers. They know that no harm is meant, and that such gestures are merely signs of friendliness or affection, therefore they cannot openly show their displeasure. On the other hand, such actions in their own culture would be considered rude, intrusive and offensive and could arouse a strong dislike and even repugnance. So the mothers often stand by and watch in awkward silence, with mixed emotions, even when the fondling is by Chinese friends or acquaintances.

The matter of physical contact between members of the same sex in English-speaking countries is a delicate one. Once past childhood, the holding of hands, or walking with an arm around another's shoulder is not considered proper. The implication is homosexuality, and homosexuality generally arouses strong social disapproval in these countries.

### 7.3.3 Eye Contact

Eye contact is an important aspect of body language. One could draw up quite a list of「rules」about eye contact: to look or not to look; when to look and how long to look; whom to look at and whom not to look at. There are different formulas for the exchange of glances depending on where the meeting takes place. If you pass someone in the street you may eye the oncoming person till you are about eight feet apart, then you must look away as you pass. Before the eight-foot distance is reached, each will signal in which direction he will pass. This is done with a brief look in that direction. Each will veer slightly, and the passing is done smoothly. In conversations with people who know each other, however, American custom demands that there should be eye contact. This applies to both the speaker and the listener. For either one not to look at the other person could imply a number of things, among which are fear, contempt, uneasiness, guilt, indifference, even in public speaking there should be plenty of eye contact. For a speaker to「burry his nose in his manuscript」to read a speech instead of looking at and talking to the audience, as some Chinese speakers are in the habit of doing this, would be regarded as inconsiderate and disrespectful. In a conversation, a person shows that he is listening by looking at the other person's eyes or face. If the other person is speaking at some length, the listener will occasionally make sounds like 「Hmm」「Umm」, or nod his head to indicate his attention. If he agrees with the speaker, he may nod or smile. If he disagrees or has some reservations, he may slant his head to one side, raise an eyebrow, and have a quizzical look. Staring at people or holding a glance too long is considered improper in English – speaking countries. Even when the look may be one of appreciation—as of beauty—it may make people uneasy and embarrassed. Many Americans traveling abroad find the stares of the local people irritating. They become extremely self–conscious and often end up quite indignant about the 「rudeness」of the people there, not realizing that the practice may be quite common in the country and may be nothing more than curiosity. Many English-speaking people in China have been heard to complain about this. The difference in interpreting a simple eye gesture was a lesson in cultural diversity that we would not easily forget. For example, Chinese avoid long direct eye contact to show politeness, or respect, or obedience, while North Americans see eye contact as a sign of honesty and a lack of eye contact or shift eyes as a sign of untruthfulness. Though speaking the same language, the British, unlike the Americans, believe that looking someone directly in the eye to be a mark of rudeness until a more familiar relationship is established. An American businesswoman told a story that they (Americans) felt as if the British were hiding something because none of them would look them in the eye throughout the presentation. The failure of the British to look her in the eye almost 「ruined the relationship and suck the deal,」she said,「I understand it now, but I still don't like it.」

The amount of eye contact varies greatly among cultures. For example, in business meetings, the French will demand at least some direct eye contact. To refuse to meet someone's eyes is an unfriendly gesture. Compare this to the attitude of Japanese, who believe that the less eye contact, the higher the level of esteem. To divert eyes from a business colleague is a sign of respect and reverence. Rules about eye–language are numerous and complex. What has been mentioned gives a good idea of this; we shall not go further into detail.

## 7.3.4　Facial Expression

As the most expressive part of the body, the face is probably the single most important source of non-verbal communication. It is capable of conveying several emotions simultaneously. The face not only can communicate a great deal, but also seemed to be the type of non-verbal behavior that people are able to control. However, facial expressions should be interpreted in cultural context and with caution. Take smiles and laughter for example, smiles and laughter usually convey friendliness, approval, satisfaction, pleasure, joy and merriment. This is generally true in China as well as the English-speaking countries. However, there are situations when some Chinese laugh, which will cause negative reactions by westerners. Other facial expressions also vary from culture to culture. For instance in some US businesses, it is considered acceptable to swear, and yell, but not to cry. But for the Japanese in situations of strong emotion it is considered acceptable to smile or laugh, but not to cry.

### 7.3.5　Gestures

Gesture is the expressive movement of a part of the body, especially the hand and the head. People talk with their hands, but what they mean depends on their culture. As with verbal language, non-verbal codes are not universal. Same gestures have different meanings in different cultures. The forefinger near lips with the sound「shah」, which is a sign for silence in UK and America, means disapproval, hissing in China. In different cultures different gestures are used for the same meaning. For coming here, Chinese gesture is a hand extended toward the person, open palm, fingers crooked in a beckoning motion; the American is a hand extended toward person, close hand, palm up, with forefinger only moving back and forth. For Americans, the Chinese coming-here gesture is like good-bye gesture. Many Chinese would see American coming-here gesture as offensive. The same is true with some commonly used gestures. The OK sign (the circle formed with the thumb and first finger), which has the similar meaning in most of Western Europe, is a vulgar insult in Greece, an obscene gesture in Brazil, Mediterranean countries and Southern Italy, and can mean「you're worth nothing」in France and Belgium. Like hand movements, head movements differ from one culture to another. In Bulgaria, for example, people may nod their heads to signify no and shake their heads to signify yes. So gestures can be very confusing inter-culturally. But there are some gestures that have widely understood meanings. For example, foot-shaking, finger-tapping and fidgeting with a tie or hair usually signify nervousness or boredom; a clench fist typically indicates hostility or aggression.

Specialists in the study of body movement emphasize that no single gesture carries meaning in and of itself. The gestures just discussed do not always mean the same thing. To understand a person's meaning, pay attention to all the cues they are sending and the context in which the cues occur, not to just a single gesture. When one communicate in a certain language, it is generally advisable to use the non-verbal behavior that goes with that particular language.

### 7.3.6　Posture

The way people carry themselves communicates volumes. People from different cultures learn to sit, to walk and to stand differently. The impact of culture on non-verbal communication is so strong that even people with great experience in cross-culture communication might be unaware of how meaning of a non-verbal act varies from culture to culture. The wife of a former president of the United States was said to have shocked her Arab hosts by crossing her legs during a public meeting, which is an indecent posture in Arab culture. Posture offers insight into a culture's deep structure. For instance, in the United States where being casual and friendly is valued; people often fall into chairs and slouch when they stand. In many European countries, such as Germany, where lifestyle tends to be more formal, a slouching posture is considered a sign of rudeness and poor manners. Similarly, in Japan, the formality is important and the Japanese value the ability to sit quietly. They might see the Americans fidget and shift as an indication of lack of mental or spiritual balance.

But there are similarities. For instance, even in North America, swinging a foot in interview makes negative impression. Also, people respond unfavorably to standing with weight back on heels and hands in pockets at work place or sitting with feet up on the desk in office. And slouching or leaning on the lectern in business presentation may make the audience feel that the speaker's ideas area as careless as his or her posture. Generally, standing erect, shoulders back, head held high display confidence, energy, and self-assurance, which gains more attention from the audience. And a relaxed posture, a comfortable seating position, uncrossed arms, and lack of stiffness indicate openness with no communication obstacles. on the other hand, abrupt movements, shifting seating positions, uncrossed arms or legs may signal defiance, disinterest or an unwillingness to listen. Women in many settings will often hold their arms closer to their bodies than men. They will also keep their legs close together and seldom cross them in mixed company.

## 7.4 Application of the Body Language in Negotiation

Good negotiators know how to use body language to their advantage. They also know how to read other people's body language to gain the upper hand. Crossed arms, raised eyebrows, wandering eyes—they all mean something. Pay attention and you'll be surprised about what you might learn about what is really going on in the negotiation regardless of what is being said with words.

### 7.4.1 Body Language Affects Negotiation

Body language and attitudes: body language research has catalogued 135 distinct gestures and expressions of the face, head, and body. Eighty of these expressions were face and head gestures, including nine different ways of smiling. These gestures and expressions provide insight, into the attitude of the originator. Simultaneous physical signals often reinforce each other and reduce the ambiguity surrounding the message. For example, eagerness is often exhibited with the simultaneous physical displays of excessive smiling along with frequent nodding of the head. Common attitudes communicated nonverbally during negotiations can be grouped into positive attitudes and negative attitudes and these attitudes can be manifested by gestures.

(1) Positive attitudes: positive attitudes indicated by body language may signal a sincere effort to achieve win-win results.

(2) Gestures: be particularly careful when you are interpreting or using gestures. A gesture that means one thing in one society can mean something completely different in another.

There is a good chance that you will encounter differing interpretations whenever you are negotiating with someone from another part of the world. Even if the other party is from the United States, some of these differing interpretations may remain as part of the person's heritage.

①Shaking your head up-and-down means「yes」in the United States and left-to-right means「no」. In some parts of the world the meanings are just the opposite.

②The hand signal for OK in the United States is an obscene gesture in some societies.

③The thumbs-up gesture is a positive sign in most of the world, but in some cultures is considered a rude gesture.

④The V-shaped hand gesture with the index finger and middle finger may mean victory or peace in the United States, but in some countries it could be interpreted as an obscene gesture.

### 7.4.2　How to Understand Body Language in Negotiation

Learning the language of nonverbal communications is almost as difficult as acquiring fluency in a foreign language. Reading body language is perhaps the most powerful form of human communication. And armed with the right information about reading body language, you can almost read people's minds. In addition to studying your own gestures and the meaning you are conveying, you must also become aware of what your counterpart is conveying.

Many skeptics argue that it is difficult to tell what someone is thinking by singling out one gesture—and they are right. A single gesture is like a single word; its true meaning is difficult to understand out of context. However, when gestures come in clusters, their meaning becomes clearer. For example, while a person's fidgeting may not mean much by itself, if that person is avoiding eye contact, holding his hands around his mouth, touching his face and fidgeting, there's a good chance he is not being totally honest.

For example: involuntary hand movements can be particularly telling. People often touch their nose, chin, ear, arm or clothing when they are nervous or lack confidence in what they are saying. When asked why they cross their legs, most people say they do so for comfort. Although they are being truthful, they are only partially correct. If you have ever crossed your legs for a long period of time, you know that this position can become painfully uncomfortable. Studying what you and your counterpart in the negotiation process are not saying is critical to achieve a win-win outcome.

# Case Study

Mr. Herb Cohen is a world-famous negotiator and once held the position of negotiation adviser for the former American presidents Carter and Reagan. He was often invited by some transnational companies or governmental agencies to negotiate with other parties on their behalf as well as asked to make speeches all over the world. The fee for his presence is usually extremely high—always hundreds of thousands or millions of dollars—an astronomical number.

One day, a clerk in Mr. Cohen's office received a telephone call from a large information technology company in California's Silicon Valley. The caller was a female executive who wanted to know the fee for a speech by Mr. Cohen at a public conference in San Francisco. According to the routine practice, the telephone conversation began with the usual formulas, such as how long the speech would be, who would be in the audience and finally a question like 「What is the fee for the speech?」The office clerk would make a quotation of 「astronomical numbers」as usual even though it might scare 10% of the inquirers away. However, this time, what the female executive said on the other end of the phone was so extraordinarily brilliant that it made Mr. Cohen treat her with increased respect. She did not ask directly, 「How much does Mr. Cohen want to charge for his speech?」or 「How much do we have to pay?」Instead, she asked with discreet gentility, 「Well, what is an appropriate gift to Mr. Cohen in token of gratitude?」A gift in token of gratitude? What did it mean? The office clerk got muddled even though he knew such brilliant words apparently and simply implied that she intended to pay a little symbolic feel, but he still quoted a standard charge of an astronomical figure.

To his surprise, his counterpart did not sound a bit surprised or dissatisfied at all in her response—she did not say, 「Who does he think he is? Whoever he is, he is not entitled to charge such a high price!」On the contrary, she said with delight. 「I know he is completely entitled to charge such a high price. In addition, our vice CEO heard a speech by Mr. Cohen, and he said that Mr. Cohen is worth more than twice as that fee. If we had had that much money, we would have felt fortunate happy and lucky to give that sum to Mr. Cohen!」Then she said with a little shame, 「But unfortunately our budget allows only this sum of money.」

Can you guess whether her words would work?

Six months later, Mr. Cohen appeared on the platform of the Sheraton Hotel in San Francisco.

## Exercises

(1) What kinds of persuasion tactics and techniques were used by the female executive in the IT company so that the world famous negotiator Mr. Cohen abandoned his extremely high standard quotation and accepted the speech fee she could afford?

(2) Under what circumstances should we ask closed questions in business negotiations? Under what circumstances should we ask open-ended questions in business negotiations? Try to justify your answers with respective examples.

(3) Under what circumstances should one answer questions asked by one's counterpart selectively? Under what circumstances can one give an irrelevant or ambiguous answer? Please

illustrate your point.

(4) Why shouldn't one hasten to cut in or refute a statement of one's counterpart? What else should one pay attention to while listening to a statement?

(5) What should one pay attention to when one gives a statement? Try to illustrate your point.

(6) How can one demonstrate the principles and techniques of argument in a tit-for-tat negotiation? Practice the argument techniques on the topic you have chosen by yourself in a group-to-group debate (Divide the class into two groups: Group A and Group B).

(7) Try to apply appropriate forms of body language in the course of the argument in the group debate, and observe what kinds of body language your counterpart uses.

# Chapter 8　International Business Contract Negotiation

## 8.1　Conclusion and Guarantee of a Contract

### 8.1.1　Characteristics of an International Business Contract

(1) It is an agreement between parties from different countries or regions.

As they are from different countries or regions, the parties involved in signing the contract have to be governed or regulated by the laws prevailing in their counterpart's country or region. For example, frozen ducks to be exported to Islamic countries must be butchered in the way stipulated by the local laws. In addition, since the contracted items are shipped across a border and are subject to customs regulations, more complicated issues are inevitably concerned, including formalities of coming into or going out of customs: import or export licenses, payment settlement and international protection of industrial property rights.

(2) The laws of all the parties involved are binding.

The stakeholders in an international business contract are individuals, legal entities (corporations) or institutions from different countries or regions. According to the principle of national jurisdiction, the behaviors of the parties to the contract and the clauses in the contract signed by them must conform with the laws of the countries or regions they are from. Additionally, the location of the contract signing is important. The reason is that the signing site of the contract usually determines which country's laws are adopted to settle any disputes and to establish how arbitration is carried out. According to international convention, the court or arbitration organization may make the adjudication or arbitration based on the law of the country where the contract is signed should any dispute arise. To avoid unnecessary trouble, it is wise to stipulate in which country or region disputes should be settled and which laws or arbitration authority should be adopted.

(3) The international treaties and trade practices are binding.

An international business contract reflects the interaction of cross-border economic activities. It is inevitably under the control of relevant international multilateral or bilateral treaties and must be in accordance with international trade practices. In the above case, the interpretation of the trade term CIF by the International Chamber of Commerce was adopted and the liabilities, expenses and division of the risks the importer and exporter must face were determined in line with these practices.

(4) It is affected by international political relationships.

An international business contract involves economic interactions between different countries. Therefore, the political relationship between these countries or regions as well as subtle geographic political factors may have positive or negative impacts on the implementation of the contract. For example, the American Congress once prevented China's National Off shore Oil Corporation (CNOOC) from acquiring CHEVRON, the ninth largest oil company in the US with the contention that this would damage America's national security. This is a typical example of how an international political relationship affects business activities.

### 8.1.2 Types of International Business Contracts

(1) Classified by the Contract Signatories

①Contract between the governments of different countries or regions: for example, multilateral or bilateral agreement, etc.

②Contract between legal entities from different countries or regions: for example, the sales contract between corporations from two countries.

③Contract between the government and legal entities of different countries or regions: for example, a purchasing agreement between the government of country A and a corporation of country B.

④Contract between an individual and a legal entity from different countries or regions: for example, a car rental agreement between a car rental company in country A and a tourist from country B.

⑤Contract between individuals from different countries or regions: a housing rental agreement between the owner of an apartment or house in country A and a tenant from country B.

(2) Classified by the Trading Items

①sales or purchase contract

②technological trade contract

③joint venture contract and contract for cooperation

④processing trade contract

⑤finance and loan contract

⑥equity transfer contract

⑦project construction contract

⑧labor exportation contract

⑨international lease contract

⑩international contracted operation contract

(3) Classified by the Forms of the Contract

①oral contract

Anoral contract or agreement is an arrangement or promise made by the parties concerned through verbal means such as conversation in person or via telephone. Article 10 of the Contract Law of the People's Republic of China and Article 11 of the United Nations Convention on Contracts for the International Sale of Goods (UNCCISG) both recognize the legal status of an oral contract. Verbal contracts are convenient and quick, but can not provide necessary evidence in case of disputes and this makes it difficult to identify where the responsibility lies. Therefore, a verbal contract is usually suitable only in cases where the contracting parties know each other well and have regular business transactions within a short time span and maintain a simple business relationship.

②written contract

A written contract is an arrangement made between the contracting parties in written form. A written contract is the major form for international business contracts. It is evidenced in writing and thus it is easy to tell which party is responsible in case of any dispute. Therefore, written contracts are usually used in deals which involve a large amount of money, complicated contents and a long time span of implementation and payment.

Common forms of written contracts are listed below:

a. Formal contract, also known as agreement: this contains full terms and conditions and complete clauses.

b. Simplified contract, also called a letter of confirmation, memorandum and order, etc. After the negotiating parties have reached an agreement through correspondence or face-to-face bargaining, one party writes down the terms and conditions of transaction briefly, making two copies, which are signed and sent to the other party for confirmation. After the other party receives and signs them, they will send one copy back, keeping one themselves, and then the contract goes into effect.

c. Electronic contract: an electronic contract is the ratification in software or by means of electronic communication, such as telegraph, telex and email, of a statement that regulates behaviour among the contracting parties. Though it is not a formal document with signature or seal, this form of contract is in conformity with the United Nations Convention on Contracts for the International sale of Goods and carries legal force.

(4) Classified by the Relationship Between the Contracting Parties

①Direct contract: the contracting parties all have direct interests in the deal and they sign the contract themselves.

②Agency contract: also referred to as contract for intermediation, this form is signed by a third party on behalf of one of the parties with direct interests in the deal.

## 8.1.3 Procedure for Formatting a Contract

The formation of international business contracts is a legal activity among the contracting parties in which they bargain and reach an agreement over the contract terms and conditions. The procedure involves two steps: offer and acceptance.

(1) Offer

The offer is a proposal or requirement a contracting party addresses to other specific parties for forming an economic contract. The party who makes the offer is called the offeror.

①An effective offer must conform to the following points:

a. It expresses the intention of the offeror to the other parties to the contract.

b. It contains the major clauses of the standard contract.

c. It comes into effect upon reaching the offeree.

d. The offeror cannot withdraw the offer once it is accepted by the offeree.

②Making an offer is a legal action, which means that within the stated time of the validity of the offer:

a. The offeror has the obligation to acknowledge the acceptance and sign the contract with the offeree.

b. The offeror should not make the same proposal and sign a contract with a third party.

c. The offeror may not withdraw, modify or limit the offer unless the notice of withdrawal reaches the offeree before or at the same time as the original offer.

③The offer shall lose its binding force in one of the following cases:

a. If the offeree's notice of refusal reaches the offeror.

b. If the offeror withdraws the offer legally.

c. If the offeree fails to make an acceptance within the time of the validity of the offer.

d. If the offeror makes substantive modification to the offer.

(2) Acceptance

An acceptance is a statement made or other action by the offeree indicating assent to an offer. It is usually stated in either the oral or the written form. A contract is concluded at the moment when an acceptance of an offer becomes effective in accordance with the UNCCISG. The offeree must carry out the obligations stated in the contract.

①An effective acceptance must satisfy the following requirements:

a. The acceptance must be made by the offeree.

b. The declaration of an acceptance must be in precise accordance with the offer.

c. An acceptance must be made within the time of validity of the offer.

②An acceptance may be withdrawn if the withdrawal reaches the offeror before or at the same time as the acceptance would have become effective.

The formation of an international business contract is a process in which the parties involved exchange their ideas about an offer and an acceptance. In reality, sometimes, only a single exchange may settle the case, that is, one party makes an offer and the other then accepts it, and a contract is concluded. But most cases tend to require several rounds of exchange; that is, after a chain process of ⌈making an offer... countering the offer... making a new offer...⌋.

## 8.1.4　Guarantee of the Contract

A contract guarantee refers to measures necessary to ensure the implementation of the contract. These measures may be taken by one of the contracting parties or by a third party in response to a contracting party's request, because there are many risks and uncertainties in cross-border business activities.

Six major modes of international business contract guarantee are available, including: guaranty guarantee, mortgage guarantee, down payment guarantee, lien guarantee, deposit and penalty guarantee, lien guarantee, deposit and penalty guarantee.

(1) Guaranty Guarantee

With guaranty, the guarantor and the creditor agree that if the debtor falls to perform on his debt, the guarantor or surety will perform on the debt or bear the liability in accordance with the agreement. A guarantor should be a third party having dealings with the debtor that promote their common interests, so the guarantor may be an entity such as a loan bank, holding company or higher-level department responsible for the work involved. In international business, a letter of credit, factoring, letter of guarantee and standby L/C all fall into this category.

(2) Mortgage Guarantee

A mortgage guarantees that a debtor or a third party can not transfer possession of the property, making possession of the said property the obligatory right of the creditor. When the debtor does not perform on the debt, the creditor shall be entitled to have the right to keep the said property to offset the debt or have priority in satisfying his claim out of proceeds from the auction or sale of the said property pursuant to the provisions of a contract guarantee bond. The debtor or third party prescribed in the guarantee bond shall be the mortgagee, the property offered to guarantee shall be the collateral, which may be immovable properties, such as a house or other land fixtures, a machine, a vehicle or other property owned by the mortgagor. When entering into a mortgage contract, the mortgagor and the mortgagee shall agree that, when the mortgagee is not satisfied at the date of expiration of the time limitation for the debt performance, the ownership of the collateral is to be transferred to the creditor.

(3) Deposit Guarantee

The contracting parties may agree that one party will pay a deposit to another party as guarantee. After the debtor performs on the debt, the deposit may offset any remaining amount owed, or may be returned If the party who pays the deposit does not perform on the debt, he shall not be entitled to have the deposit returned; if the party who accepts the deposit does not perform on his obligations involved in the debt, he shall return twice the amount of the deposit. If both parties are negligent, resulting in an invalid contract, the deposit should be returned. The amount of the deposit shall be determined by both parties, but shall not exceed 20 percent of the target amount of the master contract.

(4) Lien Guarantee

The lien means that the creditor possesses the property of the debtor according to the agreement of the contract, if the debtor does not perform the debt pursuant to the time limitation agreed in the contract. In international trade, this form of guarantee is popular in dealings with transportation, warehousing or processing businesses that have right to alien on the said property. If the debtor fails to effect payment or pays less than agreed, the creditor shall be entitled to the right to have a lien on the said property to keep the said property to offset or have priority in satisfying the claim out of proceeds from the amount realized from the auction, or sale of the said property.

(5) Penalty Guarantee

A penalty is a form of financial punishment one has to bear if one fails to honor a contract or implements the contract but in an improper way. The party who breaks the contract should pay a penalty to the other party in accordance with the contract even though the other party incurs no damage. Therefore, a penalty is a mandatory guarantee.

There is no international standard regarding the amount of the penalty. Some industries have their standards, and if so, then the respective standard must be followed. If there is no industrial standard, the parties shall determine the amount of the penalty.

## 8.2 Modification, Termination and Assignment of Contracts

### 8.2.1 Modification of the Contract

A contract may be modified if the parties reach a consensus through consultation. If the circumstances under which the contract is performed undergo changes, the parties to the contract shall modify certain clauses or provide supplements to the contract. As Airbus was unable to make the delivery on time, it revised the contract to extend the delivery time by half a year. This is a typical example of modification of a contract.

Modification of a contract shall be partial, involving alteration of only a few individual clauses, while the principal contract remains unchanged.

### 8.2.2 Termination of the Contract

A contract may be terminated if the parties to the contract reach a consensus through consultation before they begin to perform their obligations or before the contract has been fulfilled.

Sometimes, changing circumstances make it impossible or unnecessary to perform the contract. In such cases, the parties to the contract may decide to rescind the contract, before the contract expires, through legal procedures or under the conditions or procedures stipulated in the contract itself.

When Airbus failed to deliver the ordered aircraft to S Company the second time, S Company had to give up the second batch of A380 jets; that is, to rescind the contract. The reason why S Company wanted to rescind the contract was mainly to reduce the loss incurred when they could not update their fleet as a result of the 「delayed performance of the contract-waiting for the delivery」.

If a contract or part of a contract has not yet been performed, its performance shall be terminated after the rescission. If it has been performed, a party to the contract may, in light of the performance and the character of the contract, request that the performance be completed, that the original status be restored or that other remedial measures be taken, as well as that proper compensation be made to offset the losses.

However, the rescission of a contract does not mean the termination of all rights and obligations of the contract. In reality, mutual legal obligations terminate only after the party responsible pays the required penalty fee, or compensates for any losses the other party may have suffered.

### 8.2.3 Circumstances That Allow Altering and Rescinding a Contract

(1) A contract may be altered or terminated if all the parties to the contract agree.

Since the contract is established as the outcome of the parties' agreement, any alteration to it or rescission should also be made after the parties reach a consensus through consultation. Neither party may unilaterally modify or rescind the contract. To do so is an illegal act. In addition, if the modification or rescission is made in a way that it may damage the interests of the state or the public citizenry of one party, the government agencies or citizens concerned in the relevant countries may take legitimate action to stop the modification or rescinding of the contract.

(2) It is impossible to perform the contract because of a force majeure.

A force majeure or act of God refers to an irresistible force, that is, natural circumstances or events that are unpredictable or unexpected and inevitable that prevents someone from doing what they have officially planned or agreed to do. A force majeure usually manifests itself in the form of natural disasters, such as flood, earthquake, or tsunami, or social chaos, such as war, government instability, and strikes. Because a force majeure is totally beyond the expectations of the parties to the contract, they may alter or rescind the contract when they are thus prevented from performing the contract.

(3) One party to the contract fails to perform the contract within the agreed time period. Three major circumstances exist in this respect:

①One party expresses explicitly or indicates through its acts, before the expiry of the performance period, that it will not perform the principal debt obligations.

②One party to the contract fails to perform the contract at the due date, thus affecting severely the projected interests of the other party, making it unnecessary for the affected party to have the first party implement the contract.

③One party to the contract delays in performing its principal debt obligations and fails, after being urged, to perform them within a reasonable time period.

Under these circumstances, one party has the rights to modify or rescind the contract in accordance with legal procedures and to ask the party in breach of the contract to pay a penalty or take other remedial measures to compensate losses incurred due to the breach of contract.

### 8.2.4 Procedures for Altering and Rescinding a Contract

There are two common approaches to altering or rescinding a contract:

(1) All the parties reach a consensus through consultation to alter or rescind a contract.

If all the parties to a contract agree through consultation to modify or end a contract, they may carry it out via the same procedure used in establishing the contract. First, the party that asks for a modification or rescission of the contract makes a proposal and then waits for the other party's reply within the agreed time period. Once the other party accepts the proposal, the modification or rescission becomes effective immediately; if the other party does not accept, the modification or rescission is null and the original contract is still valid.

(2) One party notifies the other party that it proposes to rescind the contract.

Due to a force majeure or corporate bankruptcy and the like, one party to the contract has the right to modify or rescind the contract, but has to give notice to the other party. If the other party does not agree, the party with the fight to do so may ask for arbitration or appeal to the court for a judgment.

Two points need attention in the process of modifying or rescinding the contract:

①Some form of written notice or agreement shall be used to notify the other party of the modification or rescission of the contract.

②A proposal of or response to a modification or rescission of a contract shall be made within the time limit stipulated by the relevant law or contract.

### 8.2.5 Assignment of Contracts

(1) Implications of Contract Assignment

The assignment of a contract means the change of the subject of (or the party to) a contract. In other words, for certain reasons, one party to a contract withdraws from the legal relationship involved in the original contract and assigns its rights and obligations under the contract together to a third party with the consent of the other party, but the contents and terms of the original contract remain the same.

(2) Difference Between Contract Assignment and Contract Modification

The assignment of a contract does not change the contents of the contract, but only changes the subject (one of the parties involved).

The modification of a contract does not change the subject of (or parties to) the contract, but only changes the contents or provisions of the contract.

(3) Conditions for Effective Assignment of a Contract

The assignment of a contract shall become effective under the following conditions:

①A creditor assigning its rights shall notify the debtor. Without notifying the debtor, the assignment shall not become effective to the debtor.

②If the debtor assigns its obligations, wholly or in part, to a third party, it shall obtain consent from the creditor first.

③The assignment of certain special contracts, such as corporate merger and acquisition, joint venture and cooperation, must be approved by the relevant higher-level authorities; otherwise, the assignment is not effective.

④The assignment of a contract must be made according to the provisions of the laws. If it is against the laws, policies and the public interest of the parties' home countries, the assignment is not effective.

In addition, it is required in some countries that in concluding a contract, the parties shall have appropriate civil capacity of rights and civil capacity of conduct and the transaction between them shall fall into the scope of their respective business. For example, an Italian travel agency plans to accept the assignment of a merger and acquisition of a contract from an Italian oil company with a Russian oil company, but the contract may not be allowed to be assigned by certain Russian government agencies because this Italian agency shall be viewed as a company whose business scope is not in line with the nature of the business stipulated in the contract.

## 8.3 Authentication and Notarization of a Contract

Contract identification and certification is a contract administration mechanism by which a government or government-authorized statutory contract administration institution, in response to the contracting parties requests, reviews, evaluates and certifies the legitimacy, feasibility and authenticity of a contract in accordance with the relevant laws, rules and policies in the contract country or territory.

Procedure for arranging contract identification and certification:

(1) To file an application for contract identification and certification with the authorities.

In certain circumstances, there may be a request for a contract to be formally identified and certified. After signing a contract, the signatories may feel it necessary to voluntarily submit an application to an industry and commercial administration department at the site of signing or implementing the contract, with expenses shared by all the parties concerned. If only one party to the contract asks for contract identification and certification, the same procedure shall be followed, but the party asking for the identification and certification must bear the expenses. The application may be submitted through an agent in accordance with the law as well, and the applying party or parties must then pay an agency fee in addition to the identification and certification charges.

(2) To submit the relevant documents.

When one party or all the parties apply to an identifying authority, they must submit a number of documents related to the contract as evidence, including original and duplicate copies of the contract and business licenses, certification data for the corporate legal representative or the principal, and other certification materials required by the authority.

(3) To go through the formalities.

After receiving the application and documentary evidence (usually a contract for a large project) mentioned above, the Administration Department for Industry and Commerce shall carry out the identification and certification. Then, the contract shall be signed by the authorized officer in charge of the identification and certification and affixed with the seal of the Administration Department for Industry and Commerce.

In international business endeavors, it is necessary for the parties to have their contract, especially one for a large project, identifies and certifies to ensure that it is legitimate and will be performed afterwards. For some common international trade contracts, it is generally not necessary that they are identified and certificated unless the two sides or one side really deems it necessary.

Contract notarization is a judicial superintending procedure in which a public notary or a state notarization department, upon application by any party concerned, reviews and verifies a contract and then attests to its validity according to law, to its authenticity and legality in all respects, and thus renders it legally authentic as evidence of a deal.

Procedures for handing contract notarization:

(1) The party concerned shall file an application with the authorities.

In applying for notarization, a contracting party or contracting parties shall go personally to a notary office in the place where the contract is signed to make an application verbally or in writing.

(2) The party concerned shall submit relevant documents.

When filing an application, the party or parties shall submit to the authorities a business license or ID card (the passport), original and duplicate copies of the contract, and other relevant documents or statements.

(3) The party concerned may entrust an agency with the notarization.

If the application affair is entrusted to an agent, documents certifying the power of attorney shall be presented, indicating the commitment and extent of authority entrusted to the agent.

(4) The notary office examines and verifies the contract.

After receiving an application, the notaries must examine the status of the parties concerned and their ability to exercise the rights and to perform the obligations required, and must examine the authenticity and legality of the facts and relevant documents, with regard to all aspects of the contract and of the parties who are applying for a testimonial.

(5) The notary office shall give a testimonial or refusal.

After the thorough examination, notaries shall prepare notarized documents in accordance with the format prescribed or approved by the relevant authorities, if the contract in question satisfies the notarization conditions and requirements. After notarized documents have been processed, an additional copy of the documents shall be kept on file. In accordance with the needs of the persons concerned, duplicates may be prepared, which shall be issued to the persons concerned together with the original documents. The notary office shall refuse to give a testimonial to false or illegal statements and documents, and shall not prepare notarized documents if the contract fails to meet the requirements. However, when the notary office refuses to accept an application of the party concerned for notarization, it shall explain, verbally or in writing, to the party concerned the reason why his/her application is rejected.

(6) The party concerned may make an appeal.

In the event that the party concerned is not satisfied with the rejection made by the notary office, or thinks that the notary has handled the notarization affair improperly, he may make an appeal to a judicial administrative department at the locality where the notary office is located or to the judicial administrative department at a higher level, and the department that accepts the appeal shall make a binding decision.

## Case Study

In 1999, a private company in Zhejiang, China (hereafter called Company A) negotiated a deal with a chemical engineering company in Singapore (hereafter called Company B) for the export of chemical engineering raw material. Company A was not allowed to deal in import and export business at that time. Therefore, the company entrusted a state-owned foreign trade corporation in China (hereafter called Company C) with the import transaction. Company A and C signed an agreement that Company C shall act as the import agency of Company A and sign an import contract as a buyer directly with Company B. It was stipulated that the payment should be made by Telegraphic Transfer (T/T) upon the delivery of the goods. In reality, Company C and B did not have any direct negotiation and contact. After the arrival of the goods in Shanghai, Company A collected the goods. But right after that, their statutory representative died in a traffic accident. The company stopped its operation immediately and went into bankruptcy soon after. However, the company had not yet effected the payment. It was not until September 2003 that Company B filed a lawsuit against Company C, demanding that Company C pay the total price in accordance with the signed contract. Because the agency agreement Company C produced could not be convincing enough to prove that Company A and B closed the deal directly, and moreover, Company A was broke, at last, the dispute over the payment could only be resolved through consultation between Company B and Company C.

## Exercises

(1) What will happen if the negotiation is concluded earlier than the optimum time, or if the best time to conclude the negotiation is missed?

(2) What should be done if the terms and conditions given by one party do not fall into the other party's scope of closing prices?

(3) How should a party respond to an ultimatum delivered by its counterparty?

(4) What factors should be considered when an international business contract is signed?

# Chapter 9   Personal Styles and Negotiation Modes

## 9.1   Negotiators' Personal Styles

(1) Understand the Personalities of your own and Your Counterpart

In negotiation, another decisive factor crucial to outcomes of negotiations is negotiators' personal styles. Negotiations are human activities; therefore, negotiator's behavior during negotiation is the result of his psychological activity. A negotiator's own personality, due to his cultural background, educational level, personal experiences, may bring about unexpected and sometimes even surprising result to negotiations. A party weak in power may gain more and win final success of negotiation simply because of negotiators' high assertiveness, while a negotiator of low assertiveness may make things difficult for its own party and give up possible gains. Many a case has demonstrated the conclusive function of negotiators' personality. It is therefore essential for negotiators to understand their counterparts' personality and possible linkage between one's personal style and his customary action in negotiation.

However, it is not unusual that quite a number of people in negotiation do not seem to have a good view of their own personalities although they often stress the necessity of having a better comprehension of others' personality. As a result of the ignorance, quite a few negotiators are able to neither perceive the progress of a negotiation nor explain the result of the negotiation, a problem which can be resolved if they know more or less about their own personal profiles. However, a good understanding of people's personalities is not easy. Some psychologists point out that there are actually 6 different kinds of personalities in display during a negotiation between two negotiators because each negotiator may have three coatings of personalities: the first one is his real personality; the second one is what he assumes and the last one is the personality that he actually shows during the negotiation. What sides of his personalities will be shown is determined by the negotiation settings and his objectives. Understanding the fact that people can play different roles during negotiation is important for us because we will make more efforts to understand each other, which is conducive to the success of negotiations.

(2) Negotiators' Personal Styles and Some Interesting Findings

Because of the complexity of people's personalities, experts have carried out various researches on the subject. A personal style check designed by K. W. Thomas and R.H. Kilmann makes it feasible for those who want to find out their own personal styles (do the personality test in the exercises). The test, according to degree of one's assertiveness and cooperativeness in negotiation, divides personal styles into five modes: competing, collaborating, compromising, avoiding and accommodating, arranged from highest assertiveness to lowest assertiveness and highest cooperativeness to lowest cooperativeness.

The results noted from the repeated tests have revealed the following findings:

firstly, one's personal profile consists of all these five modes. However in the five modes, there is one style which is primary and closest to one's nature, and one style which is a backup to the primary one and the least likely styles. It can be inferred from the tests that people's personalities are multi-sided. In most cases, a person's behavior is controlled by his primary style and in some other situations his actions can be explained by his backup styles. For instance, a person whose primary style is compromising often has avoiding style as his backup one. Sometimes a person may unexpectedly turn to his least likely style and acts like a totally different person. For example, a person of avoiding style or accommodating style may behave as a person of competing style, a situation which happens when the person is cornered or pressed too hard.

Secondly, one's living environment and cultural background are by far the most important factors in shaping one's personality. From international perspective, people from the same country influenced by their culture and traditional customs tend to follow an identical pattern of personal styles, which has been proved correct repeatedly by the personal style checks mentioned above. For instance, the Americans tend to be competitive and most of the Chinese (about 85%) are of compromising and avoiding styles.

Thirdly, the personal style check also reveals a shocking result—few Chinese students are of collaborative style. The research result should be a warning to China's education workers since cooperation has been regarded as an indispensable element in today's economic development, therefore it is of significance that spirit of collaboration is advocated and encouraged among Chinese students.

## 9.2　Negotiators' Personal Styles and AC Model

Different personal styles play decisive roles in negotiators' attitudes in negotiation, and express the degree of negotiators' assertiveness and cooperativeness in negotiation, two primary factors in relation with personal styles and negotiation outcomes. The following Figure 9-1 shows how personal styles combine different degree of assertiveness and cooperativeness.

The model clearly shows the location of each personal style in the figure and their combination of different degrees of assertiveness and cooperativeness. Competing style and accommodating style are at the high ends of assertiveness and cooperativeness, and avoiding style is neither assertive nor cooperative, thus is the least recommended style for negotiations. Compromising style, corresponding to its middle position, is inclined to take middle way and seek balance between different people. Collaborating style combines highest degree of both assertiveness and cooperativeness and should be recommended as the most suitable personal style for negotiations.

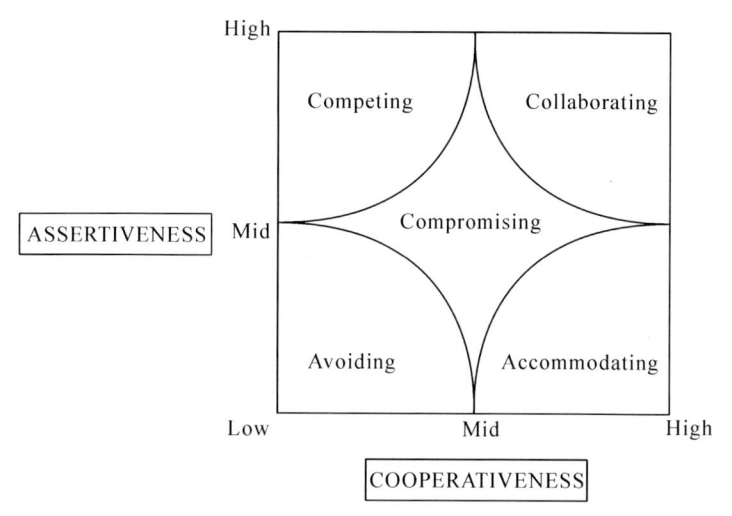

Figure 9-1  Negotiators' Personality and AC Model

The degree of a negotiator's assertiveness and cooperativeness depends on their personalities. What determines assertiveness and cooperativeness? The key determinants of assertiveness and cooperativeness are specified below.

(1) Assertiveness Depends on Stakes and Power.

Stakes are expressed as long or short-term interests or underlying desires and issues articulated for negotiation.

Power is an estimate of the pressures one may bring to bear to induce the other to do something or prevent them from doing something. Relative power is an estimate of one's power diminished by the other's power.

The higher degree the stakes and power are, the more assertive the negotiators are. It is foreseeable that when a negotiation becomes so crucial that any drawback will mean great losses, people involved will naturally appear firmer and tougher. The degree of assertiveness will rise accordingly. When a negotiator's estimation of his relative power is stronger, he will not give up effortlessly and make easy concession.

The combination of stakes and power assists negotiators in making tactical decisions: adopting high, medium high or low assertive stance.

(2) Cooperativeness Depends on Alignment of Interests and Relationship.

Alignment of interests means how much the two parties share common interests, which varies from convergent, through mixed to divergent. When two parties share most of their common interests, the cooperation happens naturally. When two parties' interests are in complete divergence, the chance of cooperation is slender. The reality is that negotiating parties' alignment of interests can hardly be in complete convergence or divergence, but rather mixed, otherwise there should be no negotiation happening.

Relationship depends on trust between the two parties and negotiating atmosphere. Trust encourages cooperation. Mutual trust also contributes to sincere and open negotiation atmosphere, which in turn enhances cooperation between negotiating parties.

Alignment of interests and relationship jointly determines negotiators' degree of cooperativeness ranging from high, medium to low.

## 9.3 Personal Styles vs. Negotiation Modes

In negotiation, it is imaginable that the result of a negotiation depends greatly on the personalities of negotiators if regardless of other factors. Let's assume that a negotiator of competing style talks with a person of the same style and most probably the talking would end up quarreling furiously. However, when he negotiates with a person of accommodating style, the situation would be favorable to him. He may not feel so comfortable talking with a person of avoiding style because he tends to reach his goal by direct and short-cut way, whereas the latter tends to express himself in the way of beating-around-the-bush or implied way, which often makes persons of competing style rather frustrated and thus loses control of himself. It can be inferred from the description that the most suitable personal style for a negotiator is collaborating style and the least preferable style is avoiding and accommodating style.

Each of the five personal styles acts differently in negotiations and produces different effects on the negotiation process and its outcomes. Each of the five styles expresses a negotiation mode. Please look at Table 9-1 and study the negotiation modes and their related personal styles.

The table exhibits the five personality styles connecting with negotiation modes from the aspects of approach, issues, information, condition, differences, strategy, solution, relation, time, modes, request, and assistance. To sum up the commonality of the modes of each personality style, we may draw a sketch of the five personalities related with negotiation. Competing style of persons tends to use high pressure such as dead-line, ultimatum and sanctions. They show little concern to others' interests and force the other party to surrender to their demands. As for collaborating kind of persons, as they are so named, cooperation is an outstanding feature in their negotiating activities. They show concerns and understanding to both parties' interests, difficulties and satisfactions, which explain the reason why they can share information, trust others and offer help needed in negotiation. Seeking middle ground is the representative feature of compromising style. They cooperate with others on some items but refuse to collaborate on other items. They treat assistance, information and trust as commodities; hence they look for trades with others. 「I won't give you anything unless you can provide me with what I want」is the typical feeling of compromising style. Avoiding style of persons is never willing to cooperate with others, nor do they state their consent or objection openly. They resist passively often by finding excuses, or changing topics or leaving the matters to others. People of accommodating style are the other extreme of competing style. They habitually cater to other's desires and requests. Harmony is their motto. They avoid hurting feelings, damaging relationship and disturbing peaceful atmosphere, so they try to be very helpful and care a lot about other's ideas.

Table 9-1　　　　　　　　**Personal Styles vs. Negotiation Modes**

| Modes | Competing | Collaborating | Compromising | Avoiding | Accommodating |
| --- | --- | --- | --- | --- | --- |
| Approach | press own goals | get both concern out | work on a few items | postpone, delay | ask for the other's views |
| Issues | stress own position | identify issues | stay in stated bounds | ask/say little, withdraw | accept the other's views |
| Information | exaggerate | share information | look for trades | be irrelevant | be tentative, modest |
| Condition | demand | build commonalties | give some to get some | don't appear | don't press own ideas |
| Differences | override the other's views | work out differences | split difference | change the topic | concede |
| Strategy | threaten | create new options | stay calm | hand off to another | stress communication |
| Solution | use subterfuge | seek joint satisfaction | be professional | claim limited authority | avoid hurting feelings |
| Relation | exploit vulnerability | trust the other | moderately trust | straddle | seek harmony |
| Time | time pressure | give time needed | seek middle ground | discuss a minor item | avoid rejection |
| Modes | competing | collaborating | compromising | avoiding | accommodating |
| Request | little concern for the other | high mutual concern | half beats nothing | passively resist: yes, but | other must be satisfied firstly |
| Assistance | give no help | ask and give help | give modest help | claim need to consult | be very helpful |

## 9.4　Application of Personality Checks

「What is the right type of lover for you?」When asked the question. most of people would feel that their privacy is invaded. But actually the question is not interested in your lover at all. The only thing it wants to find out about is your personality.

The first personality test was developed by the American army in 1917 to filter out weak recruits. Psychometric tests have been used alongside interviews in western countries for more than 50 years. Compared with traditional ways of assessment, such as question-and-answer formatted tests and interviews, psychometric tests make the process of selection from thousands of candidates quicker and easier since they use the same yardstick to measure the result of every interviewee. With a rising number of graduates going for a falling number of jobs, organizations began to see psychometric testing as a cheap, reliable alternative to the expensive, time-consuming interview. Now, for example, nearly half of UK firms, 46 percent, will use psychometric tests to select trainees, compared with just 17 percent in 2000.

Today the tests are becoming alarmingly sophisticated and are edging towards probing the 「dark side」: pathology and personality disorders. Increasingly, tests are being used to try to detect promising young graduates who may, later in life fly off the rails (go crazy) or to stop psychopaths (having mental disorder) getting recruited. In the future, interviewees could even be given a swab to reveal the genetic and biological markers of personality, a kind of genetic screening.

The psychometric tests were brought to China by foreign-funded enterprises in the late 1990s. The growth of managerial roles and the mass media stimulated the use of psychometric tests. But it is foreign ventures that are the most frequent users. Jia is from a foreign-funded logistics company in Beijing. He says his company uses both Intelligent Quotient (IQ) test and Emotional Quotient (EQ) test in recruitment. The IQ and EQ judge the interviewee's language, analytical and cognitive ability. Candidates must select from 300 adjectives, those that best describe themselves and the kind of character they would like to be. Their selection, when analyzed with special software designed by psychologists, reveals their personalities. Since personality affects one's attitudes towards work, it is very important for employers to know about their potential employee's personality before hiring them. That is why most international companies place so much emphasis on the test as part of their recruitment strategy. Nowadays, many sackings result from poor working attitudes.

However, there are problems with the tests. For starters, it is possible to fake it—even the test producers agree on this. But they have made it as hard as possible. For example, look at whether you agree or disagree with the following two statements:「New ideas come easily to me」and「I find generating new concepts difficult」. How long did it take you to realize that they both could ask about the same personality of a person? Jia thinks that in fact most candidates will not lie, since it can only end in misery because even if someone passes the test by cheating, he might suffer in the future if he gets a job that does not fit his true personality. That could be worse than if he did not get the job at all.

While the debate rages continue, however, the most important thing is to adopt a professional attitude to psychometric tests so that neither employees nor employers will suffer. The golden rule is then, that a psychometric test should never be used as the sole basis of selection, but should always be followed by interviews.

## Case Study

RJR Nabisco was having a bad year with its stock performance. The CEO of the company, Ross Johnson thought that this was an opportune time to attempt a leveraged buyout to increase the shareholder's value of the stock. He, and his management group, entered into negotiations with the board of directors' special committee that had been assigned with the particular task of finding ways to maximize the shareholder value.

Since he was the CEO of Nabisco, Johnson was confident because of his close ties to the company; his buyout attempt would be the proverbial「no-brainer」. He outstepped his confidence and found the banana peel instead. His over-confidence led him to fall into the trap of making assumptions and jumping to an erroneous conclusion.

His first mental lapse was to assume that his company connections would automatically give him the「go-ahead」to make the buyout happen. He made the second mistake of assuming that his investment bankers would simply have to put the financing in place, and that the RJR board of directors would also give him the power main financial partner, Shearson Lehman Hutton, US/share.

The initial offering meant that his management team would only have to put up 20 million US dollars or 8.5% of the total offer. If the board acceded to this offer then Johnson's management team would receive 18% of the company's total equity. Johnson was also insisting that the 18% would be divided equally amongst the 15,000 personnel who were employed for RJR Nabisco. However, he neglected to mention that in reality, only six names actually appeared as the real beneficiaries of the transaction—a real but unintentional「Oops!」

So stroked by his over-confidence in closing the buyout he moved ominously close to the waiting banana peel because he wasn't paying attention to several occurrences that were transpiring in the meantime. First, the board never discussed or made any concessions with Johnson or his financiers. Johnson also never even conceived there were any other players who might also be interested in buying Nabisco. In truth, he had so alienated the board with his attitude that they eventually awarded the buyout bid to an investment banking firm, Kohlburg, Kravis, and Roberts (KKR) for 109 million US dollars.

KKR's bid was actually lower than Johnson's bid. The board was so ticked off at Johnson that they took the loss instead because they appreciated KKR's negotiation flexibility, and believed that KKR would have a more positive influence on the company rather than Johnson's「arrogance and overconfidence」. So the moral of the story is that when you become overconfident and full of yourself, just remember there's almost always a banana peel lying there in wait.

# Exercises

This case was so classic that the book *Barbarians at the Gate* was a business best-seller. What factors beyond the「over-confidence」do you think lead to the final result of the deal?

# Chapter 10  Different Cultures and Business Negotiation

## 10.1  Definition of Culture

Of the more than 160 definitions of culture, some conceive of culture as separating humans from non-humans, some define it as communicable knowledge, and some as the sum of historical achievements produced by man's social life. All of the definitions have common elements: culture is learned, shared, and transmitted from one generation to the next. Culture is primarily passed on from parents to their children but also transmitted by social organizations, special interest groups, government, schools, and churches. Common ways of thinking and behaving that are developed are then reinforced through social pressure. Culture is also multidimensional, consisting of a number of common elements that are interdependent. Changes occurring in one of the dimensions will affect the others as well.

Culture is also defined as an integrated system of learned behavior patterns that are characteristic of the members of any given society. It includes everything that a group thinks, says, does, and makes—its customs, languages, material artifacts, and shared systems of attitudes and feelings.

The most fundamental component of national culture consists of value. Value are broad preferences for one state of affairs above others. Values are acquired in the family during the first years of our lives, further developed and confirmed at school, and reinforced in work organizations and in daily life within a national cultural environment. Values determine what we consider to be good and evil, beautiful and ugly, natural and unnatural, rational and irrational, normal and abnormal. Values are partly unconscious and because of their normative character, hardly discussible. We cannot convince someone else that his/her values are wrong. It is essential that negotiators share the national culture and values of the country they represent, because otherwise they will not be trusted by their own side.

Other components of national culture are more superficial—that is, visible, conscious, and easy to learn, even by adults. They include symbols—words, gestures, and objects that carry a specific meaning in a given culture. The entire field of language consists of symbols; and a culture group's language can be learned by outsiders. Besides symbols, a culture has its collective habits or rituals, ways of behavior that serve to communicable feelings.

Those involved in international negotiations will have developed a professional negotiation culture, which considerably facilitates the negotiation process. This professional culture, however, is more superficial than their national cultures: it consists of commonly understood symbols and commonly learned habits more than shared values. Different types of negotiators will have their own kind of professional cultures: diplomats, bureaucrats, politicians, business people, lawyers, engineers etc. Negotiations are easier with people from other countries sharing the same professional culture than with those who do not.

For success in international negotiations, it is important for parties to acquire an insight into the range of cultural values they are going to meet in the negotiations. This includes an insight into their own cultural values and the extent to which these deviate from those of the other side (s). Such insight will allow them to interpret more accurately the meaning of the behavior of the other side (s).

In the occidental culture, oneself consciousness is emphasized whereas in the oriental culture group consciousness is stressed. Loyalty to central authority and placing the good of a group before that of the individual is held valuable. The different focuses in the two types of cultures have even led to misunderstandings. In Western societies there has been a perception that the subordination of the individual to the common good has resulted in the sacrifice of human rights; however on the other hand it may explain the economic success of Japan and the Newly Industrial Economics etc.

A Dutch expert Gilt once conducted a research on self-consciousness of managers in selected countries and areas from the major parts of the world.

References indicate American value individualism the most, which is manifested in their daily life and social activities, taking the example of the rewarding system in sport competition. If the price for the champion is 150,000 USD, then anti-globalization protestors, led by Jose Bove, attempted to destroy a McDonald's restaurant that was under construction in the town of Millau in southern France, causing 120,000 USD worth of damage. Bove's subsequent brief imprisonment only served to strengthen his cause in France, on the face of it, the farmers were protesting about the loss of traditional food production and the dominance of multinational corporations, symbolized by McDonald's. But in the French media and political circles the issue was more fundamental. It was about the protection of French gastronomy, French industry, and the French way of life from the invasion' of Anglo-Saxon free trade and multinational corporations. McDonald's has brought an element of American culture to France. Its menus and even the names of its products represent a challenge to the French diet and language, both of which are treated with great respect in France. Of course, compared to the vast array of international cultural influences, both now and in the past, the 「McDonald effect」 is barely significant. The incident in Millau does, however, illustrate the enduring role of culture in people's lives even in a world where globalization is breaking down barriers between nations.

Clearly, the incident in Millau was an illegal act by a group of angry protestors anxious to protect their traditional markets and way of life. Many of France's younger generation and more cosmopolitan citizens would have taken a different view and most people would have deplored the farmers' actions. However, multinational enterprises like McDonald's have become increasingly sensitive to the host country's cultural environment when expanding abroad in recent years, adapting to different work practices and laws as well as different consumer tastes and concerns. Not only is there still significant cultural variation between countries, but differences in national economic and political systems have also remained remarkably persistent.

## 10.2　Cultural Change

Globalization has far-reaching consequences for the way people live their lives. Not only does it bring opportunities for international travel and allow the local supermarkets to stock goods from around the world, it also exposes people to unfamiliar cultures and practices. Cultural changes can be regarded both positively and negatively. There is a view that the world's cultures are converging and that 「western」 or American culture is becoming dominant: examples cited to distinguish this 「dominance」 include the prevalence of western dress, fast food, and the English language. However nothing is ever quite straightforward as it seems. Whilst some degree of cultural convergence has taken place, there is also evidence of cultural diversity. For example, a European citizen enjoys a much more varied choice of cuisine today than he or she would have fifty years ago. It is also curious that neighbouring countries such as the UK or France, or even neighbouring communities in a single country, still retain their distinctive cultural identities after many centuries of coexistence. Even the ubiquitous English language may not be quite as widely spoken as is commonly imagined.

Culture is often influenced by religious beliefs. Only a few years ago it might have been argued that religion was becoming less important in the western world. This can hardly be claimed today. Sometimes, these religious traditions represent important differences of outlook and beliefs, including their perspectives on political issues and business practices. In reality, therefore, it is by no means certain that cultural convergence predominates over cultural diversity. What is certain, however, is that the study of culture leads to fascinating insights into the complexities of the business environment.

Akio Morita, the founder of Sony Corporation said, 「Grammar and pronunciation aren't as important as expressing yourself in a way that matches the way Westerners think, which is very different from our thought process. So when you're in America you must be clear, and when you return to Japan you must be vague. It's more difficult than you can imagine.」

A significant part of every manager's job is the role of negotiator. That role can involve activity across the boundary of the organization, such as buyer-seller negotiations, or within the company, such as negotiating performance expectations with an employee. Underlying every negotiation that takes place in an international context is the process of cross-cultural communication.

(1) Cross-Cultural Communication Process

Communication is the act of transmitting messages, including information about the nature of the relationship, to another person who interprets these messages and gives them meaning (Berlo, 1960). Therefore, both the sender and the receiver of the message play an active role in the communication process. Successful communication requires not only that the message is transmitted but also that it is understood. For this understanding to occur, the sender and receiver must share a vast amount of common information called grounding (Clark and Brennan, 1991). This grounding information is updated moment by moment during the communication process. Probably all of us have noticed how people who have extensive common information can communicate very effectively with a minimum of distortion. For example, hospital emergency room personnel depend on sharing a great deal of information, such as medical jargon and the seriousness of the situation, in order to communicate complex messages efficiently.

Cross-cultural communication is significantly more demanding than communicating in a single culture because culturally different individuals have less common information. They have less grounding because of differences in their field of experience (Schramm, 1980). The term cultural field refers to the culturally based elements of a person's background (e.g. education, values, attitudes) that influence communication.

(2) Language

One obvious consideration in cross-cultural communication is the language being used. Language is a symbolic code of communication consisting of a set of sounds with understood meanings and a set of rules for constructing messages. The meanings attached to any word by a language are completely arbitrary, but cultural conventions control the features of language use. For example, the Japanese word for cat (neko) does not look or sound any more like a cat than does the English word. Somewhere during the development of the two languages, these words were chosen to represent the animal. Similarly, the Cantonese word for the number four (sei) has the same sound as the word for death, whereas the word for the number eight sounds like faat (prosperity). Therefore, some Chinese avoid things numbered four and are attracted to number eight, although there are no such connotations for English speakers.

Although English may be becoming the lingua franca of international business, culturally based conventions create differences even between English speakers. In Britain, a rubber is an eraser, to knock someone up means to call at their house, and tabling an item means to put it on agenda, not to defer it. Likewise, British people live in flats and might stand in a queue, US people live in apartments and stand in line, and Canadians live in suites and stand in a lineup.

Even when translators know the meaning of words and the grammatical rules for putting them together, effective communication is often not achieved. The diversity of languages means an important issue in cross-cultural communication is finding a common language that both parties can use to work effectively. Practically, this means that at least one of the two parties must use a second language. The end result is that cross-language communication can be as demanding for the native speaker of the language as for the second-language speaker. Both participants must devote more attention to the communication process in order to achieve an effective transfer of understanding.

(3) Communication Styles

It is important to consider the aspects of communication that transcends the specific language being spoken. In general, these communication behaviours are logical extensions of the internalized values and norms of their respective cultures. That is, culturally based rules govern the style, conventions, and practices of language usage. In some cases, a relationship to the key value orientations of individualism and collectivism is apparent.

**Explicit vs. Implicit Communication**

One way in which cultures vary in terms of communication style is the degree to which they use language itself to communicate the message. For example, in the United States effective verbal communication is expected to be explicit, direct, and unambiguous (Gallois and Callan, 1997). That is, people are expected to say exactly what they mean. In contrast, communication styles in some other cultures, such as Indonesia, are much more inexact, ambiguous, and implicit. These two styles are characterized by a bipolar typology called high-context and low-context communication styles.

On the basis of observation, a number of countries have been classified along the continuum according to whether they are primarily high or low context (Hall, 1976). In low-context cultures, the message is conveyed largely by the words spoken. In high context cultures, a good deal of the meaning is implicit, and the words convey only a small part of the message. The receiver must fill in the gaps from past knowledge of the speaker, the setting, or other contextual cues. Furthermore, high-and-low-context communication styles may actually serve to perpetuate collectivism and individualism, respectively.

For example, inindividualist cultures speech is more focused and brief, with more reference to specific goals. However, collectivist cultures speech includes more qualifiers such as maybe, perhaps, somewhat, and probably (Smith and Bond, 1999). Some support for this idea is found in comparisons of pairs of cultures.

**Direct vs. Indirect Communication**

An idea complementary to the high-context versus low-context communication styles just discussed is the degree of directness of communication. Directness is associated with individualist cultures and indirectness with collectivist cultures. A pertinent example of this difference is expressed in the indirect style in which a collectivist might say no without really saying it. Direct communication is needed at some time in all cultural groups. In collectivist cultures, politeness and a desire to avoid embarrassment often take precedence over truth, as truth is defined in individualist cultures. That is, for collectivists truth is not absolute but depends on the social situation. Therefore, the social situation is an important indicator for the appropriate degree of directness or truthfulness. Making untrue statements to preserve harmony (white lies) is probably universal (Smith and Bond, 1999).

## 10.3 Negotiation and Conflict Resolution Across Cultures

An important application of cross cultural communication for the international manager is face-to-face negotiation. All negotiations share some universal characteristics. They involve two or more parties who have conflicting interests but a common need to reach an agreement, the content of which is not clearly defines at the outset. A substantial body of literature exists about the effects of both contextual and individual factors on the negotiation process and on outcomes (see Neale and Northcraft, 1991). However, the extent to which these findings generalize across cultures is just beginning to be understood.

The study of cross-cultural business negotiation has produced a number of analytical models that identify the antecedents to effective negotiation. Consistent among them is that the outcomes of negotiation are thought to be contingent on (a) factors associated with the behaviour of people involved in the negotiation, (b) factors associated with the process of negotiation, and (c) factors associated with the negotiation situation. In general, culture probably has an indirect (contextual) effect on the outcome of negotiations by influencing all these contingency variables (Brent, 2001; Usunier, 1996).

Efforts to understand cross-cultural negotiation fall into one of three types. The first type is descriptive approaches, which are characteristics of much early study of cross-cultural negotiation. These studies involve documenting differences in negotiation processes and behaviours in different cultures. The second might be called the cultural dimensions approach (Brett and Crotty, 2008), in which the cultural effects are attributed to the cultural values and norms of knowledge structures of the participants and the social context in which the negotiations take place.

A number of efforts have been made to describe the stages of the negotiation process. Although the idea of a sequential, phased structure to negotiations might be a peculiarly Western notion, the concept is nevertheless appealing from a comparative standpoint. The Graham four-stage model seems to have the most elements in common with the other popular models. Essentially, the model suggests that all business negotiations proceed through four stages:

(1) Nontask sounding or relationship building.
(2) Task-related exchange of information.
(3) Persuasion.
(4) Making concessions and reaching agreement.

Graham (1987) suggests that the content, duration, and importance of each of these stages can be seen to differ across cultures. That is, the internalized cultural values and norms of the negotiator influence which aspect of the process is emphasized. Descriptions of the negotiation process in different cultures support the notion that different aspects of the negotiation process are emphasized in different cultures. For example, Japanese negotiators spend more time in non-task sounding or relationship building than US people, and they also emphasize an exchange of information as opposed to the persuasion tactics preferred by people from the United States. These differences are reflected in descriptions of the behavioural styles of negotiators.

Culture also seems to influence the preference that individuals have for a particular conflict resolution style. For example, some cultures prefer confrontation in the negotiation process, whereas others prefer a more subtle form of bargaining in which balance and restraint are important. France, Brazil, and the United States are typically competitive, whereas Japanese and Malaysian negotiators are characterized by their politeness, ambiguous objections, and restraint. In addition, Indians can be even more competitive in negotiations than people in United States. Japanese managers preferred a status power model in which conflicts are resolved by a higher authority. Germans preferred a regulations model in which pre-fexisting procedures or rules resolve problems. People from the United States preferred an interest model that focuses on discovering and resolving the underlying concerns of the other party to make it worthwhile to reach an agreement.

Culture also seems to influence the initial offers and concession patterns of negotiators. Some cultural groups use very extreme initial offers, such as Russians, Arabs, and Chinese, whereas others, such as people from United States, are more moderate in their initial positions. Similarly, cultural differences exist in the willingness of negotiators to make concessions. Russians, for example, seem to view concessions as a weakness, whereas other groups, such as North Americans, Arabs, and Norwegians, are more likely to make concessions and to reciprocate an opponent's concessions.

## 10.4 Cultural Dimensions and Negotiation

Research that relates dimensions of cultures such as individualism-collectivism or power distance to negotiation improves our ability to explain and predict the effect of culture. For example, the cultural dimensions of individualism and collectivism can be predictive of a preference for a particular style of conflict resolution. Characteristics of Japanese (social inequality), German (explicit contracting), and US (polychronicity) cultures were linked to conflict resolution preferences for use of authorities, external regulations, and integrating conflicts, respectively.

Cultural dimension have also been related to differences in cognitive processes related to negotiation. Japanese and US participants differed in their perceptions of conflict based on cultural differences with regard to the need to preserve harmony in negotiations. And individualist and collectivist cultures have been found to differ with regard to egocentric perceptions of fairness (self-serving bias).

Negotiation processes can be understood from a cultural dimension perspective as well. For example, negotiators from low-context cultures have been found to engage in more direct information sharing, throughout the stages of the negotiation, whereas negotiators from high context cultures engaged in direct information exchange in the earlier phases of negotiation. Recent research suggests that the need to gain information, consistent with Japanese culture, was the reason for the early initial offers by Japanese negotiators. That is, these offers were used as a means to begin information sharing (Adair et al, 2007). Cultural dimensions also relate to the outcomes of negotiation. Most often this has been studied in terms of distributive (win-lose) or integrative (win-win) outcomes. For example, Natlandsmyr and Rognes (1995) found that Norwegians had more integrative outcomes than Mexicans, based on the cultural profile of Norway that includes low masculinity, weak uncertainty avoidance, and lower power distance. And Brett and Okumura (1998) reported that, consistent with their hierarchical cultural values, Japanese achieved a lower level of joint gains in intercultural dyads.

## 10.5 Business Negotiating Styles of Different Cultures

People from different countries have different values, different attitudes and different experience. These different notions of culture yield different understandings of the culture-negotiation link. Researches and observations by most scholars indicate fairly clearly that negotiation practices differ from culture to culture and that culture can influence「negotiating style」—the way persons from different cultures conduct themselves in negotiating sessions. A competent negotiator should develop a style appropriate for his own strengths of his particular culture. The following will provide some typical negotiating styles of different countries.

**American Style**

The American style of negotiating is possibly the most influential in the world. It is characterized first by personalities which are usually outgoing, and quickly convey sincerity. Personalities are confident and positive and talkative. Generally, Americans are very direct, openly disagree and try to demand the same from counterparts. They tend to make concessions throughout the negotiations, settling one issue, then proceeding to the next. They are particularly high in the bargaining phases of negotiation, make decisions based upon the bosom line and on cold, hard facts. Thus the final agreement is a sequence of several smaller concessions. They usually ignore establishing personal relation prior negotiation. In their minds, good business relation brings about good personal relation, not vice versa. American's high individualism is manifested through their decision making process—individual has the right to make the decision. Personal responsibility is stressed.

### Australian Style

The Australians are tough breed and they enjoy competition. They encourage long-term relationships and prefer to work with people they count as friends. Being direct while negotiating, the Australian are keen to spot deception and they feel no hesitation to walk away from the table if they feel one is holding back information.

Australian will bargain, but only to a small degree. Waiting for the price to drop is an Australian pastime. Since Australian tend to dislike bazaar haggling, visiting negotiators will get better results by opening discussions with a realistic bed. The negotiating process may take more time than it would in some other deal-focused business cultures, though less than in strongly relationship-focused markets such as Japan.

Australians have well developed commercial law. Handshakes are an amenity. Signatures mean business. Because of their relatively small population and remote location, the Australians have become experienced travelers and negotiators. They research the target economies and companies in great detail, with an eye toward reducing surprises at the table. Be assured that they will know all about the prospective company and culture before the first meeting.

### German Style

German negotiators are highly prepared, low in flexibility and compromise. In other words, in particular the German preparation for negotiations is superb. They are also well known for sticking steadfastly to their negotiating positions in the face of pressure tactics. They tend toward a factual approach when conducting business. Instructions and preliminaries are brief, so be prepared to get right to the point. They always identify the deal he hopes to make, and then prepare a reasonable bid, carefully covering each issue in the deal. While selling, make straightforward presentations. They will be interested in the reasons for purchasing goods or services, rather than the image that surrounds the purchase. They observe strictly schedule, punctuality go for meetings, payments and social gatherings as well, and therefore, will not trust those who fail to keep good time. As to the time of negotiation, they take more time than Americans but perhaps less than the Japanese and most other Asians. Decisions are made after careful, thorough and precise analysis, thus risks are minimized.

Therefore, German negotiators are characterized by the following generalizations:

(1) Do their homework very well before negotiations;

(2) Make poor conversation partners as they see no points in small talk;

(3) Frankness is honesty and 「diplomacy」 can often mean deviousness;

(4) Consider formality and use of surname as signs of respect;

(5) Stick to the facts and expect organization and order in all things;

(6) Be slow at making decisions for taking time to have a consensus decision-making process.

### Japanese Style

Japanese belonging to high context culture communicate with othersin implied and roundabout way. The most effective way to achieve the purpose is to find an 「insider」 who can introduce or establish a tie between you and your Japanese partner. If there is lack of such a go-between, special business agency or government and other organizations can serve the purpose.

Japanese negotiators are famous for their ambiguous responses to proposals. They view vagueness as a form of protection from loss of face in case things go sour. They are also known for their politeness, their emphasis on establishing relationships, and their indirect use of power. To maintain surface harmony and prevent loss of face, Japanese rely on codes of behavior such as the ritual of the business cards. Japanese negotiators rarely come to the table in groups smaller than three. The negotiating communication focuses on group goals, interdependence, and many Japanese companies still make decisions by consensus. This is a time-consuming process, one reason to bring patience to the negotiating table. So quick answers to any question or problem are almost impossible. Japanese negotiators are also known for their politeness, their emphasis on establishing relationships, and their indirect ways consistent with their preference for harmony and calmness. In comparative studies, Japanese negotiators were found to disclose considerably less about themselves and their goals than French or American counterparts.

### Russian Style

Russians may be new to international commercial negotiations but they're old hands at negotiation with foreign powers. They have clear agenda and no strategy or tactics is off-limits. Russia is no place for negotiation amateurs. Generally, Russians view compromise as a sign of weakness. Often, they will refuse to back down until the other side agrees to make sufficient concessions or shows exceptional firmness. Russians' decision-making is rather bureaucratic. Even the simplest deals will take a great deal of time to analyze and decide. Numerous trips will be required for medium to large ventures. Just as the geography lies between Europe and Asia, so does Russia's attitude toward contracts. It's best to get as many details written into the document as possible. Important points must be stressed continually as the Russians tend to look at the totality rather than the details of a contract.

### French Style

French negotiators are reputed to have three main characteristics in international dealings: a great deal of firmness, an insistence on using French as the language for negotiation, and a decidedly lateral style in negotiating. That is, in contrast to the American piece-by-piece approach, they prefer to make an outline agreement, then an agreement in principle, and then headings of agreement repeatedly covering the whole breadth of a deal. The French are verbally and non-verbally expressive. They love debate, often engaging in spirited debate during business meetings, but not intense criticism to avoid direct confrontation. The French will discuss every point at length and will have a position on every topic. They think proper use of the language is a sensitive cultural issue. All contracts must be completely in French, and commonly used foreign words cannot be substituted. They consider friendship as important in doing business, so they will not place large order before trustful and friendly relation is established. French decision-making takes longer time than German and have a well-known weak point: often late or changing schedule unilaterally, but they will not forgive their partner's delay.

### British Style

The British are old hands atinternational business. Their history of negotiation in international business goes back centuries. The depth of their knowledge is without comparison. They may put a wide safety margin in their opening position so as to leave room for substantial concessions during the bargaining process.

Britain is an orderly society, punctuality is mandatory and presentations should be detailed. Englishmen always arrange appointments in advance and present an agenda as early in the process as possible. British business moves at a more deliberate pace than American business. British negotiators' style is calm, balanced, confident, cautious and not flexible. They tend to keep silent in the beginning in business talks, they are reserved rather than expressive or demonstrative in the way they communicate and start the bargaining at a point only slightly distant from the projected goal. They are not used to showing off in public and keep a distance with others. They will not confuse personal relation with business relation, so business affairs go first. They also attach great importance to protocol and ceremony, before negotiation exchange of greetings and courtesy may sometimes last for a couple of hours. This is evident in their use of understatement, low-contact body language and restrained gestures.

### Latin American Style

In Latin American contexts responsibility to others is generally considered more important than schedules and task accomplishment. People in Latin America consider relationship a very important element in doing business. If a good relationship is established between the two sides, they will not hesitate to help their counterparts. It is conceived that business people there have a poor record of credibility and commitment, because it is not unusual that they postpone payment without any reason or make use of the delaying to cut prices. Their negotiation approach relates to the patterns of high-context communication. A common term for conflict in Central America is enredo, meaning 「entangled」 or 「caught in a net」. When Latin Americans need help with negotiations, they tend to look to partial insiders rather than neutral outsiders, preferring the trust and confidence of established relationships. Thus, negotiation is done within networks, relationships are emphasized, and open ruptures are avoided.

### African Style

Many African nations have indigenous systems of conflict resolution that have endured to the present. Some of these systems are quite intact and some are fragmented by rapid social change. These systems rely on particular approaches to negotiation that respect kinship ties and elder roles, and the structures of local society in general. In Nigeria, for example, people are organized in extended families, villages, lineages, and lineage groups. A belief in the continuing ability of ancestors to affect people's lives maintains social control, and makes the need to have formal laws or regulations minimal. Negotiation happens within social networks, following prescribed roles.

In the Nigerian Ibibio context, the goal of restoring social networks is paramount, and individual differences are expected to be subsumed in the interest of the group. To ensure that progress or an agreement in a negotiation is preserved, parties must promise not to invoke the power of ancestors to bewitch or curse the other in the future. The aim of any process, formal or informal, is to affect a positive outcome without a 「residue of bitterness or resentment」. Elders have substantial power, and when they intervene in a conflict or a negotiation, their words are respected. This is partly because certain elders are believed to have access to supernatural powers that can remove protective shields at best and cause personal disaster at worst.

In other African contexts, arrange of indigenous processes exists, in which relationships and hierarchies tend to be emphasized.

## 10.6　Cross the Cultural Gap

Negotiation is a conflict-solving process. Approaches to conflict reflect underlying cultural values. In many cases, business people find that it is not easy at all to communicate with people from different cultural backgrounds. People may mistake someone as a culturally identical person, which often ends in troubles. In order to communicate effectively, negotiators should:

(1) learn to respect each other's culture;
(2) be objective about the culture differences;
(3) pay attention to the language barriers;
(4) use skills when communicating cross-culturally.

Under these thoughts, we now provide strategies to cross the cultural gap between negotiators.

### Effective Strategies

◎ **Assume You Don't Know Everything**

Test what you learn. When you travel to a foreign country, you are more likely to question your assumptions about how to appropriately interact with people than you would when you're home. You might become more sensitive to the impact of your words and behavior. You might ask more questions. This mindset can be useful for any negotiation. By taking a more honestly inquisitive and curious mindset, you are less likely to mis-communicate or misunderstand. Check your understanding, ask follow-up questions, dig for underlying rationales, and regularly summarize progress in your negotiation.

◎Acknowledge That Your Perceptions Are Limited

Share your perceptions as perceptions. In an explicitly cross-cultural situation, you are more likely to assume there is something you're missing, that you don't have all the information, or that there's a history you aren't aware of. Perhaps you will recognize that because your nationality is different, you just see things differently. Why not think more like this in your everyday negotiations?

In everyday negotiations, you are more likely to sense you are right and the other party is, well, not as right. Negotiation can succeed only when you and your negotiating partner learn how you each perceive a situation in a unique way.

◎Tell Your Story and Listen to Theirs

Keep in mind that individuals negotiate; cultures do not. Rather than assuming or projecting your understanding of someone else, share what makes you 「you」and listen to the other person's story as well. Everything he says and does communicates his story. Ask questions to learn more. At the same time, help the other party by sharing your story, what is important to you, and how you have become the negotiator you are. This kind of storytelling often takes place away from the table in an informal setting. Don't underestimate the value of these opportunities.

◎Understand Intent, but Share Impact

When words or actions surprise you—especially if they run counter to your sensibilities—attempt to understand the intent or purpose of the person. Say something like, 「I'm not sure what you're trying to achieve. It would help me if I could learn more about your goals here.」Share the impact on you of a given statement to help the other person understand and to move the conversation forward.

◎Learn About the Other Party's 「Culture」

It helps to understand the cultures—corporate, governmental, family, and so on—of the people you interact with. Knowing this can help prevent miscommunication and misunderstanding, and it can help smooth interactions. It can also demonstrate an effort to build rapport. Many negotiators extol the value of informal time spent together: 「We get more done during lunch than we do during the formal meeting.」At the same time, be careful with this knowledge. Having information about a person's culture can be misleading and even wrong when applied to a particular individual. Use this information to increase understanding, test assumptions, and increase empathy.

◎ **Monitor and Be Sensitive to Perceptions of Power and Respect**

Individuals often perceive each other through the lens of power. Awareness of this can help break through the walls that perceptions of power can create. Distrust and suspicion often follow perceptions of power, so be sensitive of this dynamic in order to improve relationships.

If you're concerned that someone distrusts you because you are in a position of power, inclusiveness may reduce distrust. Say things like,「Before we approach this problem, I want to make sure I get everyone's input.」Be more transparent and explicit about goals, agenda, and motives to help prevent misunderstanding and suspicion. Monitor whether the individual across the table feels respected. Showing respect will help you flame what you say and do in ways that build rapport.

## Case Study

Company H is a large company and its products are among the best of the same line in China. They have already extended their businesses into several regions overseas. However, the Middle East remains blank, as they have no experience in doing business with Arabs.

One day, a delegation from Dubai visited Company H. Mr. L, the chief representative of the company, received them. As the delegation was interested in the Company's products, both sides sat down for a negotiation on the products.

As the negotiation went on, Mr. L felt confused and bored because the Arabs asked for a break every hour. Then they went to the toilet to wash their hands and faces. When they came back, they knelt down to pray. As there was no towel in the toilet, the Arabs prayed with wet hands and faces. Mr. L found himself in a dilemma, because he did not know whether he should withdraw from the scene or not.

When it was time for lunch, the Arabs were treated to a rich dinner. When everyone was seated, the waitress started introducing the different dishes in English to the Arab visitors. They all looked surprised and pleased at the variety. But this did not last long. When the waitress mentioned some specially cooked pork, the smiles disappeared from all those visitors' faces and all of them looked blue—no one said a word. Quickly they stood up and left the dinner table without bidding farewell to anyone, though there were some important Chinese local guests present. The same day, the Dubai delegation left the city without notifying Company H.

A few days later, the bad news reached Mr. L—this Dubai delegation had signed a contract with their competitor—Company C, and the contract was the very one which was being negotiated between Company H and that Dubai delegation. Mr. L got a strong blame from his boss for losing the opportunity to their rival's hand.

Three days later, Mr. L took the following actions:

・Start a training program for all waitresses and persons involved in communicating with

Middle East business people, and invite some professors to give lectures on the Islamic culture and customs.

· Invite some Arabic teachers to teach the waitress simple Arabic to communicate with Arabs.

· Set up a separate dinning room with special set of dinner dishes for Arabs.

· Set up a special room close to the meeting room. This room would be used only for praying by those Middle Eastern business persons. In addition, he also put some compass and small carpets in the room.

· Prepare some small towels in the toilet for the Arabs to dry their hands before praying.

Half a year later, Company H had five customers in Middle East. All of them had visited Company H and were impressed by their understanding and respect for the Islamic culture and habits. Company H has been expanding their market share in the Middle East ever since.

## Exercises

(1) List all the conflicts in the case.

(2) What do you think of Mr. L's actions after his first failure? Which one impressed you most? Why?

(3) What is required for a modern business person with reference to a globalized economy and business? Why do you think that way?

國家圖書館出版品預行編目（CIP）資料

如何用英文進行國際商務談判 / 溫晶晶 編著. -- 第一版.
-- 臺北市：崧博出版：崧燁文化發行, 2019.10
　　面；　公分
POD版

ISBN 978-957-735-801-1(平裝)

1.商業英文 2.會話 3.商業談判

805.188　　　　　　　　　　　　　　　　108005644

| | |
|---|---|
| 書　　名： | 如何用英文進行國際商務談判 |
| 作　　者： | 溫晶晶 編著 |
| 發 行 人： | 黃振庭 |
| 出 版 者： | 崧博出版事業有限公司 |
| 發 行 者： | 崧燁文化事業有限公司 |
| E-mail： | sonbookservice@gmail.com |

粉絲頁：　　　　　網址：

地　　址：台北市中正區重慶南路一段六十一號八樓 815 室
8F.-815, No.61, Sec. 1, Chongqing S. Rd., Zhongzheng Dist., Taipei City 100, Taiwan (R.O.C.)

電　　話：(02)2370-3310　傳　真：(02) 2388-1990

總 經 銷：紅螞蟻圖書有限公司

地　　址：台北市內湖區舊宗路二段 121 巷 19 號
電　　話:02-2795-3656 傳真:02-2795-4100　　網址：

印　　刷：京峯彩色印刷有限公司（京峰數位）

　　本書版權為西南財經大學出版社所有授權崧博出版事業有限公司獨家發行電子書及繁體書繁體字版。若有其他相關權利及授權需求請與本公司聯繫。

定　　價：320 元

發行日期：2019 年 10 月第一版

◎ 本書以 POD 印製發行